# GALAXY'S EDGE

## EDITED BY MIKE RESNICK

I0520623

**ISSUE 20: MAY 2016**

Mike Resnick, Editor
Jean Rabe, Assistant Editor
Shahid Mahmud, Publisher

Published by Arc Manor/Phoenix Pick
P.O. Box 10339
Rockville, MD 20849-0339

*Galaxy's Edge* is published in January, March, May, July, September, and November.

www.GalaxysEdge.com

*Galaxy's Edge* is an invitation-only magazine. We do not accept unsolicited manuscripts. Unsolicited manuscripts will be disposed of or mailed back to the sender (unopened) at our discretion.

Available by subscription (www.GalaxysEdge.com) or through your favorite online store (Amazon.com, BN.com, etc.).

ISBN: 978-1-61242-305-0

Advertising in the magazine is available. Quarter page (half column), $95 per issue. Half page (full column, vertical or two half columns, horizontal) $165 per issue. Full page (two full columns) $295 per issue. Back Cover (full color) $495 per issue. All interior advertising is in black and white.

Please write to advert@GalaxysEdge.com.

**FOREIGN LANGUAGE RIGHTS:** Please refer all inquiries pertaining to foreign language rights to Spectrum Literary Agency, 320 Central Park West, Suite 1-D, New York, NY 10025. Phone: 1-212-362-4323. Fax 1-212-362-4562

## CONTENTS

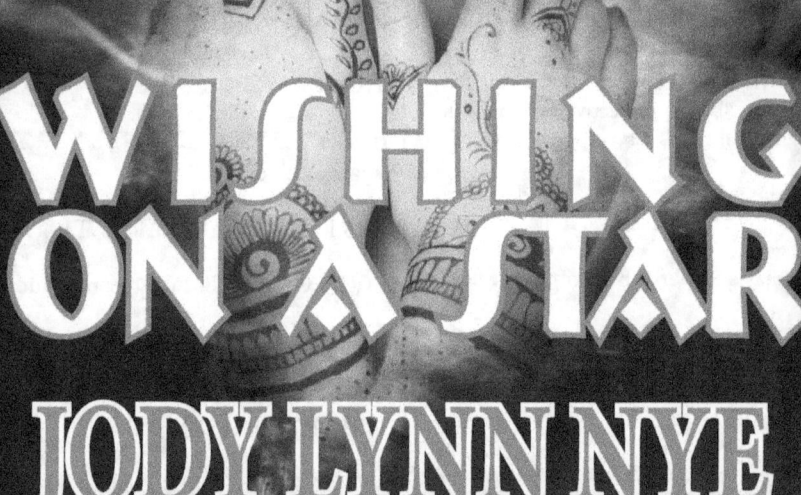

# THE EDITOR'S WORD

## by Mike Resnick

Welcome to the twentieth issue of *Galaxy's Edge*. We have new stories from Jeff Calhoun, Stewart C Baker, Tina Gower, Auston Habershaw, Jean-Claude Dunyach, Nick DiChario, Paul Di Filippo, and Zach Shephard, plus reprints from old friends George R. R. Martin, Kij Johnson, Jack MacDevitt, and Sheila Finch. In addition, we've got our regulars: book reviews by Bill Fawcett and Jody Lynn Nye, science by Gregory Benford, literary matters by Barry N. Malzberg, and the Joy Ward interview, which this issue—by popular request—reprints her excellent chat with George R. R. Martin. And finally, another installment in our serialization of Leigh Brackett's classic *The Long Tomorrow*.

✦

Worldcon this year will be held in Kansas City in August. We hope to see a lot of you there, and of course we'll have a table in the Dealer's Room.

It occurs to me that not all of you have been to a Worldcon before, so it seems appropriate to give you some hints and tips about attending your first one.

### Parties

You've probably heard endless tales about all the parties at Worldcon, and indeed most nights there will be more than fifty of them—big ones, little ones, public ones, private ones. There are all kinds of parties—the single events, the pro events, the bid parties, the hospitality suites. You'll get most of your info from various bulletin boards, and also from the twice-daily (and often thrice-daily) convention newsletter, which will be made available in most public places. Hollywood to the contrary, not all parties feature drugs, nudity, drunken behavior, and wild sex, and Worldcon parties are among those that feature none of them. These are just people visiting with old and new friends who share some of the same interests.

Every group that's bidding for a future Worldcon will have at least one party, most two, and a few every night. These are "open" parties and will be advertised all over the hotels and in the newsletters.

A number of regional conventions will also have open parties to interest you in attending their upcoming cons. Most new conventions with ambitions of becoming a major feature on the convention calendar will also have an open party to announce its existence.

Many of the major parties will be held in the Convention Center this year, but a number of smaller ones will be held in suites in the convention hotels.

The hosts for the next two Worldcons usually have open parties. In fact, next year's winner traditionally hosts the Hugo Losers Party. Frequently the previous year's host has an open "thank you" party.

Then there will be open and semi-open Hospitality Suites, including the Con Suite, which will be run by the host committee and open to all.

There will be a SFWA (Science Fiction and Fantasy Writers of America) Suite. You'll need to be a SFWA member or a member's guest to get you in the first time. If you want to return, you can probably pick up a sticker for your badge that will get you in.

There will be an ASFA (American Science Fiction Artists) Suite, usually less crowded and easier to gain entrance to.

There will be pro parties. They're not exactly open, and not exactly closed. Basically, you'll need a pro or a well-known fan to get you in some of them, but once inside they won't have to stay with you or vouch for you:

- Tor Books almost always has a party.
- Baen almost always has a party.
- Eos, DAW, Bantam, and Ace occasionally have parties.
- *Asimov's* and *Analog* will have a party, but it usually consists of renting out the SFWA suite and supplying food and drink for the writers for one evening.

Many of the semi-pro and specialty publishers will have open parties. Just check the daily newsletters for time and location (or look at the elevator walls, which are usually plastered with notices of the night's parties.)

Almost every special interest group will have a party, some private, most open.

A number of fan clubs, computer networks, and the like will have parties. First Fandom, a last-man organization consisting of anyone who can prove he was active in science fiction prior to 1938, often has a party.

Any foreign group with enough attendees from home will throw a party, usually though not always an open one. The Japanese almost always have one. So do the Australians. Others have them from time to time, including the British, the Slovakians, the Germans, and the Dutch.

There'll be fifteen to twenty rooms where fans have brought their favorite movies or TV shows, legitimate or bootlegs, and will show them to anyone who wants to watch. This won't be advertised, but just walk up and down the hotel corridors, and when you find an open door, take a peek in—it's usually a small party or a group watching videos.

And, of course, I'm barely scratching the surface. Despite the fifteen to twenty-track programming and the Hugos and the masquerade and the dealers' room and the art show and everything else, seventy percent of a Worldcon takes place from 10 p.m. until 4 or 5 a.m.

### Standing Exhibits

There will be a number of standing exhibits, open from 10 a.m. to 6 p.m. or thereabouts. Two are huge, most aren't; the two big ones are easy to find, while most of the others take some looking for.

**The Dealers' Room**, a/k/a the Hucksters' Room. It used to sell only books and magazines, but these days it sells games, CDs, toys, clothes, jewelry, videos, medieval weapons, and anything associated with SF. Probably a third of the dealers still sell books and magazines, which is a lot, since there will be about three hundred tables and a number of booths.

**Autograph sessions**—they'll be announced well in advance—are usually held in or near the hucksters' room. But those are just the "official" Worldcon autograph sessions. Most of the popular writers will also be signing at dealers' or publishers' tables as well, so that they put in from two to five hours

signing during the convention…enough time for just about anyone to get their autographs. (And if you see a writer whose work you admire in the hallways, just walk up and ask for an autograph; that's part of what they're there for. You're paying good money to attend, so don't be shy about asking for anything at all.)

**The Art Show.** Just about every major artist from Whelan to Eggleton to Giancola to Maitz to Picacio to whoever will display paintings here, as will hundreds of minor artists. The hangings will all be in the middle of the room; sculptures and other 3D pieces will be on tables lining the walls. Almost everything will have a minimum-bid price tag on it. The auction rules change from year to year, so ask how to bid at the entrance to the art show—but know that ninety percent of what you see will be sold during the con.

**Kaffeeklatsches.** These are one-hour (and occasionally two-hour) periods where you sign up to meet with your favorite writer or artist. They serve coffee and sweets, and usually there are about a dozen fans pro's. Sign up for the kaffeeklatsches you want to attend as soon as you get to the con. It's always first-signed first-seated.

**Fanzine room.** There is always a room devoted to fanzines. Usually it's a small, unpublicized room, difficult to find, but it's worth the hunt because it offers dozens of free fanzines. Not the perennial Hugo nominees, but enough to get you started.

**Fanhistorica room.** This doesn't occur every year, but it's present more often than not, and will be devoted to the history of fandom—books, photos, artifacts, famous (and incredibly valuable) old fanzines, Hugos from previous years…everything you'll want to know about SF fandom from its origins in the 1930s to the present day. Often old-time pros and fans will lead docent tours of the exhibit.

**Fan lounge.** Many Worldcons have one of these. It'll be somewhere near the dealers' and lecture rooms, and you'll find tables where you can plop down, relax, get soft drinks or coffee, read fanzines (which will be supplied), and meet other fans.

**Costume exhibit.** This doesn't occur at every Worldcon, but when it shows up it is stunning. It'll be a display of the greatest masquerade costumes of the past two or three decades, draped on mannequins.

**Photo exhibit.** Over the years SFWA's former attorney, M. Christine Valada, who was also a photographer, took black-and-white portraits of just about every pro who attends Worldcon, and there is a standing display of them every year.

**Fan photo exhibit.** Encouraged by Valada's traveling photo show, fandom now has its own portrait exhibit.

There will doubtless be more exhibits, but these are the ones that tend to show up most years. I encourage you to hunt them all up. You do yourself a disservice if you travel all the way to Worldcon, pay your money to become a member, pay even more to stay at the hotels, and then don't take advantage of all the exhibits offered.

### Special Events

Along with the regular programming, every Worldcon has its share of special events.

**Hugo Ceremonies.** This is where the Toastmaster gets to shine (if they shine at all; alas, some don't). More than a dozen Hugos will be presented in the pro and fan categories, but that's not all. Also presented are the Campbell Award for Best New Writer; the Big Heart Award; and the Seiun (Japanese Hugo) for the Best Translated Novel and Best Translated Short Fiction. There will be photo ops for everybody, and you can probably watch the Hugos and the Masquerade in your room on closed-circuit television.

**The Retro Hugos.** The Hugos began in 1952, so from time to time a Worldcon will also host the Retro Hugos, Hugo Awards for a year prior to the inception of the Hugos. This year's Retro Hugos will be for 1941.

**The Masquerade.** This used to be the biggest draw of Worldcon, but it's a mere shadow of its former self. During the 1970s and 1980s the Worldcon masquerade used to draw well more than a hundred costumes and last four or five hours. Now, thanks to Costume Con and the proliferation of minor costume conventions, the masquerade barely draws forty costumes...but it's still a fun event to attend. And if you're an author, not much gives you a bigger kick than watching a fan who spent months of effort creating a costume based on one of more of your characters.

**Opening Ceremonies.** The Toastmaster introduces the Pro and Fan Guests of Honor, who will make brief speeches. You'll be told where to find everything, and then sent off to do just that.

**Pro Guest of Honor Speeches.** There used to be just one Pro GOH, and most of the time it was a writer. These days there's usually a Writer GOH, an Editor GOH, and an Artist GOH, and each will have an hour in which to make a speech.

**Fan GOH Speech.** It probably draws a bit better than the pro speeches, which is only right and fitting. Unlike the Nebulas, Worldcon is put on by and for fans, a fact that many pros forget or are simply unaware of. Pros are an attraction, and their function is to draw more fans to the con, but never make any mistake about who the con is for.

**Hugo-Nominated Movies.** These will play free of charge sometime during the con before the winner is announced.

There may be other special events. They can be as diverse as a miniature golf tournament (1991), a pro vs. fan basketball game (1986), a trivia contest (just about every year), the world premiere of a science fiction movie (*A Boy and His Dog* in 1974; Watership Down in 1978) or the first peek at a new TV show (*Star Trek* in 1966).

### Programming

I've mentioned programming and the like, but until you run into it, I don't think any of you can truly realize the magnitude of Worldcon programming.

A typical hour will have three or four panels to choose from on science fiction, all featuring well-known writers; a pair of panels on fantasy; a panel on horror; a panel or two on science; a couple of panels on the business end of science fiction, from writing to editing to selling to reading contracts; an item or two of children's programming; a pair of panels on various aspects of fandom, from fan history to publishing a fanzine; a publisher's editorial staff telling you what they're looking for this year; a panel of critics evaluating the year's fiction; and a couple more panels or speeches on various subjects.

That's every hour, from 10 a.m. to 6 p.m. when it slows down. But you'll still have perhaps four panels an hour from then until 10 p.m., and maybe two panels after that until perhaps 2 a.m.

While all this is going on, three or four rooms will be set aside for writers to read their most recent works, and at the same time half a dozen authors will be autographing in or near the dealers' room. And of course there will be two to four kaffeeklatsches occurring at the same time.

And let's not forget the free, round-the-clock science fiction movies that will be showing in an auditorium.

That's it. Every hour. And while all this is happening, the dealers' room, the art show, and most of the other exhibits will be open as well.

Yeah, I know, it's overwhelming. Probably the best thing to do is log onto Worldcon's web page after the final schedule is posted—usually two or three weeks before the con—and make your decision as to what items you definitely don't want to miss. It can take a few hours, and why spend that time at the convention when there are so many interesting things to do?

### What to Bring

So it's your first Worldcon. What do you pack?

There is no panel or party where you won't be accepted wearing a T-shirt, shorts or jeans, and sandals...so what else you bring depends on what makes you comfortable and where you plan to go when you leave the hotel.

If you're dining out, and especially if you plan to visit some upscale restaurants, bring along the appropriate attire. If you plan to use the hotel's pool, bring a swimsuit. (The skinny-dipping days of the 1970s and 1980s Worldcons are long gone.) If you're entering the masquerade, make sure you pack your costume in a way that won't break or otherwise harm it. If you plan to participate in the Regency dance (yes, almost every Worldcon has a Regency dance, don't ask me why), you might bring the appropriate Regency costume.

If you're on any medication, bring enough to see you through the convention; it's murder trying to fill a prescription in a strange city on a weekend.

I wouldn't bother bringing a laptop. First, there's too much to do (and you're paying quite a bit to do it) to waste time with your computer—and second, most of the people you want to chat with and send e-mails to are already at the con. (And most downtown hotels in major cities will charge incredibly high connect rates, measured by the minute if not the second.)

Bring any books you want autographed. This is your one chance all year to find a great many of the major authors in the field in one place, and they're all there for your convenience. Ditto any magazines.

Bring any guidebooks you may have purchased. Why try committing them to memory?

If you're into photo memories, bring your camera, or camcorder, with enough batteries that you won't have to go out to purchase any.

Bring cash and credit cards. No one in a strange city wants to cash your checks.

Above all, bring the one item I never do without, the most important single thing you can bring (besides money): a small blank notebook—paper or electronic, makes no difference—that fits easily into a pocket.

Why?

Well, to begin with, before leaving home you'll write down the titles of all the books you're looking for in the hucksters' room, as well as the dates of all the magazines, to make searching through the dealers a little easier.

You'll want to write down the room numbers of all your friends—impossible to remember them all.

As you find out when and where the parties are, you'll want to write down the times and room numbers of each. That's dozens more numbers and times.

You'll want to jot down those events that you absolutely don't want to miss. Still more times and places.

You might also record the addresses and phone numbers of all the restaurants you want to visit (and on a busy summer weekend in a major city, almost all the better ones, inside and outside the hotel, require reservations.)

If you're a hopeful writer, you'll want to write down whatever it is you have sold, or promised to send, to which editor. Even if you're not, it helps to write down anything you promise to send/sell/trade with other fans.

If you're trading addresses, either street or e-mail, with new friends, you'll want to write them down.

So be sure you bring that blank book. You'll fill it up soon enough.

### Saving and Spending Money

Worldcon isn't cheap. There are a few ways—not many, but a few—of saving money. To wit:

**Car pool to get there.** The cheapest way to get to any Worldcon (at least, any Worldcon on this continent) is to car pool.

You'll hear stories of fans sleeping ten and twelve to a room. They are not an exaggeration, but it seems a bit excessive to me. Still, if you're traveling on a budget, it makes sense to **share a room** with perhaps two or three others.

**The price of an attending membership** goes up every few months. The initial price is about a third of the at-the-door price. If you're late buying your membership—and the lead time is two years—there's a way around this. Surf the net and find someone who has an attending membership and can't use it; it can be sold and transferred to you prior to mid-July of the year the Worldcon is held... after that, it has to be done at the door. (Example: someone who bought his membership early at $80 wants to sell; the price is currently $200 if you buy from the convention; you offer to split the difference, the seller agrees, you get an attending membership for $140, you save $60, the seller makes $60, and everyone's happy.)

If you see a second-hand book or magazine you want in the hucksters' room and it's too expensive for your budget, **make an offer**. Half the time you'll find the huckster is willing to deal.

And now a couple of proper ways to spend money:

The maid who makes up your room doesn't work a seven-day week, so for the best service, and just to be fair, **leave a buck or two** on your pillow every morning when you go out for the day, rather than leaving $10 or $15 in a lump at the end of the week.

Most parties don't want your money. But a few hospitality suites will have a bowl out with a note asking for donations. **Put a couple of bucks in**, or you may never be asked back.

That's pretty much it—a way to vote for your favorite stories, books, editors, artists, movies, and fanzines, and mingle with like-minded fans and writers at our grandest annual event.

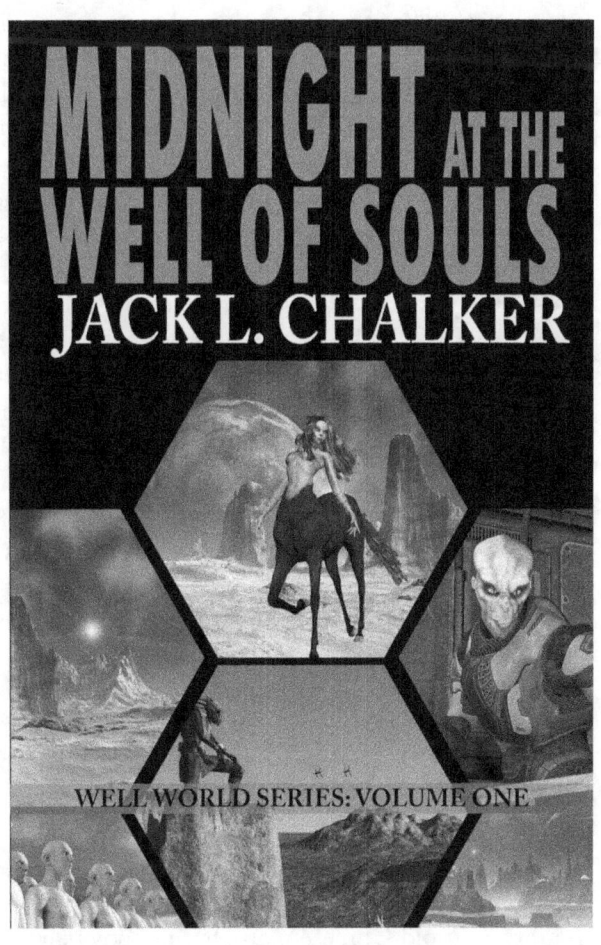

MIDNIGHT AT THE WELL OF SOULS

JACK L. CHALKER

WELL WORLD SERIES: VOLUME ONE

*Auston Habershaw's stories have appeared in* Analog *and other venues, and he is the author of a series of novels—*The Saga of the Redeemed—*that are currently out from Harper Voyager.*

# LORD OF THE CUL-DE-SAC

## by Auston Habershaw

Once upon a time, a dragon got a good deal on a modified, split-level ranch with aluminum siding and a big yard—2.9% APR for a fifteen year fixed, no points, no closing costs. Truly, his credit was mighty.

Nobody saw the dragon move in. Oh, there were signs—a torn up lawn, the scorched backyard, the smell of brimstone in the air—but no sign of the dragon itself. For a week after the closing, the neighbors in the little cul-de-sac watched as armored cars pulled up to the garage, one after another. Burly men with handguns hefted small sacks of prodigious weight into the house and gradually, after hours of labor, dumped their cargo into the empty in-ground pool out back. Milly Petersen, the dragon's direct neighbor on the right hand side, told everyone the pool glittered like the sun. There was now no way to verify this, of course, as the pool was covered over with a pretty hefty tarp once the shipments ended, and hadn't been disturbed since. Mr. Fu, the dragon's other immediate neighbor, insisted that Milly was just making it up.

"Dragons don't hoard gold. That's just in stories." He had insisted at Dr. Cohen's son's bar mitzvah that July.

Mr. Fu was often lying about things just to calm people down. He once told Jack Petersen, Milly's husband, that his chest pains were probably just gas. They hadn't been, and now Milly was speed dating at the local Pizza Palace on every third Saturday of the month.

People took Mr. Fu's comment about the dragon's swimming pool in the same vein. Nobody called him out on it (you just didn't argue with a sweet eighty-year old Chinese man), but nobody believed a word he said, either. That pool was full of gold—fifteen thousand gallons of it.

The dragon didn't go out. It didn't collect its mail. It had no listed phone number. Chessie Vormount had gone over shortly after it moved in with a housewarming gift (Gordon, her husband, still told jokes about that one). It was a basket containing a variety of products recommended at the local pet store for grooming and caring for lizard scales. The whole neighborhood had watched her walk over there, peering through their curtains, hands hovering by the fire extinguisher, waiting for her to ring the doorbell in the same way that cops waited for the bomb squad to disarm an explosive.

She rang. Nothing happened. She stood there on the front stairs in her stiletto heels and dazzling white dress for a full five minutes, just ringing. Finally, she just left the gift basket on the porch and went home. The basket went unmolested for six days. Then, one morning, it was simply gone.

The dragon, they collectively decided, wasn't social. It (or 'he', as Chessie Vormount insisted that no female of any species would be such a shut-in) probably just wanted to be left alone. This of course meant he had moved to the wrong neighborhood, since if there was one way to attract attention in a suburban cul-de-sac, it was to be the guy on the block of whom nothing was known.

Rumors snowballed around 'their' dragon. The whole town knew they 'had one.' Everybody knew about dragons, of course—ever since the Reawakening, they'd been living among humanity with relatively little trouble. Of course, when everybody said 'among humanity,' they meant that in the general sense, as in they lived on the same planet as us, like pandas and giant squid. Dragons owned private islands. Dragons lived on expansive mountain estates in Idaho. Dragons were petty warlords in sub-Saharan Africa. There was one in Hawaii that lived in a volcano.

They were *not* your neighbors.

So, naturally, the questions piled up: Why did it move here? Where did it come from? What did it want? What (who?) did it eat? Was it awake? Asleep? How did it pay the mortgage? Did it get cable? What did it keep in the garage?

To each of these was supplied an answer based largely off a cocktail of innocent conjecture and pernicious gossip. The answers also conflicted: the dragon came here because it was broke (for a dragon). The dragon ate stray cats and runaway dogs. It slept all day and only after dark did it slip out and flap over to Newark to eat homeless people. It did not have cable; it paid for premium satellite. There was a pile of human bones in the garage. And a Porsche.

Life went on. Dragons, as everybody knew, were not to be prodded. The rumors swirled, but as far as anybody knew, not a single living soul had placed a toe over the property line since Chessie Vormount had left her basket of Doc Slither's EZ Lizard Scales Disinfectant and some live mice in a pretty box and strutted home. They were curious, sure, but not suicidal. Everybody in the neighborhood bought an extra fire extinguisher, assumed any Frisbees or baseballs that went astray were lost for good, and went about their business.

Then came 2008. The bottom dropped out of the market like the trapdoor on a gallows, and suburbia was left to wriggle on the rope, gasping for air. The cul de sac went through it like everybody else. The Cohen's did okay—Rebecca went back to teaching to compensate for the hike in their rates and they quietly pushed their son to go to a state school. Mr. Fu's sixty-year-old son was laid off, so he and his family moved from upstate to live with him. Fu the Younger got a job managing an Arby's; Fu the Youngest drove a cab and went to dental school at night. Gordon Vormount lost a mint on the stock market, barely escaped a round of layoffs, and was so underwater on his mortgage he started calling himself 'Captain Nemo.'

Milly Petersen, though, lost the house. It wasn't a quick loss—not a 'rip off the band-aid and get it over with' loss. Unlike her husband's death—sudden, immediate, stunning—her home drifted away piece by piece. She passed her two little kids around to the neighbors' houses so she could work double-shifts. Chessie Vormount had the Lions Club throw a bake sale for her. She sold her car, pawned her jewelry. Jack's life insurance settlement vanished in a puff of financial vapor. The kids' college funds went next. In the end, none of it mattered. The pending foreclosure notice was pinned to her front door like the flag of a foreign nation, claiming her house—the house she and Jack had intended to live in forever—for somebody else.

The dragon's house, though, remained unchanged. It was about then that the dwarves showed up.

Milly had heard a fair amount about dwarves, and none of it good. As far as anybody could tell, they had crawled up from somewhere in the depths of the earth and began settling in old mine shafts and abandoned industrial facilities. The three dwarves that presented themselves on Milly's doorstep smelled like motor oil and were covered in grime. Their beards were matted and frizzy and, most distressingly, they wore mismatched NFL paraphernalia. One of them—wearing a Buffalo Bills knit hat and a Carolina Panthers jacket—held up a copy of the local paper's classified ads with a red circle around the "room for let" notice she had posted. He said only one thing, and that barely a word: "Eh?"

*Where were you three months ago?* Milly thought, but smoothed her sweatpants and straightened her posture. "I'm sorry, but the property will be foreclosed in a month."

She went to close the door, but one of the dwarves stuck a fat foot against the door jamb. The one with the newspaper pointed to the ad again and grunted, "Month enough time. We pay double rent, eh?"

The one that hadn't spoken grumbled something in a foreign language to the other two. Newspaper dwarf nodded.

"What did he say?"

The dwarf doffed his Bills hat. "He ask to make sure is basement room. Eh?"

Milly frowned. "Yes, I'm sorry—I don't have anything above-groun—"

The dwarves barged past her, grinning toothy grins. The third dwarf dropped a sack in her hands that had to weigh twelve pounds. She opened it on the kitchen table; it was filled with silver ingots. Two months' rent in one lump of precious metal.

The dwarves said they would move in immediately, which turned out to be exactly accurate. They had a motorcycle and sidecar in her driveway strapped with duffel bags and suitcases. Two of them brought their stuff inside and straight down into the basement while the third—the talker—filled out the rental application. He wrote in blocky, large letters, clutching the ballpoint pen as though it were a live serpent. Their names were Thondor, Jorri, and Glorin. Under "occupation," Thondor wrote "DWARVES."

The Milly Petersen of six months ago would have had an apoplectic fit at the thought of a trio of mythical creatures with no credit history squatting in her husband's old man-cave. The Milly Petersen that had resigned herself to foreclosure just wondered how she was going to deposit a bunch of silver ingots at the local bank branch.

The cul-de-sac went wild. The Cohen's actually *dis*-invited her to a dinner party. Chessie Vormount started talking with some ladies down at the grocery store that Milly was going to sell them the house. Mr. Fu started sending his grandson over with envelopes full of "helpful" coupons—"50% off air freshener"; "buy one set of children's overalls, get one free"; "free beard oil with purchase of men's grooming kit."

The rumors piled up, and Milly denied them in turn. No, the dwarves were not relatives. No, the dwarves hadn't been making shoes in the basement. No, the dwarves did not work for Disney. *No*, they were *not* her lovers.

Eventually, Rebecca Cohen and Chessie Vormount had Milly over for tea one afternoon, ostensibly to plan Milly's going away party. It was, in reality, an ambush. The two women sat at the edges of Chessie's tufted leather wingback chairs, hands clutching teacups. "What if they don't *leave*?" Rebecca said, pursing her lips. "I mean, when…you know…*after*."

"What am I supposed to do about it?" Milly shrugged. "If the bank can't get them out, that's the *bank's* problem."

"Well, that's fine for you, darling." Chessie said, tapping her manicured nails on a saucer. "But think of our property values!"

Milly threw up her hands. "Look, we've already got a *dragon* living here—how much of a difference will three dwarves make?"

The two women were persistent, though, and Milly eventually relented, just as she usually did. "Fine," she said, "I promise to talk to them."

They parted all smiles, but Milly sensed the hostility that lurked beneath Rebecca's cold hug. She didn't believe Milly would do anything. Neither did Chessie.

Milly hadn't really seen much of the dwarves since they descended into the basement. In the two weeks since they'd moved in, they only came up to watch football on the Petersen's one remaining television. Milly had taken to laying towels over the couch and chairs when they did this, since everything they touched came away stained with grease. They would sit there, wearing the wrong shirts for the game, and curse at the television in their language. At least, she *assumed* it was cursing. It sounded a lot like cursing, anyway.

The rest of the time they stayed in the basement, had pizza delivered to the basement hatch on the side of the house, and didn't bother anyone. There were times that Milly would stand at the top of the basement stairs and listen. She only ever heard their singing—a trio of *basso profundo* voices, echoing up from the depths. The basement light was never on.

It took Milly a few days, but she finally worked up the nerve to head down the stairs. She made as much noise as she could, so as not to startle her boarders. She found two of them sitting together on a pair of folding chairs. It was Thondor, in his perennial Panther's jacket, and Jorri, who was sleeveless in a Utah Jazz jersey. His arms were as thick as Milly's legs and gorilla-hairy. And filthy with oily grime. Of Glorin there was no sign.

Thondor had his copy of the lease and was reviewing it with a monocle. "Yes. You are allowed to do this."

Milly blinked. "I…I know."

They sat in their chairs and waited for her to say something. Milly looked around the room. Other than a few folding chairs and the single double bed, there was no furniture. The walls were bare. Their duffel bags and luggage were piled in one corner, right by a large stack of empty pizza boxes. "Ummm…is Glorin out?"

"Yes." Thondor nodded. "Glorin is out."

"Where did he go?"

"Out. Like you say."

"But your motorcycle is still here so—"

Jorri grumbled something in their language. Thondor nodded. "Jorri wants to know what you want. We make too much noise, eh?"

"No. Nothing like that…I just…" but Milly struggled with what to say. *My nosy neighbors want you to promise to move out.* It seemed so petty. "You know what—never mind. Sorry I bothered you."

The two dwarves muttered to one another in their language as she left. Their black, beady little eyes seemed full of hostility, though why she couldn't guess. "Turn light out when you go." Thondor said. She did, feeling guilty, as though she had invaded someone's inner sanctum.

She never saw Glorin again. He didn't come up any longer for football games. His voice was never added to the deep chorus of the dwarves that would emanate from below the kitchen. He was gone. When she asked, Thondor only said, "He is out. Like you said."

It had been a little shy of three weeks when she saw Mr. Fu mowing his front lawn. Milly was in the midst of packing for the long drive to Pittsburgh, where she and her kids were about to move from their lovely suburban home to a two bedroom apartment. Her attempts to avoid eye contact with the old man did not dissuade him from talking to her.

"You are such a lucky lady, right?" Mr. Fu said.

Milly grimaced.

"Dwarves are good luck. You'll see!"

She didn't answer. She couldn't even bring herself to look at the stupid old man. Her? Lucky? Jesus Christ.

That night was a Sunday night. Only Thondor came up from the basement for football. He had a bag of Chex Mix in his lap. He glowered at the television, munching pretzels with greasy hands.

"Thondor," Milly asked, "is Jorri okay?"

"Yes." Thondor grumbled. "He okay. Just went out."

"Out *where?*"

But the Jets fumbled, and Thondor cursed too much for the next five minutes to supply an answer.

Just like Glorin before him, Jorri never reappeared.

At the going away party, she told everybody the story of the disappearing dwarves in her basement. "Do you think…do you think they *killed* each other?"

Dr. Cohen stroked his beard. "I've read that dwarves can be violent. I mean, well, more *prone* to violent outbursts."

"That's bull." Gordon Vormount sipped his beer. "The answer's *obvious*, Milly."

Milly tried not to scowl. "Why? What's so obvious?"

"It's the dragon!" Gordon smiled at those assembled, glorying in his own revelation. "The little bastards are trying to rob the dragon, and

the dragon is eating them. Any of you ever read *The Hobbit?*"

Milly had not. Nobody else had, either. Gordon shook his head. "It's all there, Milly. You can borrow my copy."

She declined—she'd be damned if she borrowed anything from Gordon Vormount again—but she did Google it. She read over the plot synopsis after she got home. She had one too many of Chessie's cocktails in her, so she had to read it twice to be sure. "Son of a bitch!"

She stumbled down the basement stairs, shouting. "Thondor! Hey! Thondor, are you awake!"

The basement was empty. The stack of pizza boxes had expanded mightily, but otherwise the place appeared unchanged. The place smelled of oily dwarves and burned pizza. "Thondor! Thondor?"

No sign of him. Peeking through the basement window, she confirmed that the little motorcycle was still in the driveway—right next to her moving pod, just where it had always been. So he wasn't driving anywhere and his legs were way too short to bother walking…so then where the hell was he?

Milly eyed the mountain of pizza boxes. She knew they hadn't thrown out a single one since they'd been here. There were dozens and dozens of the things—probably well over a hundred, maybe even two hundred of them—all stacked to the ceiling. She grabbed one. It was heavy, like a hunk of iron; she lost her grip and dropped the thing. It landed on the ground with a clank. She opened it up.

The pizza box was filled with *gold*.

"Oh my God."

She opened another box. And another. And another. Gold—thick, heavy gold coins, gold bars, gold jewelry. Milly tore through the giant pile of pizza boxes—a full third of them was weighed down with treasure. The others were empty, presumably waiting to be filled.

And behind the pizza boxes? A door of earth and stone: it was perfectly round and inscribed with blocky runes in the hand of Thondor himself. Milly had no idea—no idea whatsoever—how the door had come to be in the corner of her basement or how the dwarves had fashioned it without her knowledge, but she did know—without any doubt whatsoever—what lay behind the door. With a boldness borne of a bit too much vodka, she grasped the handle at the center of the door and yanked. It swung open easily, silently. Beyond was a round passage about five feet in diameter, lit intermittently by bare light bulbs spliced into an extension cord which was plugged into an outlet mounted just inside the door. Milly couldn't help but wonder how they managed that part above all—since when were dwarves electrically inclined? *Tolkien didn't write anything about that, now did he, Gordon?*

The tunnel stretched out in front of her, the light bulbs only reaching so far. At the other end was the dragon's lair. And probably the charred bones of her three tenants.

At least they had paid in advance.

Milly set one foot on the threshold of the tunnel… and stopped. Her heart, she realized, was pounding so hard she could feel the impact in her throat. *Milly, at the other end of this tunnel is a dragon. What the flying hell do you think you're doing?*

She backed away, closed the door quietly, and went back upstairs.

Thondor never reappeared. Monday Night Football went unwatched.

Milly had six days to vacate the premises. Her furniture—what few pieces she was able to keep—was all covered and taped up, ready for the movers to come. The kids were gone, sent ahead to her sister's place in Pittsburgh to await her arrival. It was only Milly, an empty house, and a stack of gold coins and bars in her basement. She went downstairs several times to check on them; still there. The door, too.

Milly spent one afternoon—right after she cashed her last paycheck from her old job at the diner—and did some calculations. Gold was worth about a thousand bucks an once and, right at that moment, her basement had about a seven hundred and fifty pounds of the stuff. That was twelve million dollars, give or take. That was more money than poor Jack had earned in his entire life, all pilfered from some dragon's in-ground swimming pool over the course of two weeks by a trio of hairy midgets. And even *that* wasn't enough money to make any kind of dent in the dragon's giant pool of treasure. The damned thing probably didn't even notice it was gone. Milly took the fact that her house was still standing and not an ashen heap as evidence of that.

She lay on the cot she had rigged up in the now empty master bedroom and stared at the ceiling fan slowly whirling. Her mind spun off with it, on flights of fancy. Of her, lugging a duffel bag full of gold doubloons into the bank, thumping it on the counter, and laughing in that bank manager's smug little face. *My house, you hear me, you tubby little prick? MY HOUSE!*

The thought gave her a thrill. She could do it, too. With all that gold in her basement, she could pay off the mortgage, buy a new car, send the kids to college, and still have enough for a yearly trip to Disney World—that trip Jack had always wanted the family to take and never got the chance to. She thought of him pulling double shifts with a smile, that steely glint in his eye, *"Don't worry, baby. I'm working my way up. Everything's okay."*

But it hadn't been.

*She* could fix it. She could fix every last problem Jack hadn't been able to solve—all she needed to do was to lug up those pizza boxes, put them in sacks, and take them to the bank. That was literally *it*. There was a pool in Orlando, suspiciously mouse-shaped, that was calling to her. Palm trees swaying in the breeze, a cool drink, a chaise lounge. The laughter of children.

She got up and went downstairs. The sun was on its way down—she'd have to hurry if she wanted to make the bank today. She emptied a suitcase of all its clothes and dragged it into the basement.

The door was still there, of course. Behind it, the tunnel—naturally. Milly tried to ignore it and went straight to work, clanking gold bars out of pizza boxes and into her suitcase. Her heart thumped loudly against her ribs. Her hands shook. The skin on the back of her neck crawled; she felt eyes on her, even though nobody was there. What if…

Her mind flew off to still more fantasies. What if the dragon *did* know about the gold? What if the dragon was just waiting for her to try and steal it and then *boom*—she would vanish in a puff of flame. What if it crouched even now in its own garage, lying in wait for her rental car to cruise by and then…

Milly stopped and faced the door. For all she knew, the dragon was small enough to wriggle down that tunnel and was *right there* on the other side of the door, fiery breath at the ready. Now that she was thinking about it, there *was* a bit of a hot draft coming from that tunnel—she could feel it around her ankles. Oh God.

*You're being ridiculous,* she snarled at herself. *There's nothing there. Go on and open the door. Prove it.*

Licking her lips, hands shaking, she went over to the door and ripped it open in the same wild manner you ripped off a bandage.

Nothing. Just darkness and still air. The gold was hers if she wanted it. She just had to finish loading that suitcase. She wanted to. She *had* to.

Yet she didn't move toward the stairs. She thought of Jack's smile, the way he'd brush a stray hair from her face and kiss her on the cheek. She thought of her kids—Billy standing next to her at the funeral, eight years old and still he held her steady. Sarah, too, hugging the stuffed tiger Jack had gotten her at the mall, eyes wet but not crying. Not while Mommy could see. Later on, when she had confronted Sarah about it, the little six year old had looked up at her and said, *"I want you to be brave, Mommy. I don't want to make you cry, too."*

*Be brave.*

"Shit." Milly picked up the suitcase handle and dragged it into the tunnel.

The passage was narrow, but cleanly hewn from the earth and supported by arches of stone—though how they had gotten there, Milly had no clue. It was a pretty short walk, moving diagonally from the back corner of Milly's house to a ladder that led up to a trap door in the floor of a disused pool shed. Milly couldn't get the suitcase up the ladder—too heavy—so she grabbed one bar of gold and climbed up.

The inner walls of the shed were scorched black and the floor was a goopy morass of melted plastic piping and pool toys. There was a pile of charred black bones right by the door that made Milly yelp in horror. The nylon of a Carolina Panthers jacket had fused to the ribcage, the teal mascot giving a lopsided growl from the breastbone. This had been Thondor.

Milly froze in place, unable to advance past the body, unable to retreat now that she had seen it. Part of her, on some level, had always wondered if the dragon was *real.* Now she knew for certain, and that knowledge was too much for her. The dragon could *kill* her. She couldn't even call the cops—the time

to call the cops would have been when she found a pile of stolen gold in her basement. That time was long past.

The door to the pool shed opened as though blown by a breeze. Milly could see across the pool, still covered, and to the open back door of the house. Terror seized her; she couldn't breathe.

The dragon's voice was deep and smooth, with just a touch of sibilance. It seemed to crawl from the house and envelop her. "Mrs. Petersen, won't you please come in?"

Moving slowly, her steps soft, Milly walked across the patio, across the Frisbee-strewn yard, and up to the door. She held the gold bar up in front of her like an offering. "I'm…I'm very sorry to disturb you, but I just…" She couldn't finish. Tears welled in the corners of her eyes. She blinked them away.

When she paused at the entrance to the house, the dragon spoke again. "Come in, come in, please. Never mind the dirt."

Milly stepped inside.

All interior walls of the house had been removed, as had the floor separating the garage from the bedrooms. The house was simply an enormous shell with a chimney at one end and the garage at the other. There, coiled beside a brand-new Porche, was the dragon. A fire burned in the fireplace—the only light other than the streetlights which leaked through the venetian blinds strung over all the windows. In this light, she could see the dragon's scales were russet-gold, his claws long and black, and his wingspan must have been enormous. From tail to head, she guessed it was about fifty feet long, maybe more. Its head was an array of back-angled horns and steak-knife sized fangs. Its eyes glowed like embers and it smelled very much like burning coal and rotting eggs.

The ember eyes focused on the gold bar. "Put that on the ground, please."

Milly did as she was told. "I'm sorry."

The dragon's eyes opened wide. "For what? For the dwarves?"

"Y-yes."

The dragon leaned down so its snout was no more than a few feet from her own. She could feel its breath, hot as a furnace. "But you didn't *know.* Why should you be sorry for that?"

Milly felt tears trickle down her cheeks. She was trembling. "Please, if you'll just let me go—"

"You don't want to talk?" The dragon blinked slowly. "Whyever did you come?"

Milly took a deep breath. "There's a lot of gold in…in my basement. It's yours."

"I know. Those dwarves—quite the nuisance. Anywhere a dragon tries to build a decent horde, there they are, trying to steal it. Can't keep them out, you know—they just *sing* the blasted earth open, and there they are, putting their grubby mitts all over everything." The dragon sighed, sending out a little puff of fire that came close to Milly. "Still, it's the risk I took, moving here."

"So you aren't angry?"

The dragon's eyes widened. "Of *course* I am! Dwarves in my horde? Gah! Disgusting! Still, they're dead now, so the matter is closed."

Milly took a deep breath. "Oh, well, then I guess I'll just be going…"

The dragon's tail shifted to block her exit. "I didn't say I was done with you *yet*, Milly Petersen. I have some questions for you."

Milly said nothing. She wondered at the prospects of her running for it. How far would she get? What would happen if she jumped in the Porche? Would it barbeque its own property to stop her from speeding away? Would it need to?

The dragon pointed a claw at the gold bar. "*Why* did you bring that back?"

Milly looked down at it. She searched for the words. "Because I'm not a thief."

The dragon snorted, which caused Milly to duck for cover as a spurt of fire shot out. "What? *WHAT?*" The dragon opened its mouth wide and Milly thought she was dead until she realized this was an expression of shock. The dragon was *shocked* by her.

Milly shrugged. "It's not mine. The gold, I mean. I couldn't steal it."

"Ridiculous. You're playing a prank." The dragon's eyes narrowed. "I hate pranks. That's why I lit that boy on fire on Halloween."

Milly blinked. "Cameron Bishop? I thought he was playing with firecrackers."

"Tried to TP my lawn, the odious thing. He only *told* everyone the firecracker bit."

Milly shook her head. "How do you even know about this? You never go out!"

"I have very good hearing." The dragon said, "and I *do* go out. Just after all you people are sleeping. The last thing I need is Chessie Vormount criticizing the state of my haunch scales."

"Why would she—"

"Don't feign ignorance!" The dragon snarled. "You were there, too, you know! What kind of a thing is it to put *scale cleaner* in a welcome gift, I ask you? She thinks I'm filthy, and you *know* it! She says it all the time—that 'filthy' dragon, she says. Bah! So maybe I'm not as beautiful as I was in the old days, but that old hag isn't much better! At least I don't need to inject *poison* into my face to keep it from drooping off!"

Milly could scarcely believe she was hearing this. "You…listen to us? All the time?"

"Of course." The dragon shook its head side-to-side. "You're changing the subject! Why didn't you steal the gold! If any woman needs money, it's you! You can barely afford *Pittsburgh*, Milly! You're going to wind up living in your sister's basement, and you know what a bad influence her Peter is going to be on Billy!"

It was Milly's turn for her mouth to drop open. "That's none of your *business!*"

"You're my neighbor—of *course* it's my business. What's the point of having neighbors, then?"

"Neighbors don't pry into people's personal business!" Milly snapped.

The dragon laughed, which caused the biggest gout of flame yet. It caught one of the support beams on fire, but the dragon doused it quickly with a swat of a vast wing. "Don't give me that! It's the *exclusive* thing neighbors do. Chessie Vormount is always—"

"Chessie's not a good example!"

"Fine! Fu, then—did you know he's been trying to find you a husband?"

Milly gaped. *"What?!"*

"Oh, yes—he pulled a picture off the internet and had it printed on some cards that he hands out to handsome men he sees in the park. It has the time and address of your speed dating group—every third Saturday at Pizza Palace, right?"

Milly put her hands to the sides of her face and began to pace across the bare floor. "Oh. My. God."

The dragon nodded. "I know. That old man is completely clueless. Even *I* know you're still grieving for Jack, and I'm not even human."

Milly glared at the dragon. "Okay, that's *it*! What the hell do you want from me, anyway?" She kicked the gold bar so it slid across the floor a few inches in the dragon's direction. "There's your stupid gold, okay? I want to go home!"

"Home?" The dragon snorted again. "In case you forgot, you haven't *got* one of those, Milly. The bank shows up on Monday. What has me itching, though, is that you've got millions of dollars in gold in your basement right now, and you bring some of it back here, to *me*. Why?"

"I told you. I'm not a thief."

"Everybody's a thief." The dragon narrowed its eyes. "Children steal the vitality of their parents, workers steal the riches of their masters, masters steal the toil of their workers—that's all life is, Milly Petersen: theft. And you're here, dropping a bar of my gold on my floor. Why? To prove you're a good person? Maybe to ask for a loan?" The dragon exhaled slowly, sending a heat ripple through the air that made Milly feel like she was under a hair-dryer. "Well *forget it*. No loan for you, Milly Petersen. Not a damned doubloon."

Milly backed away. She found herself pressed against the wall. "If I *had* stolen it, would you have let me get away with it?"

"Of course not. Ha! Let *dragon gold* into general circulation? Think of the devaluation!"

Milly snorted. "At least Chessie Vormount threw me a bake sale!"

"That was just so she'd look better when it came time to elect officers for the Lions Club the following week. Another theft, Milly, only this time of your dignity for her personal gain."

That one stung. Milly took a deep breath—she'd always known Chessie wasn't a true friend, of course, but still she had been touched by the gesture, no matter how pointless it had been. "I'm going to leave now."

The dragon curled itself up and sighed. It pulled its tail away from the door. "I'd appreciate it if you returned the rest of the gold."

"Another theft? My labor for *your* money?" Milly scowled, hand on the doorknob.

The dragon showed its teeth in a vicious grin. "It *would* be neighborly of you."

Milly rolled her eyes. "Send a mover and I'll leave the door unlocked. I'm not breaking my back for you."

The dragon dipped its head in assent. Milly turned to leave, but then stopped. "I have one more question: why did you move here? You could have lived anywhere—why *here*?"

The dragon half closed its eyes. "My kind are all so self-important, so self-involved. It gets…lonely." It sighed. "I wanted to get away from my own for a while."

Milly snorted, thinking of Chessie Vormount and her heels, of Mr. Fu and his constant meddling, of the Cohens and their insular success. "You know, I don't think you actually succeeded."

Two teams of movers came the next day: one for Milly and her last few things and the other for the dragon and his gold. The neighbors all turned out, but none of them helped her pack. They were too busy asking her about the men hauling those heavy sacks from her house and into the dragon's. She feigned ignorance, waved good-bye, and shook a few superficial hands.

Then she moved to Pittsburgh. After a year, she suspected no one there on the street remembered her name. She never cared to find out.

*Copyright © 2016 by Auston Habershaw*

*Kij Johnson won the Nebula in 2009, 2010 and 2012, as well as the 2012 Hugo. This is her third appearance in* Galaxy's Edge.

# PONIES

## by Kij Johnson

The invitation card has a Western theme. Along its margins, cartoon girls in cowboy hats chase a herd of wild Ponies. The Ponies are no taller than the girls, fat and bright as butterflies, with short, round-tipped unicorn horns and small fluffy wings. At the bottom of the card, newly caught Ponies mill about in a corral. The girls have lassoed a pink-and-white Pony. Its eyes and mouth are surprised round Os. There is an exclamation mark over its head.

The little girls are cutting off its horn with curved knives. Its wings are already removed, part of a pile beside the corral.

You and your Pony ___[and Sunny's name is handwritten here in puffy girl-letters]___ are invited to a cutting-out party with TheOtherGirls! If we like you, and if your Pony does okay, we'll let you hang out with us.

"Yay!" Sunny says. "I can't wait to have friends!" She reads over Barbara's shoulder, her rose-scented breath woofling through Barbara's hair. They are in the big backyard next to Sunny's pink stable.

Barbara says, "Do you know what you want to keep?"

Sunny's tiny wings are a blur as she hops into the air, loops and then hovers, legs curled under her. "Oh, being able to talk, absolutely! Flying is great but talking is way better!" She drops to the grass. "I don't know why any Pony would keep her horn! It's not like it does anything!"

This is the way it's always been, as long as there have been Ponies. All ponies have wings. All Ponies have horns. All Ponies can talk. Then all Ponies go to a cutting-out party with AllTheGirls and they give up two of the three, because that's what has to happen if a Girl is going to fit in with TheOtherGirls. The Ponies must all keep their voices because Barbara's never seen one that still had her horn or wings after her cutting-out party.

Barbara sees TheOtherGirls' Ponies all the time, peeking in the classroom windows just before recess or clustered at the bus stop after school. They're baby pink and lavender and daffodil-yellow, with flossy manes in ringlets and tails that curl to the ground. When not at school and cello lessons and ballet class and soccer practice and play group and the orthodontist's, TheOtherGirls spend their days with their Ponies.

The party is at TopGirl's house, which has a mother who's a pediatrician and a father who's a cardiologist and a small barn and giant trees shading the grass where the Ponies are playing games. Sunny walks out to them nervously. They touch her horn and wings with their velvet noses and then the Ponies all walk out to the lilac barn at the bottom of the pasture where a bale of hay is broken open for them.

TopGirl meets Barbara at the fence. "That's your Pony?" she says without greeting. "She's not as nice as mine."

Barbara is defensive. "She's beautiful!" She knows this is a misstep and adds, "Yours is so pretty!" And TopGirl's Pony Starblossom *is* pretty. Her tail is every shade of purple and glitters with stars; but Sunny's tail is creamy white and shines with honey-colored light, and Barbara knows that Sunny's the most beautiful Pony ever.

TopGirl walks away, saying over her shoulder, "There's Rock Band in the family room and a bunch of TheOtherGirls are hanging out on the deck and Mom bought some cookies and there's Coke Zero and Diet Red Bull and diet lemonade."

"Where are you?" Barbara asks.

"*I'm* outside," TopGirl says so Barbara gets a Crystal Light and three frosted raisin-oatmeal cookies and follows her. TheOtherGirls outside are listening to an iPod plugged into speakers and playing Wii tennis and watching the Ponies play HideAndSeek and Who'sPrettiest and ThisIsTheBestGame. They are all there, SecondGirl and SuckUpGirl and EveryoneLikesHerGirl and the rest. Barbara only says anything when she thinks she'll get it right. It seems as though it's going okay.

And then it's time. TheOtherGirls and their silent Ponies collect in a ring around Barbara and Sunny. Barbara feels sick.

TopGirl says to Barbara, "What did she pick?"

Sunny looks scared but answers her directly. "I would rather talk than fly or stab things with my horn."

TopGirl says to Barbara, "That's what Ponies always say." She gives Barbara a curved knife with a blade as long as a woman's hand.

*Me?* Barbara says. "I thought someone else did it, a grownup."

TopGirl says, "Everyone does it for their own Pony. I did it for Starblossom."

In silence Sunny stretches out a wing.

It's not the way it would be, cutting a real pony. The wing comes off easily, smooth as plastic, and the blood smells like cotton candy at the fair. There's a shiny trembling oval where the wing was as though Barbara cut rose-flavored Turkish Delight in half and saw the pink under the powdered sugar. Barbara thinks, *It is sort of pretty,* and throws up.

Sunny shivers, her eyes shut tight. Barbara cuts off the second wing and lays it beside the first.

The horn is harder, like paring a real pony's hooves. Barbara's hand slips and she cuts Sunny and there's more cotton-candy blood. And then the horn lies in the grass beside the wings.

Sunny drops to her knees. Barbara throws the knife down and falls beside her, sobbing and hiccupping. She scrubs her face with the back of her hand and looks up at the circle. "Now what?"

Starblossom touches the knife with her nose, pushes it toward Barbara with one lilac hoof. "You're not done yet," TopGirl says. "Now the voice. You have to take away her voice."

"But I already cut off her wings and her horn!" Barbara throws her arms around Sunny's neck. "Two of the three, 0you said!"

"That's the cutting-out, yeah," TopGirl says. "That's what *you* do to be OneOfUs. But the Ponies pick their own friends and that costs, too." Starblossom tosses her violet mane. For the first time Barbara sees that there is a scar shaped like a smile on her throat. All the Ponies have one.

"I can't!" Barbara tells TheOtherGirls, TopGirl, Starblossom, Sunny. But even as she cries until her face is caked with snot and tears, she knows she's going to. When she's done she picks up the knife and pulls herself upright.

Sunny stands up beside her on trembling legs. She looks very small without her horn, her wings. Barbara's hands are slippery. She tightens her grip.

"No," Sunny says suddenly. "Not even for friends. Not even for you."

And Sunny spins and runs, runs for the fence in a gallop as fast and beautiful as a real pony's. But there are more of the others and they are bigger, and Sunny doesn't have her wings to fly or her horn to fight. They pull her down before she can jump the fence into the woods beyond. Sunny cries out and then there is nothing, only the sound of pounding hooves from the tight circle of Ponies.

TheOtherGirls stand, frozen, their blind faces turned toward the Ponies.

The Ponies break their circle, trot away. There is no sign of Sunny beyond a spray of cotton-candy blood and a coil of her mane torn free and fading as it falls to the grass.

Into the silence TopGirl says, "Cookies?" Her voice sounds fragile and false. TheOtherGirls crowd into the house, chattering in equally artificial voices. They start up a game, drink more Diet Coke. Soon they sound almost normal.

Barbara stumbles after them into the family room. "What are you playing?" she says uncertainly.

"Why are *you* here?" FirstGirl says, as though noticing her for the first time. "You're not OneOfUs."

TheOtherGirls nod. "You don't have a pony."

*Copyright © 2010 by Kij Johnson*

**Sail to Success**

## www.SailSuccess.com

SINCE 2012

A UNIQUE WORKSHOP FOR SPECULATIVE FICTION ON BOARD A CRUISE SHIP

# THE SAIL TO SUCCESS WRITERS' WORKSHOP
## HELD EVERY DECEMBER

# WHAT MAKES THIS WORKSHOP UNIQUE?

**MIKE RESNICK**
*Award-Winning & Bestselling Author*

**NANCY KRESS**
*Award-Winning & Bestselling Author*

**JIM MINZ**
*Editor, Baen Books*

**ERIC FLINT**
*Award-Winning & Bestselling Author*

**2016 FACULTY**

**ELEANOR WOOD**
*Top NY Literary Agent*

**JACK SKILLINGSTEAD**
*Author/Teacher. 2014 Nominee for the Philip K. Dick Award*

1. World-class faculty returning—authors and industry decision makers.

2. Guaranteed buy of a story from at least one student by *Galaxy's Edge* Magazine.

3. Evaluation of manuscripts by the head of a major SF publishing house. A writer's dream to by-pass the slush pile.

4. One-on-one meal with a faculty member.

5. Special insight into writing for the 1632 universe by its creator.

6. Evaluation by a top NY literary agent.

7. Limited to 22 students.

*All this while visiting the Bahamas (with your family?) on a luxury cruise ship.*

# STUDENT COMMENTS

"Fantastic Experience. Love the combo of Workshop and Cruise, something both my husband and I could enjoy together."

"Sail to Success provided a unique opportunity to interact with publishers, editors, and agents. That rare, small group interaction was invaluable."

"Never before have I met such a fantastic, currently relevant and easy-to-talk-to group of movers and shakers! Thanks."

"Just wanted to say thanks again for a fabulous time on Sail to Success. I had a lovely meeting with Eleanor, got requests for fulls of two different novels, Jack has passed my name on to an antho editor, got to meet Nancy and Jim and reconnect with Mike and Eric. I couldn't have asked for anything more out of the week!"

"The Workshop packed a ridiculous amount of professional knowledge into a short time period. Intense and valuable!"

"The Workshop provides a unique and wonderful opportunity to interact with outstanding faculty, learn about many aspects of the writing business, and have a lot of fun!"

# www.SailSuccess.com

Early booking pricing starting at just **$891 (or just $99/month)** ALL INCLUSIVE (includes classes, material, cruise to the Bahamas, food, entertainment and much more).

### SCHEDULE FOR SAIL TO SUCCESS WRITERS' WORKSHOP DECEMBER 2015

**Monday, December 7** — Primary Administrative Duties: Shahid Mahmud

| Start | End | Dur | Session | Type | Faculty |
|---|---|---|---|---|---|
| 6:30 PM | 6:55 PM | 0:25 | Registration | Other | Shahid Mahmud, Ron Friedman, Eva Eldridge |
| 7:00 PM | 7:20 PM | 0:20 | Introductions | Other | All |
| 7:25 PM | 8:25 PM | 1:00 | Publishing Business 101 | Business | Mike Resnick, Eric Flint, Eleanor Wood |
| 8:30 PM | 9:30 PM | 1:00 | The Importance of Character Buildiing | Writing | Jack Skillingstead, Nancy Kress |
| | | 2:45 | | | |

**Tuesday, December 8** — Primary Administrative Duties: Shahid Mahmud

| Start | End | Dur | Session | Type | Faculty |
|---|---|---|---|---|---|
| 1:30 PM | 3:50 PM | 2:20 | Nancy Kress Manuscript Critique, Part 1 | Writing | Nancy Kress |
| 4:00 PM | 5:00 PM | 1:00 | Going it Yourself and Indie Publishing | Business | Shahid Mahmud, Jack Skillingstead |
| | | | DINNER | | |
| 7:00 PM | 9:20 PM | 2:20 | Jim Minz Manuscript Critique, Part 1 | Writing | Jim Minz |
| 9:30 PM | 10:30 PM | 1:00 | Working With Magazines & Anthologies | Business | Mike Resnick, Jack Skillingstead, Eric Flint |
| 10:35 PM | 11:00 PM | 0:25 | Getting Past the Magazine Slush Reader | Business | Mike Resnick |
| | | 7:05 | | | |

**Wednesday, December 9** — Primary Administrative Duties: Ron Friedman

| Start | End | Dur | Session | Type | Faculty |
|---|---|---|---|---|---|
| 1:15 PM | 1:55 PM | 0:40 | Query Letters and Contracts | Business | Eleanor Wood, Eric Flint |
| 2:00 PM | 3:00 PM | 1:00 | The Professional Approach to Writing | Writing | Eric Flint, Nancy Kress, Jack Skillingstead |
| 3:00 PM | 3:40 PM | 0:40 | Bridge Tour | Writing | SIGN UP NEEDED |
| 3:45 PM | 5:10 PM | 1:25 | Working with Editors/Publishers/Agents | Business | Jim Minz, Mike Resnick, Eric Flint, Eleanor Wood |
| | | | DINNER | | |
| 7:00 PM | 7:40 PM | 0:40 | Developing Property Rights | Business | Mike Resnick, Eleanor Wood |
| 7:50 PM | 10:10 PM | 2:20 | Jim Minz Manuscript Critique, Part 2 | Writing | Jim Minz |
| 10:20 PM | 11:00 PM | 0:40 | Tips to Increase Productivity | Writing | Mike Resnick, Jack Skillingstead |
| | | 7:25 | | | |

**Thursday, December 10** — Primary Administrative Duties: Eva Eldritch

| Start | End | Dur | Session | Type | Faculty |
|---|---|---|---|---|---|
| 1:30 PM | 3:50 PM | 2:20 | Nancy Kress Manuscript Critique, Part 2 | Writing | Nancy Kress |
| 4:00 AM | 5:00 AM | 1:00 | The 1632 Universe: Intro and How to Write for It | Writing | Eric Flint |
| | | | DINNER | | |
| 6:45 PM | 8:00 PM | 1:15 | Sharpening Your Prose: An Exercise | Writing | Jack Skillingstead |
| 8:05 PM | 9:05 PM | 1:00 | What Type of a Writer Do You Want To Be? | Writing | Mike Resnick, Jack Skillingstead |
| 9:10 PM | 10:00 PM | 0:50 | My Funniest Publishing Story Plus Closing | Other | All |

*Zach Shephard has been published in* Intergalactic Medicine Show, Daily Science Fiction *and* Unidentified Funny Objects 4. *This is his first appearance in* Galaxy's Edge.

# TOMORROW'S FORECAST

## by Zach Shephard

SUNSHINE: "Attention! The meeting to decide tomorrow's weather is now in session."

WIND: "A good storm's what we need. One last bluster before summer."

RAIN: "Seconded!"

SUNSHINE: "You boys and your storms. You're adorable."

WIND: "Stop treating us like children. We're still legitimate weather systems at this time of year."

SUNSHINE: "Oh, please. You're moving about as much air as a clogged bagpipe. And I'm fairly certain Rain is suffering from dehydration."

RAIN: "I *am* a little thirsty..."

WIND: "If we work together, we might beat you."

SUNSHINE: "Or you might throw out your back again and spend the whole summer howling. No, I think you should take Snow's lead. She had the decency to stay home instead of dragging this out. I hereby vote for a sunny day."

BOB GRONSWICK: "Seconded."

WIND: "What the...Who are you?"

BOB: "I'm Bob. Hi."

RAIN: "This is awkward."

SUNSHINE: "Don't be rude. It's been centuries since a mortal has witnessed our meeting. What if he has something interesting to say?"

WIND: "I'm sure it'll be mind-blowing."

RAIN: "I'm dripping with anticipation."

SUNSHINE: "Hush. Tell us, Bob—what brings you here?"

BOB: "Well, I heard you arguing about the weather, so I figured I'd get my vote in for a sunny day. I'm proposing to my girlfriend tomorrow, and I want everything to be perfect."

SUNSHINE: "Oh, that is *adorable!* How could we say no?"

WIND: "This is ridiculous."

SUNSHINE: "Not as ridiculous as you thinking you can beat me this close to summer."

BOB: "Please, don't fight—I just want pleasant weather. Maybe 75 degrees, with no wind or rain."

WIND: "You know what? Fine. Rain and I will concede, but only if you'll do us some favors."

BOB: "Like what?"

WIND: "You know the forest down the road? I've been trying to blow over the tallest tree there, but it won't budge. Chop it down for me."

BOB: "Okay."

RAIN: "Ooh! And that umbrella shop in town has been a real thorn in my side. Please drop a hydrogen bomb on the building."

BOB: "Uh..."

WIND: "Or maybe just leave them a bad review online?"

RAIN: "That's good too."

BOB: "Can do."

SUNSHINE: "Wonderful! I'm so excited. Look at me—I'm glowing! Now run along, and come back as soon as you're done."

✿

SUNSHINE: "Welcome back! How'd everything go?"

BOB: "Not well."

WIND: "What do you mean?"

BOB: "It was just such a nice tree! I couldn't stand to see it go."

WIND: "So you did nothing?"

BOB: "I went to the ranger station and donated to their wind-turbine fundraiser. Does that count?"

WIND: "You didn't fell the tree, and now you're using my power to help those who protect it?"

BOB: "Huh. When you put it that way, I can see why you might be upset."

RAIN: "What about the umbrella store? Is it a crater now?"

BOB: "Um..."

RAIN: "Wait! What's that behind your back?"

BOB: "I couldn't resist! It was on sale. And look at the pattern: they're little umbrellas holding *even smaller umbrellas*. Too cute to pass up."

RAIN: "You were supposed to have a terrible experience and leave a bad review!"

BOB: "I ended up taking selfies with the umbrella and posting them on my blog. Sorry."

RAIN: "You're awful!"

WIND: "This blows!"

SUNSHINE: "Don't be so hard on poor Bob. He tried his best."

BOB: "That reminds me..."

SUNSHINE: "Yes?"

BOB: "I stopped by the museum today and visited the Egyptian exhibit. They had a jar painted with images of Ra."

SUNSHINE: "Wonderful! Did you get a picture?"

BOB: "Here."

SUNSHINE: "No! Why is the sun god's image shattered?"

BOB: "In my defense, they shouldn't have put a valuable artifact on such a wobbly pedestal. But believe me, the jar was really cool. You'd be able to see the finer details if I'd taken the picture before I dropped my nachos on the shards."

SUNSHINE: "This is inexcusable! Tomorrow you'll have no sun at all! The temperature won't rise above thirty degrees!"

WIND: "And there'll be wind!"

RAIN: "And rain!"

SUNSHINE: "Get out of our sight, Bob! And may your proposal be miserable!"

BOB: "Okay—it's done. They were pretty pissed, and tomorrow's forecast is now calling for a blizzard."

SNOW: "Fantastic!"

BOB: "You're sure you can hold up your end of the bargain?"

SNOW: "Don't worry, darling—December is my month. You'll have a white Christmas, no matter what the others say!"

*Copyright © 2016 by Zach Shephard*

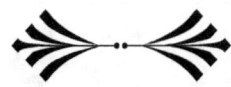

*Nick DiChario is a Hugo, Campbell, and a World Fantasy Award nominee, as well as the author of two award-nominated novels. This is his third appearance in* Galaxy's Edge, *the first in a new series of modern-day Italian folktales he's been writing.*

# STITCHES

## by Nick DiChario

Mara and Odo married when they were sixteen years old in the small Italian village known as *il villaggio di Ombri.*

Mara was a childish romantic who dreamed of love, one of seven children who wanted to be swept away to a castle on the sea. Odo was an only child who had come late to his parents—strong, confident, mature for his age, eager to start his own family and prove himself capable in the world.

Odo, like his father, like many of the other men in the village, grew up fishing on the Mediterranean at his father's side. Now that he was married, he needed to borrow money from the bank to buy his first dory, one of the small fishing boats the locals called *le pescherecce.* So one day Odo and his father walked into the bank while the other fishermen in town gathered outside on the sidewalk and waited.

When the two men emerged, Odo's loan secured, the men patted him on the back and led him to the tavern for his first official tankard of *birra* as a man. It was a ritual all the young fishermen went through. They cared little for the sports and games, music, dancing, parties, and fast cars that seemed to captivate the young people in other towns. It was dories they wanted—*le pescherecce.* In *il villaggio di Ombri,* it was not the *signorine* who turned boys into men, but rather the bankers who gave them the loans for their first boats. So it was with Odo.

✧

The young couple moved into Odo's grandfather's house, which had been empty since the old man died. Although it was little more than a shack, to Mara it was the castle she'd always dreamed of, and Odo saw it as the foundation of his new life. They did what they could to make the house their own. Mara and her mother fashioned new drapes and curtains, and coverings for the musty old furniture, while Odo and his father repaired shutters, loose boards, and replaced the sagging shingles on the roof.

Mara was an excellent seamstress. Her mother had begun teaching her to sew from the moment Mara could hold a needle and thread in her tiny fingers. Now she would be expected to make money and contribute a small amount to the household income as Odo struggled to earn a wage from his daily catch.

One afternoon while working, Odo and his father found Grandfather's old fishing net in the ramshackle shed behind the house. Odo was excited to discover it and promised to begin patching and knotting the ancient nettle-hemp rope. "*Nonno* would be proud of you," Odo's father said. "As I am."

✧

One might think that the life of fishing families was the same for everyone, wrought with the daily demands of a fishing economy, up before dawn, catching fish at sea in the morning and selling their catch at the market in the afternoon, and then cleaning and maintaining boats and equipment until nightfall. But the families that shared these lives filled them with small rituals that made their days unique, personal, and special unto themselves.

Mara and Odo woke together each morning and dressed in the darkness of their small bedroom, the smell of brine and ancient wood in the air. Mara prepared breakfast while Odo made coffee on the stove. After breakfast they went out together to launch the dory. Mara carried an old fishing rod she'd found among Odo's grandfather's belongings, and Odo carried the gear he would need for the day.

When they reached the dock, Mara baited the hook and cast the line in a graceful, sweeping arc into the sea. If she caught two fish in the morning for their supper, Odo wouldn't need to take two fish out of his nets before he went to the market.

"Happy fishing," Odo said to Mara.

"Happy fishing," Mara answered.

Then they kissed lightly on the lips and separated.

But here, too, is where their hearts divided—Mara the romantic and Odo the conqueror. Mara's lips trembled for fear that she might never see him again.

*This kiss, on this morning*, she couldn't help thinking, *might be the last. A storm or some other horror at sea could steal my Odo away forever.*

"Don't worry," Odo said, tasting her fear. "There's no danger for a good fisherman on the sea. No matter what happens out there," he motioned vaguely at the line where the sea met the horizon, "I will always come home to you. I promise." Then he took her hand and placed it over his chest where she could feel the steady, reassuring beat of his heart.

The kiss shared, the promise delivered, their ritual complete, Odo climbed aboard his dory and shoved off.

But the last part of the ritual belonged to Mara alone. She held Odo's heartbeat in her hand long after they waved goodbye. She squeezed it down so far into the palm of her hand that she would be able to hold it there all day, feel it beating gently under her skin, until Odo returned safely home. This was how she knew he was alive and well even when they were apart, separated by the sea.

⚙

One day a storm blew in while the men were out fishing. As soon as the sky darkened and the rain began to fall, the women ran to shore to wait for their husbands to return home. They clutched each other's hands and shivered as thunder sounded and lightning struck, as gusts of wind blew back their hair in swirling strands and snapped their skirts like flags.

Slowly the dories returned, one by one, bobbing like drunken buoys on the chopping waters. One by one the wives broke the chain of hands, ran to their husbands, hugged them and wept with relief as the men stepped out of their boats. All the other couples walked away until only Mara and her mother-in-law remained gazing out at the crashing waves.

Finally, another dot appeared on the water, laboring its way to shore, listing drunkenly. By the time the dory reached the dock, Mara could see there was only one man aboard.

Exhausted and drenched, her father-in-law stumbled forward. His wife ran to him and helped him walk up the shore while Mara, wringing her hands, stood and watched. The old man came to her and stood unsteadily in the wind. He was a broken mast, his face grim and sad, longer and older than she'd ever seen it.

"Daughter," he said. "I'm so sorry. I don't know how to tell you. Odo. The fishing was bad in the harbor. He went farther out than anyone else hoping to fill his nets. He knew better, but he was fearless. My Odo. I tried to hail him when the sky darkened, but he was too far out. I went after him, but the storm blew me back in. I couldn't reach him. I'm sorry."

Mara allowed herself to be led back to her house, where her in-laws wanted to stay with her and comfort her in her grief, and perhaps be comforted themselves, but she asked them to leave after a time.

"Don't worry," Mara said, hoping to reassure them. "My Odo is not dead."

"You must face the truth," the old man said. "It will be easier for you if you do."

"Did you see his boat go down?" she asked. "Did you see him drown?"

He shook his head sadly. "No, but I'm no stranger to storms on the Mediterranean. The sea has taken him. We take what we want from the sea, and then there comes a time when the sea takes what it wants from us. This is the way of things. You're not the first wife to suffer such a loss, and you won't be the last."

"I'm sorry you feel that way," she said. Mara knew what her in-laws could not have known, what she could not begin to explain to them. She still felt the soft beat of Odo's heart in the palm of her hand. Odo was alive. "Odo promised me he'd always come home no matter what happened at sea. I believe him. He'll be back."

⚙

That night, Mara slept the deep and dreamless sleep of the dead, *il sonno dei morti*, and woke before dawn with the thump of Odo's heart still in her hand. She decided to keep their rituals as much as she could and carried the grandfather's fishing rod to shore. She baited her hook and cast the line out to sea. The storm had passed. The sky was clear. She could see for miles. She watched the fishermen launch their dories one at a time into the soft blue waves. There was no sign of Odo, but Mara was not worried.

For three mornings it went like this. She woke with Odo's heartbeat in her hand, set out before dawn to cast her line, watched the boats come and go, and caught nothing. Her mother visited bearing food and more sewing work than usual to help Mara keep her mind off the tragedy. But there was no tragedy in Mara's mind, and she was happy for the extra work. Odo would be pleased when he returned to find that she'd earned some money for the household while he was away. She looked forward to showing him her full purse.

Her in-laws came to check on her, their eyes red with strain, their faces lined with grief, urging her to leave the house on the seashore and return to her parents' home where she could get on with her life. The rescuers had found no sign of Odo or his dory and had given up the search.

"It's over," her father-in-law said. For the first time Mara noticed how the sea and the wind had hardened his face, how thin and tough was his brow, the roughly tanned neck and ears, the deep crows' nests at the corners of his eyes, his hard, dry lips and tawny complexion. The fisherman's life had made him so handsome! *Odo will look like this someday*, she thought, hiding her smile.

On the third day, Mara caught three fish. This was a good omen. If the fish were returning to the harbor, Odo might be, too. She went back to the house to clean the fish and prepare a meal just in case Odo was home in time for dinner. But when she gutted the belly of the first fish, a human toe fell out.

She recoiled from it. The toe looked like Odo's big left toe, large-knuckled and bent slightly inward. No. It couldn't be. Could it? She looked down at her palm, felt Odo's heartbeat there, thumping gently just under the surface of her skin. Alive. He was still alive. He must be!

She wiped her brow and went to work on the second fish. And an ear fell out. *That could be anyone's ear*, she thought, although the lobe was long, like Odo's. When she gutted the third fish, a human finger fell out. It was Odo's finger. His wedding ring was still wrapped around it.

Her hands trembled. She dropped the knife. How does one make sense of a thing like this? The mind begins to construct scenarios. Mara's mind went swiftly to work. Perhaps things were not as bad as they seemed. Odo had told her that he would return to her no matter what happened at sea. Maybe he was trying to come home inside the fish.

Mara ran to shore with the rod, cast the line again, and in a short time caught more fish. She brought them inside and cut them open and found Odo's ear and kidney. She ran out again, cast her line, but no more fish would bite.

She began to fear that the fish with Odo inside would escape her—she would never be able to catch them all with a single line—so she went to the grandfather's shed and dragged out his tattered old fishing net. There were gaping holes in it, but Odo had begun repairing it using the clove-hitch and sheet-bend knots his father had taught him, and she was sure she could catch many fish in it.

She hauled the heavy net out to the dock and cast it into the sea. Its stone sinkers and thick ropes weighed it down. It took all her strength to throw it out and tow it back in. But she was determined.

Mara caught dozens of fish this way. Frantically cut them open. Found pieces of her husband's arms and legs and torso. Found his lips and nose and elbows. All day long she sliced open fish after fish and ran out to catch more. She set the pieces of Odo out on her worktable like a puzzle waiting to be assembled.

She dragged in as many fish as she could, worked tirelessly through the night, searching for more of her husband, finding his eyes and neck and ankles and feet, finding bits of flesh and bone. While she worked, tiny fish bones pricked her fingers, turning her hands into crimson pincushions. By the end of the night, she reeked of fish and was sodden with blood and guts and scales.

Finally, her adrenaline spent, she collapsed from exhaustion and slept for a long time.

And then, when she woke, she began stitching.

There would be no hiding the stitches, of course. There were so many pieces of Odo, and none of his parts fit as well as they had before, the fish having taken so much and returned so little. In many places, Mara's seams were deep and wide and, for lack of a better word, grisly. But when Mara finished her work, there was no doubt it was Odo. The round cheeks. The sunken, serious eyes. The thin lips and strong chin. His chest and back and legs were mostly ragged thread, although she'd done her best to weave in his flesh and bones where she could. The legs were uneven (she'd caught only one knee). He would walk with a limp, no doubt.

She was sorry about the stitches in his head, which made his face look a bit like a patchwork quilt, but there was no helping it considering what she'd had to work with. Anyone who knew good sewing would understand what a difficult job it had been and how well she'd done putting Odo back together.

But how to make him rise? He lay on her work-table no more animated than a slab of meat. She hadn't caught his heart, but she could still feel his heartbeat in her palm, so she knew he was alive. How was she to get Odo's heart from her hand into his body?

She lifted her husband's hand and squeezed it. "Odo, please, tell me what to do!"

That was when he moved. His eyes blinked, his legs twitched, and his muscles rippled and popped.

"Odo!" Mara cried. "You're alive! I *knew* you were alive!"

But when she let go of his hand to hug him, he fell dead again. She snatched up his hand once more and watched the life flow back into his body. She had to hold his hand, press his heart into his palm, to make him come alive. That was the secret! That was the key! Each morning Odo had handed his heart to her for safekeeping, so she could hand it back to him if he ever needed it again. Now that time had come. Hand to hand. Heart to heart. *Amore a amore.*

Mara helped Odo sit up, and then stand, and then walk. He seemed to understand her when she spoke, although there was no expression on his face, no sparkle in his cold, steady eyes, and he could not answer her. All he could do was move his jaw slowly, uselessly mimicking her.

No matter. Odo was alive. And Mara had given him life. He'd tried so hard to come home to her, just as he'd promised, and now they were reunited. Surely he would get better in time. She couldn't wait for her mother to see him, and Odo's parents, and the people in the village.

✧

Mara dressed Odo in his finest clothes. She wanted him to look his best when they walked together hand-in-hand into *il villaggio di Ombri*. She could

not wash the stink of rotting fish from his body, but she didn't think that anyone would care about that once they saw him. Wasn't it more important that he'd returned? A little stink would be nothing to the people of the village, who were accustomed to the smell of fish and rot.

As they made their way down Main Street, windows and doors flew open, people gawked, parents gasped and hid their children, shopkeepers talked in hushed, urgent tones. Word spread quickly through the village.

While Mara went about her shopping in the market, she smiled and talked to her husband as she bought squash and potatoes and flour, handing bags to Odo to carry, failing to notice the horror etched in the eyes of others, all the while holding her husband's hand to keep his heart beating.

Odo, with his cold, dead gaze and lifeless motions, looked no more alive than a marionette. The stall-keepers turned their noses at his horrible stench. The same people who spent all day with the smell of decapitated fish filling their nostrils, with overflowing buckets of viscera spilling from their *carrettini* into the gutters at their feet, their aprons soaked in blood, how could they turn up their noses at Odo?

Odo's parents had heard the news and arrived at the market just as Mara finished filling her bags. They rushed over to her.

"Daughter," Odo's father said, grabbing her shoulders. "What have you done?"

"Isn't it wonderful? Odo lives!"

"Dear God," Odo's mother said. "That's not Odo. Whatever it is, it's not alive. It's a monster. Can't you see that?"

Mara shook her head. *What's wrong with these people?* "I thought you would be pleased. This is your son. My husband. Don't you recognize him? You should be grateful he's come back from the sea."

"He hasn't come back from the sea," her father-in-law said, tears clouding his eyes. "He's come back from the *dead*. It's not natural. It's not right. I don't know how you've done it, but this...this...*thing* is not our son. Can't you smell it? You must return it to the sea."

"No! How can you say that?" She jerked away, tugging Odo along with her. "Come, Odo."

The other people began to scold her. "You blind fool!" they shouted. "He belongs to the dead! Give him back!"

She started to run. Odo stumbled. His legs were stiff and uneven, and he didn't seem to understand her urgency. "Hurry!" she cried. Odo dropped the bags. The potatoes rolled out onto the street. The flour bag broke into a mound of snow.

The people shouted after her: "Wicked girl! *Ragazza malvagia!* Stop them! Don't let them get away!"

The villagers rushed her and yanked her husband's hand out of her grip. Odo fell limp, as boneless as an eel. She screamed, but they held her down as the men carried Odo to the docks, laid him in a dory, and sailed him out to sea. The same men who once congratulated him when he'd secured the loan for his dory. The same men who once patted him on the back and bought him his first tankard of *birra*. Now they took him out to bury him at sea.

Her in-laws tried to calm her, but she was hysterical until a doctor arrived with a syringe and gave her a shot. Then the world spun out from under her in a dark, shadowy wave, and pulled her down into unconsciousness.

✧

Mara woke in her old bed at her parents' house, in the room she once shared with her two younger sisters. Her mother was watching over her, a look of kind concern on her face. She might have been crying. It was hard to tell. People who lived by the sea always looked as if their eyes were damp.

She brushed back Mara's hair and forced a weak smile. "Welcome home, *mia figlia*. You'll live with us now. We've moved your sisters upstairs so you can have this room to yourself."

Mara didn't answer. The house was too crowded before she'd married Odo. Giving her a room of her own was a burden to the family. But she didn't care. It wouldn't be for long. Her life was over. Odo's heartbeat was gone from her hand. It was the first thing she'd noticed upon waking. There was no chance of his coming back to her again. It was too late. He was dead.

"You're a young girl," her mother went on. "You have a long life ahead of you. Odo would have wanted you to be strong and carry on."

Not true. Odo would have wanted her to be with him, or he would never have tried so hard to come back to her. It was the outside world that had kept them apart. What was left for her now? She would be no more than a stray dog in this village, shunned and pitied. Mara had no intention of living in a world where Odo's heart no longer beat for her.

That night, she waited until everyone fell asleep, and then she slipped out of the house and returned to her castle by the seashore. She put on her wedding dress, went to the ramshackle shed, and hauled the grandfather's old fishing net onto the dock. There she wrapped the net around her shoulders and gazed up at the luminous moon glow that set the water unnaturally afire. She looked down at her hand one last time. Squeezed it into a fist. Closed her eyes. Waited to feel the beat of Odo's heart.

Nothing.

There was no more for her to do, then, but go to her husband.

She jumped into the sea. The stone sinkers and heavy ropes dragged her down to the bottom and trapped her under the net. Mara felt much like she did when she'd been drugged at the market, only this time it was the shadow of the Mediterranean that closed in over her head, and she would not be waking in her old bedroom ever again.

✧

The next day, a freighter picked up Odo out in the shipping channel. He clung, barely breathing, to a buoy as the sea captain hauled him aboard. It was a miracle he'd been found at all let alone found alive. His head was badly cut, his body bleeding from horrible gashes, and he fell in and out of consciousness as the ship's doctor tended his wounds.

Odo's rescue was, at first, joyous news to everyone in *il villaggio di Ombri*, but when Mara's body was discovered under the dock, it quickly became an impossible tragedy to bear. By mutual and silent consent, the villagers chose not to speak of the day Mara brought Odo's ghoul to the market, thinking it would be better for Odo never to hear such a story, and, no doubt, frightened at how much the stitches in Odo's head resembled those Mara had given him.

When he was well enough, Odo returned to fishing. Because he no longer had a dory of his own, he'd go out each morning with his father. They'd sell their catch in the afternoon, and work together until nightfall. Life must go on. Life did go on. Odo was a practical man by nature. Soon, when his father was ready to retire, he purchased the dory and married Mara's sister, Mina.

Mina was a year younger and looked very much like Mara. But the differences soon became apparent to Odo. Mina was a size smaller than Mara in all aspects—eyes, nose, ears, mouth, body, and spirit. She was neither as quick-witted nor as interested in the personal rituals that had been so important to Mara. Although Mina was a good cook, and adept with a broom, she had no facility with needle and thread.

Odo missed Mara's childlike attachment to romance, which Mina did not possess. He yearned for the taste of fear on Mara's trembling lips. Mina had neither the imagination nor inspiration to fear. It was Mara, he realized, who'd possessed the secrets in her heart that made him want to rise out of bed every morning and fight for their lives together rather than just live another day of it.

As the days and months and years marched on, Odo began to wonder if he was somehow living a diminished copy of his life, just as he'd acquired a diminished copy of Mara. Each morning during the first few seconds of wakefulness, he felt as if he were on the cusp of rising into a new reality. This new reality was a kind of enlightenment waiting for him, an explanation that would reveal the grand delusion he'd been laboring under for so long. In these moments, he was sure he was about to wake not from sleep, but from death itself into the truth of all existence. But the moments always passed quickly, a mere whisper away.

Such flashes continued to haunt him as the children grew, as he walked his son to the bank to secure the loan for his first dory, and as he married off his daughters one by one. The moments continued to haunt him as the grandchildren visited and scrabbled about the house like stone crabs, and Mina grew stooped and round of shoulder, and Odo became too old to fish on the sea. For whatever reason, he was living a shadow of his life, and the people in it were silhouettes, while his true life waited just out of reach.

Eventually, Odo took to sitting for long hours on the dock, his grandfather's fishing rod perched beside him, waiting for the fish to bite. As time went on he'd sit longer and longer into the night, hypnotized by the constellations and the sound of the sea sloshing dark circles around him, convincing him to fall asleep until morning. During his darkest moments, Odo could feel the barest hint of a heartbeat in the palm of his hand, and he often wondered if it was Mara somehow calling to him.

Then, one lonely night, as the sun fell into the Mediterranean, as the moon climbed high above it, as the fog rolled in, Odo heard a soft creaking sound echo across the water. He knew the sound of a dory better than any other sound in the world, but it was unusual for a fisherman to be out so late at night, especially without a lamp. He peered into the darkness for a while but could see nothing through the fog, so he finally stood and walked to the edge of the dock.

A man never forgets his first dory, no more than he forgets his first love. The curve of its spine, the way the prow breaks the waves, the flaking patches of paint on the hull, even the sound it makes in the water. Each dory speaks its own language. There was no doubt in Odo's mind. This was his first beloved *il peschereccio.*

The dory crept closer, seeming to move of its own will. There was no motor propelling it, no oars lapping in the waves. But he saw someone sitting tall, still as a ghost, draped in the chill night fog. Odo stared at the figure through the gloom until he was sure his vision hadn't betrayed him. Then the strength drained from his legs, and he dropped to his knees. The dory slid gently, silently to the dock and stopped in front of him.

"Mara, is that you?" Odo asked, his voice trembling. "Dear God, is it really you? How can it be?"

Mara stood and stared into his eyes. She was as young and beautiful as the day they'd married. In fact, she was wearing her wedding dress. But there was something different about her, too. Her face was expressionless. She seemed little more than a body, a fluid statuette, and her eyes were cold, dark, deep, and empty, like the sea itself. And she carried the faint but unmistakable odor of death.

Mara reached out and took Odo's hand in hers. Her touch chilled him to the bone and sent him shivering, and then Odo felt the heartbeat in his palm come alive and throb wildly under his skin.

"Come with me, Odo," she said in her watery voice. "It's time for us to be together again."

*My love*, Odo thought, *my true life has come for me at last.*

✿

In *il villaggio di Ombri*, it's said that when the people take what they want from the sea, there comes a time when the sea takes what it wants from the people. So no one was surprised when, one morning after the fog lifted from the shores of the Mediterranean, Odo was gone from the dock, never to be seen again.

*Copyright © 2016 by Nick DiChario*

*George R. R. Martin has won four Hugos and has been a Worldcon Guest of Honor. These days he is arguably the bestselling SF and fantasy writer of all time, and one of the bestselling writers in the world.*

# FAST-FRIEND

## by George R. R. Martin

Brand woke in darkness, trembling, and called out. His angel came to him.

She floated above him, smiling, on wings of soft gauze gold. Her face was all innocence, the face of a lovely girl-child, softness and light and wide amber eyes and honeyed hair that moved sinuously in free-fall. But her body was a woman's, smooth and slim and perfect; a toy woman fashioned on a smaller scale.

"Brand," she said, as she hovered above his sleep-web. "Will you show me the fast-friends today?"

He smiled up at her, his dreams fading. "Yes, angel," he said. "Yes, today, I'm sure of it. Now come to me."

But she moved back when he reached for her, coy, teasing. Her blush was a creeping tide of gold, and her hair danced in silken swirls. "Oh, Brand," she said. Then, as he cursed and reached to unsnap his web, she giggled at him and pouted. "You can't have me," she said, in her child's voice. "I'm too little."

Brand laughed, grabbed a nearby handbar to pull himself free of the web, then whipped himself around it toward the angel. He was good in free-fall, Brand; he'd had ten years of practice. But the angel had wings.

They flowed and rippled as she darted to one side, just beyond his reach. He twisted around in midair, so he hit the wall with his legs. Then, immediately, he kicked off again. The angel giggled and brushed him with her wings as he flew by. Brand hit the ceiling with a thump and groaned.

"Ooo," she said. "Brand, are you hurt?" And she was at his side, her wings beating quickly.

He grinned and put his arms around her. "No," he said, "but I've got you. Since when is my angel a tease, eh?"

"Oh, Brand," she said. "I'm sorry. I was only playing. I was gonna come to you." She was trying to look hurt, but despite her best efforts, a tiny smile escaped the corner of her mouth.

He pulled her to him, hard, and pressed her strange coolness against his own heat. This time there was no reluctance. Her delicate hands went behind him, to hold him tight while he kissed her.

Floating, nude, they joined, and Brand felt the soft caress of wings.

☼

When they were finished, Brand went to his locker to dress. The angel hovered nearby, her wings barely moving, her small breasts still flushed with gold.

"You're so *pretty*," she told him, as he pulled on a dull black coverall. "Why do you hide, Brand? Why can't you stay like me, so I can see you?"

"A human thing, angel," he said, hardly listening to her chatter. He'd heard it all before. His boots made a metallic click as they pulled him to the floor.

"You're beautiful, Brand," the angel murmured, but he only nodded at her. Only angels said that of him. Brand was close to thirty, but he looked older; lines on a wide forehead, thin lips set in a too-characteristic frown, dark eyes under heavy eyebrows, and hair that curled tight against his scalp in sculptured ringlets.

When he was dressed, he paused briefly, then opened a lockbox welded to the locker wall. Inside was his pendant. He took it out and stared. The disc filled his hand, a coolness of polished black crystal with a myriad of tiny silver flakes locked within. The pale silver chain it hung from curled up and away, and floated in the air like a metal snake.

He remembered then how it had been, in the old days, under gravity. The chain was heavy then, and the crystal stone had a solid heft to it. Yet he'd worn it always, as Melissa had worn its twin. And he wanted to wear it now, but it was such a nuisance in free-fall. Without weight, it refused to hang neatly around his neck; instead it bobbed about constantly.

Finally, sighing, he slipped the chain over his head, pulled the crystal tight against his neck, then twisted the chain and doubled it over again and again. When he was finished the stone was secure, now more a choker than a pendant. It was uncomfortable. But it was the best he could do.

The angel watched him in silence, trembling a little. She'd seen him handle the black crystal before. Sometimes he'd sit in his sleep-web for hours, the stone floating above him. He'd stare into its depths, at the frozen dance of the silver flecks, and his face would grow dark, his manner curt. She avoided him then, lest he scold her.

But now he was wearing it.

"Brand," the angel said as he went toward the door panel. "Brand, can I come with you?"

He hesitated. "Later, angel," he said. "When the fast-friends come, I'll call you, as I promised. Right now you stay down here and rest, all right?" He forced a smile.

She pouted. "All right," she said.

Outside was a short corridor of gray metal, brightly lit; the sealed airlock to the engine compartment capped one end, the bridge door the other. A few other closed panels broke the spartan bleakness: cargo holds, screen generators, Robi's room, Brand ignored them, and proceeded straight to the bridge.

Robi was strapped in before the main console, studying the banks of viewscreens and scanners with a bored expression. She was a short, round woman, with high cheekbones and green eyes and brown hair cut space short. Long hair was just trouble in free-fall. The angel had long hair, of course, but she was just an angel.

Robi favored him with a wary smile as he entered. Brand did not return it. He was a solo by nature; only circumstances had forced him to take on a partner, so he could complete the conversion of his ship. Her funds had paid for the new screens he'd installed.

He moved to the second control chair and strapped himself down, his expression businesslike. "I'll take over," he said. Then he paused, and blinked. "The course has been altered," he stated. He looked at her.

"A swarm of blinkies," Robi said, trying her smile again. "I changed the program. They're not far out of our way. A half-hour standard, maybe."

Brand sighed. "Look, Robi," he said, "this isn't a trap run." His hands moved over the controls, putting new patterns on most of the scanners. "We're not bounty hunting, remember? We're going to the stars, and coming back. No detours."

Robi looked annoyed. "Brand, I sold my *Unicorn* to invest in this scheme of yours. A bounty or two would be nice, in case the gimmick doesn't work, you know. And we're going out to the Changling Jungle anyway, so we might as well bring a dark or two with us, if we can trap some. That swarm is right on top of us, nearly. A couple darks have got to be nearby. So what's the harm?"

"No," Brand said, as he wiped off the program she'd fed into the ship's computer. "We're too close to fool around." He checked the console, reprogramming, compensating for the swerve she'd fed in. The newly christened *Chariot* was two weeks out from the orbital docks on Triton, where she'd been overhauled. A few short hours ahead, out toward the dark, the Changling Jungle swung around the distant sun, a man-made trojan to Pluto.

"You're being stubborn and unreasonable," Robi told him. "What do you have against money, anyway?"

Brand didn't look up. "Nothing. The idea will work. I'll have all the money I need then. So will you. Why don't you just go back to your room, and dream about how rich you're going to be."

She snorted, spun her chair around, unstrapped, and kicked off savagely. If it had been possible to slam a sliding panel door, she would have done that too.

Brand, alone, finished his reprogramming. He hardly thought twice about the argument. Robi and he had been arguing since they'd left Triton; about bounties, about the angel, about him. It didn't matter. Nothing mattered, nothing but his idea, the Jungle ahead, and stars.

A few hours, that was all. They'd find fast-friends near the Jungle. Always there were fast-friends near the Jungle. And somehow, Brand knew he'd find Melissa.

Unconsciously, his hand had gone to his neck. Slowly, slowly, he stroked the cool dark crystal.

☼

Once they'd dreamed of stars together.

It was a common dream. Earth was teeming, civilized, dull; time and technology had homogenized it. What romance there was left was all in space. Thousands lived under the domes of Luna now. On Mars, terraforming projects were in full swing, and new immigrants flooded Lowelltown and Bradbury and Burroughs City every day. There was a lab on Mercury, toehold colonies on Ceres, Ganymede,

Titan. And out at the Komarov Wheel, the third starship was a-building. The first was twenty years gone, with a crew who knew they'd die on board so their children could walk another world.

Yes, it was a common dream.

But they were most uncommon dreamers.

And they were lucky. They were born at the right time. They were still children when the Hades Expedition, bound for Pluto, came upon the blinkies. Then the darks came upon the Hades Expedition.

Twelve men had died, but Brand felt only a child's thrill, a delicious shiver.

Three years later, he and Melissa had followed the news avidly when the Second Hades Expedition, the lucky one, the one with the first primitive energy screens, made its astonishing discoveries. And a crewman named Chet Adams became immortal.

He remembered a night. They'd walked hand in hand, up a winding outside staircase atop one of the city's tallest towers. The lights, the glaring ceaseless lights, were mostly below. They could see the stars, sort of. Brand, a younger, smooth-faced Brand with long curling hair, wrapped his arm around Melissa and gestured.

Up. At the sky.

"You know what this *means?*" he said. The news had just come back from Hades II; dreamers were everywhere. "We can have the stars now. All of them. We won't have to die on a starship, or settle down on Mars. We're not trapped."

Melissa, whose hair was reddish gold, laughed and kissed him.

"You think they'll find out how it's done? How the darks go ftl?"

Brand just hugged her and kissed her back. "Who cares? I suppose ftl ships would be nice. But hell, we can have more now. We can be like *him*, like Adams, and the stars can all be ours."

Melissa nodded. "Why fly an airplane, right? If you could be a bird?"

For five long years they loved, and dreamed of stars. While the Changling Jungle swelled, and the fast-friends sailed the void.

☼

Robi returned to the bridge just as Brand activated the main viewscreen. Surprise flashed across her face. She looked at him and smiled. Above, the picture was alive with a million tiny lights, pinpoints of sparkling green and crimson and blue and yellow and a dozen other colors. Not stars, no; they shifted and danced mindlessly, constantly, blinking on and off like fireflies and making the scanners *ping* whenever they touched the ship.

She floated herself to her chair, strapped down. "You kept my course," she said, pleased. "I'm sorry I got so angry." She put a hand on his arm.

Brand shook it off. "Don't give me any credit. We're dead on. The blinkies came to us."

"Oh," she said. "I might have known."

"They're all around us," he said. "A huge swarm. I'd guess a couple cubic miles, at least."

Robi looked again. The viewscreen was thick with blinkies in constant motion. The stars, those white lights that stood still, could hardly be seen. "We're going right into the swarm," she said.

Brand shrugged. "It's in our way."

Robi leaned forward, spread her hands over the instruments, punched in a few quick orders. Seconds later, a line of flashing red print began to run across the face of her scanner. She looked up at Brand accusingly. "You didn't even check," she said. "Darks, three of them."

"This is not a trap run," Brand said, unemotionally.

"If they come right up to us and ask to be trapped, I suppose you'll tell them to go away? Besides, they could eat right through us."

"Hardly. The safe-screen is up."

Robi shook her head without comment. The darks would avoid a ship with its safe-screen up. So, naturally, you couldn't trap them that way. But Brand wasn't trapping this time.

"Look," Brand said.

The viewscreen, suddenly, was empty again; just a scattering of stars and two or three lost blinkies winking a lonely message in blue and red. The swarm was gone. Then, with equal speed, it came into sight again. Far off, growing smaller; a fast-receding fog of light.

Brand locked the viewer on it; Robi upped the scopes to max magnification. The fog expanded until it filled the screen.

The blinkies were fleeing, running from their enemies, running faster than the *Chariot* or any man-built ship had ever gone or could ever hope to go, unaided. They were moving at something close to light-speed; after all, they were mostly light themselves, just a single cell and a microscopic aura of energy that gave off short, intense bursts of visible radiation.

Despite the lock, despite the scopes, the viewscreen was deserted less than a second after the blinkies began to run. They'd gone too far, too fast.

Robi started to say something, then stopped. Instead she reached out and touched Brand by the elbow, squeezing sharply. Up in the viewscreen, the stars had begun to dim.

You can't see a dark, not really, but Brand knew how they looked, and he'd seen them often enough in his imagination and his dreams. They were bigger than the blinkies, vastly bigger, almost as big as a man; pulsing globes of dark energy, seldom radiating into the visible spectrum, seen only by the drifting flakes of living matter trapped within their spheres. But they did things to the light passing through them: they made the stars waver and dim.

As they were dimming now, up on the screen. Brand watched closely. Briefly, oh so briefly, he thought he saw a flash of silver as a flake of darkstuff caught the tired sunlight and lost it again. The old fear woke and clutched at his stomach. But the dark was keeping its distance; their safe-screens were up.

Robi looked over at Brand. "It's begging," she said, "it's practically begging. Let's drop screens and trap it. What's the harm?"

Brand's face was cold. Irrational terror swirled within him. "It knows," he said, hardly thinking. "It didn't go after the blinkies. It senses something different about us. I tell you, it knows."

She gave him a curious stare. "What's wrong with you?" she asked. "It's only a dark. Come on. Let me trap it."

Brand mastered himself, though the fear was alive and walking, the Hades fear, the trapper's companion. Creatures of energy, the darks ate matter. Like the blinkies they swept clean the scattered dust and gas on the fringes of solar space. And they moved through blinkie swarms like scythes, carving tunnels of blackness in those living seas of light. And, when they found a lonely chunk of nickel-iron spinning through the void, that too was food. Matter to energy, converted in a blinding silent flash. An incandescent feast.

A hundred times Brand had faced the fear, when he sat before his computer and prepared to drop his screens. When the ship was naked, when the screens were down, then only the mindless whim of the dark said if a trapper lived or died. If the dark came slow, moving in leisurely towards its sluggish steel meal, then the trapper won. Once the dark was in range, the safe-screens would blink on again, covering the ship like a second skin. And, further out, the trapping screens would form a globe. The dark would be a prisoner.

But if the dark moved *quickly*....

Well, the blinkies ran at light-speed. The darks fed on the blinkies. The darks ran faster.

If the dark moved quickly, there was no way, no defense, no hope that man or woman or computer could raise the screens in time. A lot of trappers died that way. The First Hades Expedition, screenless, had been holed in a dozen places.

"Let me trap it," Robi said again. Brand just looked at her. Like him, she was a trapper. She'd beaten the fear as often as he had, and she had luck. Still, maybe this time that luck would change.

He unstrapped, pulled himself up, and stood looking down on her. "No," he said. "It's not worth the risk. We're too close. Leave the dark alone. And don't change course, you hear, not five feet. I'm going down to angel."

"Brand!" Robi said. "Damn you. And don't bring that thing up here, you understand? And...." But he was gone, silently, ignoring her.

She turned back to the viewscreen and, frustrated, watched the dark.

✿

Asleep, awake, it never mattered. The vision would come to him all the same. Call it dream, color it memory.

There were four of them, inside Changling Station, on the wheel of rebirth. It was a doughnut, the Station; brightly lit, screened. Around it, in all directions, ships—trapper ships with their catch, bait ships hauled by timid trappers, supply ships out from Triton, couriers from Earth and Mars and Luna with commissions for the fast-friends. And derelicts.

Hundreds of ill-fit hulks, holed, abandoned, empty, filling up the Jungle like hunks of cold steel garbage.

Between the ships moved the fast-friends.

The airlock where they donned their spacesuits had had a window in it; it was a large, empty chamber, a good place for long looks and last thoughts. Brand and Melissa and a fat blonde girl named Canada Cooper had stood there together, looking out on the Jungle and the fast-friends. Canada had laughed. "I thought they'd be different," she said. "They look just like people, silly naked people standing out in space."

And they did. A few stood on the hulls of derelicts, but most of them were just floating in the void, pale against the starlight, small and stern and awesome. Melissa counted fourteen.

"Hurry up," the government man had said. Brand hardly remembered what he looked like, but he remembered the voice, the hard flat voice that whipped them all the way out from Earth. They were the candidates, the chosen. They'd held to their dream, they'd passed all the tests, and they were twenty. That was the optimal age for a successful merger, the experts said. Some experts. Adams, the first-merged, had been nearly thirty.

He remembered Melissa as she put on her suit, slim and clean in a white coverall zipped low, with her crystal pendant hanging between her gold-tan breasts in the imitation gravity of the spinning Station. Her hair was tightly bound. She'd kept it long, her red-blonde glory, to wear between the stars.

They kissed just before they put on helmets.

"Love you," she said. "Love you always." And he repeated it back to her.

Then they were outside, them and Canada and the government man, walking on the skin of Changling Station, looking down into the Pit. The arena, the hole in the doughnut, the energy-screened center of the whole thing, the place where dreams came true.

Brand, young Brand, looked down at where he'd have to go, and smiled. There was nothing below but stars. He'd fall forever, but he didn't mind. They'd share the stars together.

"You first," the government man said to Melissa. She radioed a kiss to Brand, and kicked off toward the Pit.

She didn't get far. There were darks in there, three of them, trapped and imprisoned. Once she was beyond the screens, one came for her. The sight was burned deep in Brand's memory. One moment there was only Melissa, suited, floating away from him towards the far side of the Station. Then light.

Sudden, instantaneous, quick-dying. A flash, nothing more. Brand knew that. But his memory had elaborated on the moment. In his dreams, it was more prolonged; first her suit flared and was gone and she threw back her head to scream, then her clothes flamed into brilliance, and lastly, lastly, the chain and its crystal. She was naked, wreathed in fire, adrift among the stars. She no longer breathed.

But she lived.

A symbiote of man and dark, a thing of matter and energy, an alien, a changling, a reborn creature with the mind of a human and the speed of a dark. Melissa no longer.

Fast-friend.

He ached to join her. She was smiling at him, beckoning. There was a dark waiting for him, too. He would join it, merge. Then, together, he and Melissa would run, faster than the starships, faster than light, out, out. The galaxy would be theirs. The universe, perhaps.

But the government man held his arm. "Her next," he said. Fat Canada kicked free of the place where they stood, hardly hesitating. She knew the risks, like them, but she was a dreamer too. They'd tested and traveled with her, and Brand knew her boundless optimism.

She floated towards Melissa, chunky in her oversize suit, and reached out her hand. Her radio was on. Brand remembered her voice. "Hey," she said, "mine's slow. A slow dark, imagine!"

She laughed. "Hey, little darkie, where are you? Hey, come to mama. Come and merge, little…"

Then, loudly, a short scream, cut off before it started.

And Canada exploded.

The flash was first, of course. But this time, afterwards, no fast-friend. She'd been rejected. Three-quarters of all candidates for merger were rejected. They were eaten instead. Except, this time, the dark hadn't enveloped her cleanly. If it had, then, after the instant of conversion, nothing would have been left.

But this dark had just sheared her off above the waist. Her legs spun wildly after the explosion of violent depressurization. Her blood flash-froze.

It was only there for a second, less than a heartbeat, a pause between breaths. Then another flash, and emptiness. Just Melissa again, her smile suddenly gone, still waiting.

"Too bad," the government man had said. "She did well on the tests. You're next."

Brand was looking across at Melissa, and the stars behind her. But his vision was gone. Instead he saw Canada.

"No," he'd said. For the first time ever, the fear was on him.

Afterwards he went down into the Station and threw up. When he dreamt, he woke up trembling.

Brand left Robi with her dark, and sought the comfort of his angel.

She was waiting for him, as always, smiling and eager for his company, a soft-winged woman-child. She was playing in the sleep-web when he entered, singing to herself. She flew to him at once.

He kissed her, hard, and she wrapped her wings around him, and they tumbled laughing through the cabin. In her embrace, his fears all faded. She made him feel strong, confident, conquering. She worshiped him, and she was passionate, more passionate even then Melissa.

And she fit. Like the fast-friends, she was a creature of the void. Under gravity, her wings could never function, and she'd die within a month. Even in free-fall, angels were short-lived. She was his third, bred by the bio-engineers of the Jungle who knew what a trapper would pay for company. It didn't matter.

They were clones, and all alike, more than twins in their delicate sexy inhuman angelic simplicity.

Death was not a threat to their love. Nor fights. Nor desertion. When Brand relaxed within her arms, he knew she'd always be there.

Afterwards, they lay nude and lazy in the sleep-web. The angel nibbled at his ear, and giggled, and stroked him with soft hands and softer wings. "What are you thinking, Brand?" she asked.

"Nothing, angel. Don't worry yourself."

"Oh, *Brand*." She looked very cross.

He couldn't help smiling. "All right then. I was thinking that we're still alive, which means Robi left the dark alone."

The angel shivered and hugged him. "Ooo. You're scaring me, Brand. Don't talk of dying."

He played with her hair, still smiling. "I told you not to worry. I wouldn't let you die, angel. I promised to show you the fast-friends, remember? And stars, too. We're going to the stars today, just like the fast-friends do."

The angel giggled, happy again. She was easy to please. "Tell me about the fast-friends," she said.

"I've told you before."

"I know. I like to hear you talk, Brand. And they sound so *pretty*."

"They are, in a way. They're cold, and they're not human anymore, but they are pretty sometimes. They move fast. Somehow they can punch through to another kind of space, where the laws of nature are different, a fifth dimension or hyperspace or what-you-will, and..."

But the angel's face showed no comprehension. Brand laughed, and paused. "No, you wouldn't understand those terms, of course. Well, call it a fairyland, angel. The fast-friends have a lot of power in them, like the darks do, and they use this power, this magic, for a trick they have, so they can go faster than light. Now, there's no way we can go faster than light without this trick, you see."

"Why?" she asked. She smiled an innocent smile.

"Hmmm. Well, that's a long story. There was a man named Einstein who said we couldn't, angel, and he was a *very* smart man, and..."

She hugged him. "I bet *you* could go faster than light, Brand, if you wanted." Her wings beat, and the web rocked gently.

"Well, I want to," he said. "And that's just what we're going to try to do now, angel. You must be smarter than you look."

She hit him. "I'm *awful* smart," she said, pouting.

"Yes," he laughed. "I didn't mean it. I thought you wanted to hear about the fast-friends?"

Suddenly she was apologetic again. "Yes."

"All right. Remember, they have this trick, like I said. Now we know they can move matter—that's, well, solid stuff, angel, like the ship and me and you,

but it's also gas and water, you see. Energy is different. The darks are mostly energy, with only little flakes of matter. But the fast-friends are more balanced. A lot of smart men think that if they could examine a dark they could figure out this trick, and then we could build ships that went fast too. But nobody has been able to figure how to examine a dark, since it is nearly all energy and nearly impossible to hold in one place, you see?"

"Yes," the angel lied, looking very solemn.

"Anyway, the fast-friends not only move energy and little flakes of matter, they also move what once were the bodies of the human members of the symbiosis. You don't understand that, do you? Hell, this is... ah, well, just listen. The fast-friends can only move themselves, and whatever else they can fit inside their energy sphere, or aura. Think of it as a baggy cloak, angel. If they can't stuff it under their cloak, they can't take it with them."

She giggled, the idea of a baggy cloak evidently appealing to her.

Brand sighed. "So, the fast-friends are sort of our messengers. They fly out to the stars for us, real fast, and they tell us which suns have planets, and where we can find worlds that are good to live on. And they've found ships out there, too, in other systems, from other kinds of beings who aren't men and aren't fast-friends either, and they carry messages so that we can learn from each other. And they keep us in touch with our starships, too, by running back and forth. Our ships are still real slow, angel. We've launched at least twenty by now, but even the first one hasn't gotten where it's going yet."

"The fast-friends caught it, didn't they?" the angel interrupted. "You told me. I remember."

"Yes, angel," he said. "I don't have to tell you how surprised those people were. A lot of them were the sons and daughters of people who'd left Earth, and when their parents left there were no fast-friends, and they hadn't even found out about the blinkies yet, or the darks. But now the fast-friends keep all the ships in touch by running back and forth with messages and even small packages and such. Once we have colonies, they'll link them too."

"But they're crippled," angel prompted.

"For all their speed," Brand continued, smiling, "the fast-friends are strangely crippled. They can't land on any of the planets they sail by; the gravity wells are deadly to them. And they don't even like to go in much further than the orbit of Saturn, or its equivalent, because of the sun. The darks and the blinkies never do, and the fast-friends have to force themselves. So that's one drawback.

"Also, frankly, a lot of men want to travel faster than light themselves. They want to build ships and start colonies. So whoever finds a way to do what the fast-friends do, so that regular men can do it without having to merge and maybe die, well, they'll make a lot of money. And be famous. And have stars."

"You'll do it, Brand," the angel said.

"Yes," he said. His voice was suddenly serious. "That, angel, is why we're here."

"No."

The word had haunted him, its echoes rolling through his dreams. He'd thrown away his stars, and his Melissa.

He couldn't force himself to go back to Earth. Melissa was gone, off to the stars on her first commission, but he loved her still. And the dream still gripped him tightly. Yet he would not get another chance. There were more candidates than darks, and he'd failed his final test.

He worked in Changling Station for a while, then signed on a supply run from Triton to the Jungle and learned to run a ship. In two years, he saved a substantial amount. He borrowed the rest, outfitted a derelict drifting in the Jungle, and became a trapper.

The plan was clear then. The government wouldn't give him another chance, but he could make his own. He'd prowl until he found a dark, then trap it. Then he'd go outside and merge. And he'd join Melissa after all. Brand, fast-friend. Yes, he would have his stars.

A good trapper could support himself in fine style on four catches a year. On six he gets rich. Brand was not yet a good trapper, and there were months of fruitless, lonely search. The blackness was brightened only by the far-off lights of distant blinkie swarms, and the firmness of his vision, and Melissa.

She used to come to him, in the early days, when she wasn't out among the stars. He'd be on his tedious prowl when suddenly his scanners would flash

red, and she'd be there, floating outside the ship, smiling at him from the main viewscreen. And he'd open the airlock and cycle her in.

But even in the best days after, the very early ones, it wasn't the same. She couldn't drink with him, or eat. She didn't need to; she was a fast-friend now, and she lived on stardust and blinkies and junk, converting them to energy even as a dark did.

She could survive in an atmosphere, and talk and function, but she didn't like it. It was unpleasant. The ship was cramped, and it was a strain to keep her aura in check, to keep from converting the molecules of the air that pressed on her from every side.

The first time, when she'd come to him in Changling Station, Brand had pulled her lithe body hard against him and kissed her. She had not resisted. But her flesh was cold, her tongue a spear of ice when it touched his. Later, stubborn, he'd tried to make love to her. And failed.

Soon they gave up trying. When she came to his ship in those months of hunt, he only held her hard, slick hand, and talked to her.

"It's just as well, Brand," she told him once, in those early days. "I wanted to make love to you, yes, for your sake. I'm *changed*, Brand. You have to understand. Sex is like food, you know. It's a human thing. I'm not really interested in that now. You'll see, after you merge. But don't worry. There are other things out there, things that make it all worthwhile. The stars, love. You should see the stars. I fly between them, and, and… oh, Brand, it's glorious! How could I tell you? You have to feel it. When I fly, when I punch through, everything changes. Space isn't black anymore, it's a sea of color, swirling all around me, splashing against me, and I'm streaking right through it. And the *feeling*! It's like… like an orgasm, Brand, but it goes on and on and on, and your whole body sings and feels it, not just one little part of you. You're *alive*! And there are things out there, things only the fast-friends know. What we tell the humans, that's only a little bit, the bit they can understand. There's so much more. There's music out there, Brand, only it isn't music. And sometimes you can hear something calling, far away, from the core stars. I think the call gets stronger the more you fly. That's where the first-merged went, you know, Adams or whatever his human name was. That's why the older fast-friends sometimes vanish. They say it's wearying after a while, playing messenger for the humans. Then the fast-friends go away, to the core stars. Oh, Brand, I wish you were with me. It would be the way we dreamed. Hurry, love, catch your dark for me."

And Brand, though strange chills went through him, nodded and said he would.

And finally he did.

For the second time the fear came. Brand watched his scanners as they shrieked of dark proximity. Five times his finger paused over the button that would kill his safe-screens. Five times it moved back. He kept seeing Canada again, her legs a-spin. And he thought of the Hades I.

Finally, his mind on Melissa, he forced the button down. The dark came slowly. No need to hurry, after all. This was no light-fast blinkie swarm; just dead metal creeping through the void.

Brand, relieved, trapped it. But as he put on his spacesuit, the fear hit again.

He fought it. Oh, he fought it. For an hour he stood in the airlock, trembling, trying to put on his helmet and failing. His hands were shaking, and he threw up twice. Finally, slumped and beaten in the fouled lock, he knew the truth. He would never merge.

He took his catch back to the Changling Jungle for a bounty. The Station offered its standard fee, but there was another bidder, a middle-aged man who'd run an old supply ship out here on his own. As dozens did each year. Brand sold the dark to him, to this hopeful, unqualified, test-failing visionary. And Brand watched him die.

Another derelict, abandoned, joined the Jungle, floating in a crowded orbit with all the other hulks, the debris of other dreams.

Brand sold his dark again, to Changling Station. A month later, when Melissa returned, he told her. He'd expected tears, a storm, a fight. But she just looked at him, strangely unmoved. Then he asked her to come back to him.

"Maybe we can go back to Earth," he said. "We'll stay in orbit, and the scientists can look at you. They might be able to un-merge you, or something. They'll certainly welcome the opportunity. Maybe you can tell them how to build ftl ships. But we'll be together." His words were a child's hopeful gush.

No," Melissa had said, simply. "You don't understand. I'd die first."

"You said you loved me. Stay with me."

"Oh, Brand. I did love you. But I won't give up the stars. They're my love now, my life, my everything. I'm a fast-friend, Brand, and you're only a human. Things are different now. If you can't merge, go back to Earth. That's the place for men, for you. The stars belong to us now."

"*No!*" He shouted it to keep from weeping. "I'll stay out here then, and trap. I love you, Melissa. I'll stay by you."

Very briefly, she looked sad. "I'll visit you, I guess," she said. "When I have time, if you want me."

And so she did. But as the years went by, the visits came less often. Brand, more and more, hardly knew her. Her gold-tan body turned pale, though it kept the shape of a twenty-year-old while he aged. Her streaming red-blonde hair became a silvered white, and her eyes grew distant. Often, when she was with him in orbit near the Jungle, she wasn't there at all. She talked of things he could not understand, of fast-friends he did not know, of actions beyond his comprehension. And he bored her now, with his news of Earth and men.

Finally the talk stopped. There was nothing left but memories then, for Melissa did not come at all.

✧

Robi rang him on the intercom, and Brand dressed quickly. "Now," the angel said eagerly. "Can I come now?"

"Yes," he told her, smiling again his fond, indulgent smile. "I'll show you the fast-friends now, angel. And then I'll take you to the stars!"

She flew behind him, through the panel, up the corridor, into the bridge.

Robi looked up as they entered. She did not look happy. "You don't listen, do you? I don't want your pet on the bridge, Brand. Can't you keep your perversions in your cabin?"

The angel quailed at the displeasure in Robi's voice. "She doesn't like me," she said to Brand, scared.

"Don't worry, angel, I'm here," he replied. Then, to Robi, "You're scaring her. Keep quiet. I promised to show her the fast-friends."

Robi glared at him, and hit the viewscreen stud. It flared back to life. "There, then," she said savagely.

The *Chariot* was in the middle of the Jungle. Brand, counting quickly, saw a good dozen derelicts nearby. Changling Station was low in one corner of the screen, surrounded by trapper ships and screens. Near the center was a larger wheel, the spoked and spinning supply station Hades IV, with its bars and pleasure havens.

Floating close to Hades, a group of fast-friends were clustered, six at least, still small and white at this distance. There were others visible, but they were closest. They were talking, even in the hard vacuum of the solar fringe; with a simple act of will, the fast-friends could force their dark aura up in the range of the visible spectrum. Their language was one of lights.

Robi already had the *Chariot* headed toward them. Brand nodded toward the angel, and pointed. "Fast-friends," he said.

The angel squealed and flew to the viewscreen, pressing her nose against it. "They're so *little*," she said as she hovered there, her wings beating rapidly.

"Increase the magnification," Brand told Robi. When she ignored him, he strapped down beside her and did it himself. The cluster of fast-friends doubled in size, and the angel beamed.

"We'll be right on top of them in five minutes," Brand said. Robi pretended not to hear.

"I don't know about you, Brand," she said in a low serious voice, so the angel would not hear. "Most of the men who buy sex toys like that are sick, or crippled, or impotent. Why you? You seem normal enough. Why do you need an angel, Brand? What's wrong with a woman?"

"Angels are easier to live with," Brand snapped. "And they do what they're told. Stop prying and get on the signal lights. I want to talk to our friends out there."

Robi scowled. "Talk? Why? Let's just scoop them up, there's enough of them there…."

"No. I want to find one, a special one. Her name was Melissa."

"Hmpf," Robi said. "Angels and fast-friends. You ought to try having a relationship with a human being once in a while, Brand. Just for a change of pace, you understand." But she readied the signal lights as she talked.

And Brand called, out across the void. One of the fast-friends responded. Then vanished. "She'll come," Brand said firmly, as they waited. "Even now, she'll come."

Meanwhile the angel was flitting excitedly around the bridge, touching everything she could reach. Normally she was not allowed up here.

"Calm down," Brand told her. She flew down to him, happy, and curled up in his lap.

"What are the fast-friends doing?" she asked, with her arms around him. "Are they going to tell us their trick, Brand? Are we going to the stars yet?"

"Soon, angel," he said patiently. "Soon."

Then Melissa was there, caught in the viewscreen. Brand felt a chill go through him.

Her skin was milk-white now, her hair a halo of streaming silver. But otherwise she was the same. She had the firm curves of a twenty-year-old, and the face that Brand remembered.

He shooed the angel from his lap, and turned to the console. He hit some buttons.

Outside, the stars began to flicker. The bright dot of the distant sun dimmed. The hulks of the Jungle, the Hades wheel, Changling Station; all darkened slightly. Only Melissa and the other fast-friends were unchanged.

Caught within the globe.

Robi smiled, and started to speak. Brand silenced her with a look. His signal lights called Melissa. When she acknowledged, he cut the safe-screens to let her through.

He met her in the corridor after the airlock had cycled her in. Robi stayed up on the bridge.

They stood ten feet apart. They did not touch or smile.

"Brand," Melissa said at last. She studied him with ice-blue eyes, from a cold and steady face, and her voice had a husky quality he had not remembered. "You… what are you doing? We are not… not darks. To be trapped." Her speech stumbled and halted awkwardly.

"Have you forgotten how to talk, Melissa?" Brand said. As he spoke, the bridge panel slid open behind him. The angel flew out and hovered.

"Oh," she said to Melissa. "You're *pretty*."

The fast-friend's eyes flicked to her quickly, then dismissed her and went back to Brand. "Some, I've forgotten. Ten years, Brand. With stars, the stars. Not… *I'm* not a human now. I'm elder now, an elder fast-friend. My… my call comes soon." She paused. "Why have you screened us?"

"A new kind of screen, Melissa," Brand said, smiling. "Didn't you notice? It's *dark*. A refinement, just developed back on Earth. They've been doing a lot of screen research, and I've been following it. I had an idea, love, but the old screens were no good. This kind, well, it's more sophisticated. And I'm the first one to realize the implications."

"Sophisticated. Implications." The words sounded odd, foreign, alien on Melissa's tongue. Her face looked lost.

"We're going to the stars together, Melissa."

"Brand," she replied. For a moment her voice had an almost-human tremor. "Give it up, Brand. Give up… me. And stars. They… they're old dreams, and they've gone sour on you. See? Can't you see?"

The angel was swooping up and down the corridor, coming closer to Melissa each time, clearly fascinated by the fast-friend, but afraid to come too close. They both ignored her.

Brand was looking at Melissa, at the dim, far-off reflection of a girl who'd loved him once. He shook it away. She was just a fast-friend, and he'd get his stars from her.

"You can take me to the stars, Melissa, and other men after me. It's time you fast-friends shared your universe with us poor humans."

"A drive?" she asked.

"You might…"

But the angel interrupted him. "Oh, let me, Brand. Let me tell her. I know how. You told me. I remember. Let me talk to the fast-friend." She'd stopped her wild circles, and was floating eager between them.

Brand grinned. "All right. Tell her."

The angel spun in the air, smiling. Her wings beat quickly to underscore her words. "It's like horses," she told Melissa. "The darks are like horses, Brand said, and the fast-friends are like horses with riders. But he's got the first chariot, and the fast-friends will pull him." She giggled. "Brand showed me a picture of a chariot. And a horse too."

"A star chariot," Brand said. "I like the image. Oh, it's a cartoon analogy, of course, but the math is sound. You can transport matter. Enough of you, locked into a dark screen, can transport a ship this size."

Melissa floated, staring, shaking her head slowly back and forth. Her silver hair shimmered. "Stars," she said softly. "Brand, the core… the songs. Freedom, Brand. Like we used to talk. Brand, they won't… no running… they won't let us *go*… can't *chain* us."

"I have."

And the angel, emboldened by Melissa's sudden stillness, flew up beside her. In a childish, tentative way, she reached out to touch, and found the phantom solid. Melissa, her eyes on Brand, put an arm around her. The angel smiled and sighed and moved closer.

Brand shook his head.

And the angel suddenly looked up, childish pique washing across her face. "You fooled me," she said to Brand. "She's not a horse. She's a person." Then, brightly, she smiled again. "And she's so *pretty*."

There was a long, long silence.

☼

The bridge panel slid shut behind him. Robi was waiting. "Well?" she asked.

Wordlessly Brand kicked himself across the room, strapped down, and looked up at the viewscreen. Out in the darkness, in the screen-dimmed gloom, Melissa had rejoined the other fast-friends. They spoke with staccato bursts of color. Brand watched briefly, then reached up to the console and hit a button.

The stars flared cold and bright, and the flanks of Hades shone.

Before Robi had a chance to speak the fast-friends had vanished, spinning space around them, moving faster than the *Chariot* ever would. Only Melissa lingered, and only for a second. Then emptiness, and the derelicts around them.

*"Brand!"*

He smiled at her, and shrugged. "I couldn't do it. We would never have been able to let them outside the screens. They'd be animals, draft animals, prisoners." He looked sheepish. "I guess they're not. Not people either, though, not anymore. Well, we always wanted to meet an alien race. How could we guess that we'd create one?"

"Brand," Robi said. "Our investment. We have to go through with it. Maybe we can use darks?"

He shook his head. "No. We couldn't get them to understand what we wanted. No. Fast-friends or… nothing, I guess."

He paused, and looked at her. She was staring up at the viewscreen, with an expression that shrieked disgust and exasperation. "I'll make it up to you," Brand said. He took her hand, gently. "We'll trap. We're well equipped."

Robi looked over. "Where's the angel?" she asked, and her voice sounded a shade less angry.

Brand sighed. "In my cabin," he said. "I gave her a necklace to play with."

*Copyright © 1976 by George R. R. Martin*

*Stewart C Baker is a Writers of the Future winner (v32), and has appeared in* Starship Sofa, Flash Fiction Online, Nature Physics, *and elsewhere. This is his second appearance in* Galaxy's Edge.

## JUST ANOTHER NIGHT AT THE ABANDONED DRAFT BAR AND GRILL

### by Stewart C Baker

This was, by Alexandra's count, the sixty-seventh time she had been tortured, murdered, hacked to pieces, and shoved into Jim's refrigerator for him to find when he got home from his overseas deployment, and she was really starting to get annoyed.

"It's like this jackass of a would-be author doesn't even know what women *are*," she snarled, jabbing the ice cubes in her drink until they broke down into slush. "Like he thinks we're just some kind of…of…"

Wong the Inscrutable and François—her companions as always on nights like this—avoided her eyes as she looked around for the right phrase. François (AKA African Henchman #1) was fiddling with the inside of the boxy contraption he always had with him. He'd come from a Francophone sci-fi serial before being co-opted by their current author, Alex knew, had been a genius engineer on some kind of super-massive spaceship. Wong (who Alex thought was probably original, since he was so underdeveloped he wasn't even fully corporeal) stroked his pet rat with his one solid arm, glowering into the middle distance from under his painfully stereotypical peasant hat.

"Plot devices," she finished with a sigh and tossed down half the drink in one gulp.

Things hadn't always been this way. Alex remembered her first writer, the one who had created her from nothing. Alex knew the novel she'd been in back then was far from perfect—her struggles to be accepted at the corporation felt extremely dated, and she'd been a little too stereotypical-self-made-woman—but at least she'd had some say in how her story had happened. And *anything* was better than the fridge.

"Do you know what my line is?" She asked, her voice raw. "The only line I get before I'm taken out?"

Out of the corner of her eye she saw François grimace, but the liquor spurred her on. Her most insipid smile on her face, she giggled vapidly, then, in a sing-song voice, repeated the line: "co-ming!"

"That's it! All I get is a single word, delivered with the stagecraft and nuance of a dead rat! No offense, Wong."

Wong stroked the rat again and made a motion somewhere between a shrug and a nod. In all the years they'd been stuck here, Alex had never known him to speak or stand or do anything else, although to be fair he didn't really have a functional mouth. Or legs.

François, though, looked up with a grin. "Mam'selle, I know just how you feel. I myself do not even *get* a line—I merely open the door and shove the ice pick straight into your eye. And poor Wong, of course, appears only in the background, lurking in the window of an unmarked van across the street, the last thing you see before you die. He does not even get to feed your remains to his beloved rat. Maybe in a finished story he would play a large role as villain, but, well.... And let us not even speak of Jim."

Alex snorted at that. She'd never even seen her "boyfriend" Jim, wasn't sure he even existed to the author beyond the name—never mind that he would no doubt be the hero of whatever story lay beyond the first aborted scene.

"More to the point," François continued, "you know that it pains me almost as much as it does you to go through this barbarous charade, this...idiotic, endless abattoir of an opening scene." He patted the top of the box. "And I know that you will feel almost as happy as I do when I say that with this device complete, we need not suffer it a single time more."

The crushed ice in Alex's drink sloshed as she slammed her cup on the table, hopeful despite herself. "It reaches through the fourth wall and strangles him?"

"No." François frowned. "That would kill us too, since he is writing us."

"Oh." Alex took another drink. *At least it would be permanent*, she added in the privacy of her own head. She thought Wong looked disappointed, too, though of course it was impossible to tell.

François continued, undeterred. "It is something even better than that. The device will change his frame of reference; he will be able to see storytelling from entirely new points of view. *And* it will increase his motivation and ambition a hundredfold! No more will we be forced to endlessly act out an opening scene. No longer will we be stuck in endless white rooms free of description. And if my calculations are correct—" His voice dropped to a whisper, as if he were afraid to speak too loud— "this will give him the energy to finish the first draft entirely."

"We could move on," Alex said. "Be in newer, better stories—ones written by people who actually know how stories *work*."

François grinned. "You must agree, Mam'selle, that things could hardly get worse."

"Do it," Alex said. "Get us a story set somewhere other than in a delusional never-was 1960s middle-America. Get us a story where we're all active participants, where we have unique and interesting lives. Get us," she hissed, "a story where I do not get fucking *murdered* and *stuck in a fridge*."

"Wong?" François asked, looking to the other man.

Wong did the shrug/nod thing again, but his eyes were wet with emotion, and his hand was clutching Ratso so tightly that the little rat squirmed and tried to escape.

"*Bien*," François said. "We shall give it a try."

He flipped switches and pushed buttons and spun dials on the back of the box, which started to hum quietly. There was a sudden crackle, and the air filled with the smell rain makes just before it falls.

François let out a low whistle. "That was fast. He must have just been sitting down to write. Brace yourselves, everyone!"

Alex grimaced. Already she could feel the story-world pulling at her, tearing away at her control, at her identity. She had just enough time to gulp the last of her drink, the alcohol burning its way down her throat, before the familiar surroundings of the bar faded into blackness.

✿

It was a dark and stormy night in the fabled and legendary city of ELLAAAAAHKRA [*replace this with real name later*], home of storied magical spell-slingers and sword-users and heroic fighters [*fighters* is vague pick a better class title like paladin or something?]. There were also a number of dwarves, who were short in stature and savage in nature like the savages of Africa [*fix this later since it is fantasy*] had beards like flowing rivers. Also there were elves, with magical and legendary powers and strange clothing and who had strange mysteries in their eldritch eyes as they gazed up at the dark black night with its glimmering stars and nine enormous fabled moons [*what would this do to the tides? find that out so the setting is SUPER realistic and authentic*].

Ah'lek isan D'aruh, the pure half-elven priestess dressed in a beautiful gown [*need a better description of her clothes, worldbuilding is important!*], was awaiting her lover, the powerful and handsome human heroic paladin Jim, who was known as a smiter of evil and a protector of women, and who would later come to be the biggest and truest savior of the kingdom of [*spoilers? ask mom what she thinks*]. Ah'lek stood on the rooftop of the Holy Magical Legendary Temple of Anarchical Moon-God W'onG, admiring his numerous moons with their craters and magic-giving abilities. It was like a prayer for her, only she did not pray with words. She went into a trance, envisioning with her mind the holy face of Moon God W'onG, his holy moon-like yellow skin.

Suddenly there was a scream from the street a few streets over from the temple. It sounded like a girl maybe. Ah'lek knew only she could help the girl so she leaped into action, her magical katana singing its own praises with glory and righteousness. She was very scared but she knew Jim would be here to save her soon. All she had to do was last until then. She screamed blood-curdling murder in her beautiful voice when suddenly she saw that it was one of the evil black dwarves riding on a rat the size of an elephant [*no elephants in the fantasy world? better description*] holding an axe that was almost as big as his beard but not quite because he had a very big beard.

"Jim!" she shouted. "I cannot do this by myself! I need your powers to defeat this evil black dwarf on his giant rat! Please help me now! I am scared!"

From the other street over she thought she heard a reply, but before she could make it out the dwarf and his rat tragically knocked her to the ground and killed her by crushing her into tiny pieces with its

giant rat claws which were so sharp not even her magical katana could withstand it without being broken. Her last thought as the claws sliced through her attractive and beautiful face was that at least Jim would be able to avenge her because he was such a good warrior.

[Okay this is going really good so far maybe push through to the next scene and I can fix all this later in edits! Or maybe once I finish writing the whole novel I could just rewrite it a few times from scratch. I heard that's a good way to really get into my characters heads, so I bet I could make it more empathetic to women that way. But there's a lot of dialog in the next scene from the dwarf when Jim starts to fight him so I'd better rewatch Lord of the Rings a couple more times before I try to tackle it.]

*Copyright © 2016 by Stewart C Baker*

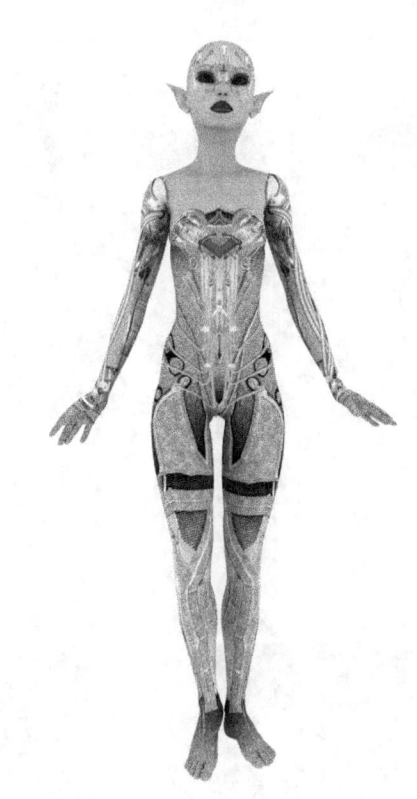

"Of all Heinlein's books, . . . Double Star is
one of my three favorites."—*Connie Willis*

ROBERT A.
HEINLEIN
DOUBLE
STAR

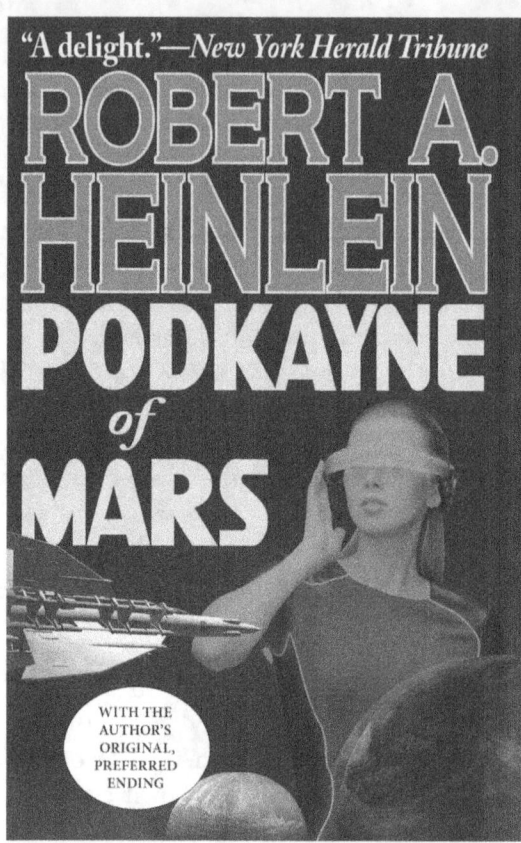

"A delight."—*New York Herald Tribune*

ROBERT A.
HEINLEIN
PODKAYNE
of
MARS

WITH THE
AUTHOR'S
ORIGINAL,
PREFERRED
ENDING

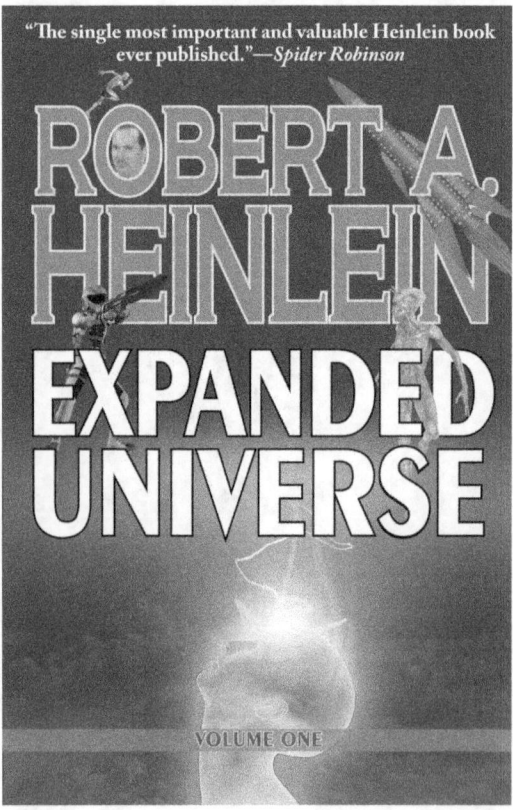

"The single most important and valuable Heinlein book
ever published."—*Spider Robinson*

ROBERT A.
HEINLEIN
EXPANDED
UNIVERSE

VOLUME ONE

"This is the book I've always wanted from Heinlein."
—*John Bruni, GoodReads*

ROBERT A.
HEINLEIN
EXPANDED
UNIVERSE

VOLUME TWO

# OVER THE
# WINE-DARK
# SEA

## HARRY TURTLEDOVE

ORIGINALLY WRITING AS H. N. TURTELTAUB

---

# THE
# GRYPHON'S
# SKULL

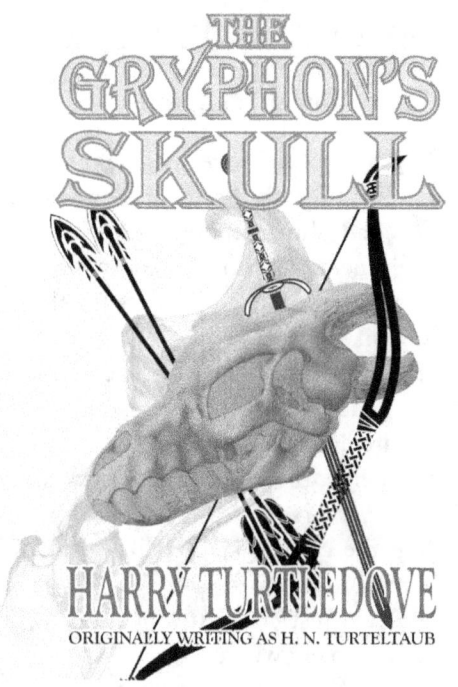

## HARRY TURTLEDOVE

ORIGINALLY WRITING AS H. N. TURTELTAUB

---

# THE SACRED
# LAND

## HARRY TURTLEDOVE

ORIGINALLY WRITING AS H. N. TURTELTAUB

---

# OWLS TO
# ATHENS

## HARRY TURTLEDOVE

ORIGINALLY WRITING AS H. N. TURTELTAUB

*Jeff Calhoun is a Cincinnati fan and writer. This is his second appearance in* Galaxy's Edge.

# THE GETTYSBURG GAME

## by Jeff Calhoun

"Why did you give the knights fifteenth-century plate armor?" demanded Morgan Hunt, founder and CEO of Ares VR Entertainments. "Don't you know King Arthur lived in the sixth century? Knights in those days wore chainmail."

"The Arthurian Age is mostly legendary," Leigh Roberts reminded him. "So it doesn't matter how the knights are dressed."

"It does to me. The Ares brand is synonymous with historical accuracy."

"Spare me the commercial. A little romanticism just might sell more games."

"Our sales are just fine. Anyone looking for romanticism can go elsewhere."

"I know for a fact you can be very romantic," she reminded him with a smile.

*Only when I've had too much to drink,* Morgan thought. "Just read some actual history before you go back to your computer."

Her smile disappeared. "This project consumed a year of my time. Because of our relationship I turned down some lucrative job offers in the meantime. I could take my design elsewhere…"

"Do that and I'd sue your pretty ass off. The idea for the game was mine."

"I used to live with a lawyer, and he might enjoy taking you to court. This isn't over." Her holographic image vanished, leaving him alone in his home office.

With a sigh he allowed the chair to massage the tension from his neck and back. His stomach growled, reminding him that he'd skipped breakfast, so he ordered a burrito and coffee and his robot glided off to the kitchen. Then he checked his inbox, finding the usual unsolicited submissions from designers he didn't know. He deleted them without a second thought until he saw one with the subject heading "Reality First." Curious, he opened it.

"Greetings, Mr. Hunt," said the hologram of a smiling clean-shaven man with high cheekbones and long iron-gray hair tied in a ponytail. "My name is Martin Blackfeather, and I am the chairman of Reality First. Our group was founded for a twofold purpose: To inform the public of the dangers of excessive virtual reality use and to seek legislation to combat this grave threat to public health.

"VR use has been linked to schizophrenia and other mental disorders. No deaths have been reported, but it is only a matter of time. As a successful publisher of VR entertainments, we thought you would like to contribute to our cause and mitigate the public relations nightmare that will surely result when such a tragedy occurs."

Morgan chuckled, thinking of Prohibition, the War on Drugs, and other failed crusades launched for the betterment of society. As he closed and deleted the message his robot returned with breakfast. While he ate he received an e-mail he was not expecting for several months.

After his own design team shamefacedly informed him that the Shiloh and Antietam Games would not meet their scheduled release dates coinciding with the upcoming Civil War Bicentennial, Morgan reluctantly contracted the Gettysburg project to an independent group he knew only from VR industry newsfeeds which gave them high marks.

Apparently the reviews were well-deserved as the game appeared ready for a preliminary run. Morgan downloaded it into his player and perused the instructions. Then he retired to his couch and donned his headset which covered his eyes and ears. He periodically cleaned the room so that no smells reached his olfactory senses. The couch made him feel like he floated in deep space, waiting for the pseudo-neurons to feed images from the program directly into his brain via his implant…

Then found himself marching on dirty, swollen bare feet along an unpaved road, his throat parched from dust. The soldiers around him reeked of body odor and tobacco, and save for an occasional barked command they marched in silence while birds sang in the trees lining a nearby ridge.

An Enfield rifled musket and horse collar bedroll weighed heavy on his shoulder. He wore a butternut jacket with two faded blue chevrons on either sleeve. *Would've preferred to be an officer, then I'd have boots, or better yet a horse,* he thought peevishly with a glance at the captain riding beside him. His wide-brimmed hat helped shield his eyes from the morning sun's glare, but that brought to mind another criticism: *July 1st 1863 started out overcast and drizzly in southern Pennsylvania; the sun didn't break through until after the battle started.*

He fell out of step after stepping on a pebble. "Straighten that line, Corporal!" the captain snapped. "We must look sharp now that we're on Yankee soil."

"Sorry, sir, but these rocks are damn hard…"

"Y'all ain't talking to some field hand, boy!" a sergeant reprimanded him sharply after spitting out a wad of tobacco.

*All I said was "damn,"* Morgan thought before remembering that many nineteenth-century Americans were righteously offended by any "bad word." At least the game's characters were behaving true to type.

"Patience, lad," the officer said with a sympathetic glance at Morgan's feet. "General Heth can shoe the whole division once we take this town up ahead."

"Amen to that, sir!" Morgan replied, getting into the spirit of the game. His suspicion that he was in Henry Heth's division was confirmed. He tensed for the first crack of carbine fire from Union General John Buford's hastily-erected pickets. He didn't have to wait long.

The Confederates quickly formed skirmish lines and returned fire, but they had to reload their Enfields after each shot while the dismounted Union cavalrymen continued popping away with their Sharps breechloaders and Colt .44 revolvers from their positions along McPherson's Ridge beyond the stream. Morgan wished the game had given him the option of being a Yankee and resolved to mention that during his meeting with the design team.

After two hours he found himself along the banks of Willoughby Run, leg muscles aching and his ears ringing from gunfire. Then an explosion showered him with dirt and pebbles. *That must be Buford's battery of Horse Artillery,* Morgan thought. Confederate guns positioned on Herr Ridge answered them, but the advance to the town itself would be slowed to a halt by the ensuing artillery duel. At least the stream cooled his sore feet.

"Lots of Yankee militias hereabouts," said a Confederate soldier on Morgan's left as they pushed up the wooded slopes. He ducked as a bullet grazed his hat that sported a single black feather.

"Those troops are not militia," Morgan told him. By now Buford's cavalrymen had been reinforced by Federal infantry regiments. "We are definitely facing the Army of the Potomac."

"You sure do talk funny, Corporal," his companion grinned. He was swarthy with high cheekbones and straight black hair. Morgan figured him for a Cherokee or some other Native American tribe with Confederate sympathies. "You a college man, like General Archer?"

"Maybe," Morgan returned the grin. He suddenly spotted a Union corpse wearing shoes he thought might fit him, and paused long enough to transfer them to his own bleeding feet while artillery thunder continued. *If nothing else, the design team deserves high marks for realism.* Yet Morgan felt the overall sensory pseudo-neuron effect might be too much for his average customers: Middle-aged men who led mostly sedentary lives. *Hell, my own heart-rate and blood pressure are probably spiking now.*

Morgan's company was suddenly enfiladed; bullets nicked his arm and thigh. His Cherokee companion was hit in the shoulder and collapsed with a cry of pain. "Throw down your arms, Rebs!" Yankees in black slouch hats, the distinctive headgear of the Iron Brigade, emerged from the trees. Morgan saw no reason not to drop his Enfield and raise his hands.

The Federals searched him, finding only a battered watch and a leather pouch full of corn. One of them paid considerable attention to his shoes, and Morgan feared he was about to be shot or beaten senseless for robbing Union dead. Then a moan drew their attention to the wounded Cherokee. "Hey, this one's an Injun!" one of the Federals said. "Damn Sioux killed my cousin's whole family in Minnesota last year." He brutally kicked the wounded man before pointing his rifle at the Native American's bleeding head. "Looks like he's trying to escape, boys." His comrades laughed while their sergeant looked away.

Morgan saw a chance. He grabbed the nearest black hat's rifle and drove his elbow into the man's chin. Stunned, the Federal released his weapon which Morgan instantly appropriated. In one fluid motion he shouldered the rifle, aimed at the soldier who threatened the Cherokee, and fired. As the man fell, Morgan used the rifle's bayonet to spear the closest Federal and use his body for a shield to block any shots aimed his way.

Just then other Confederates joined the fracas, firing into the surprised black hats. The surviving Yankees retreated. Morgan knelt to lift up his wounded squad-mate. "Can—!" he grunted. "Can one of you help me get him to the rear?" A gray-clad trooper slipped the wounded man's other arm about his own shoulder. Morgan nodded his thanks and together they hobbled off.

The Confederate lines were less than half a mile away. Their medical services were about what Morgan expected—dirty knives, whiskey for anesthetics, and somewhat sober doctors. He deposited his wounded comrade before a tent bearing a red cross, but not before hearing the Cherokee weakly say, "Thank you."

"Better put something on those flesh wounds, Corporal," said an orderly. "Else they get infected." Before Morgan could protest, the man helped him remove his blood-stained jacket, tunic, and trousers then applied alcohol to the nicks which stung like a swarm of bees. Morgan wondered if infectious diseases were widely known at this point in history.

He stumbled weakly out of the tent to find a spot unoccupied by more seriously wounded and plopped on the ground like a sack of potatoes with his bedroll behind his head. Then his stomach began growling. *Must be dinnertime*, he thought. *This game is taking too damn long!* Add the intense pain factor and Morgan deemed the Gettysburg Game totally unacceptable.

*Time to pull the plug.* The termination code given in the instructions was the name of an author from the previous century who wrote a novel about the actual battle. "End program. Shaara!"

Nothing changed. The moans of the wounded continued as did the echo of gunfire in the distance. "Malfunctioning exit code!" he swore aloud, ignoring glances from the nearby wounded. He tried yanking off his headset, and succeeded only in removing his virtual reality slouch hat. "What the hell?" It seemed he had no choice but to finish playing the game. Weariness and frustration took their toll...

He awoke with a start. It was dark, probably after midnight, and shadows danced about the lamplight

as Longstreet's Corps arrived for the battle. He'd never slept during a game, and the idea was disturbing, but not enough to prevent him from drifting back to sleep.

He awoke once more as a booted foot kicked him. "On your feet, Corporal! We're moving out." He looked up at a bearded sergeant wearing a gray tunic and a dark blue kepi, probably a battlefield souvenir.

Still sore, Morgan struggled to his feet. "What's going on, Sarge?" he asked, falling into character.

"Heard talk 'bout a flanking move around the Yankees south o' here. We're gonna be fightin' alongside some Texas boys."

Morgan gathered his gear knowing that he was to be part of John Bell Hood's assault on Devil's Den which would culminate at the epic battle of Little Round Top. *At least for this fight I've got a pair of shoes,* he thought with a sigh.

Hours of marching and countermarching followed as Hood and his fellow division commander Lafeyette McLaws sought to confound Union observers on the ridges ahead. This maneuver would double the distance their men had to travel and bring them to the attack positions east of the Emmitsburg Road this afternoon when the summer heat would be most intense. The soldiers in the ranks had no idea why they were being moved around and grumbled constantly. Though he knew what was happening, Morgan felt the tedium as well. *Hurry up and wait—the age-old soldier's complaint.* It suddenly occurred to him that *this* is what constituted a realistic battle game. Were the designers trying to make some kind of statement? *If so I damn well get it, so can we please end this?*

An artillery barrage thundered. Officers raised swords and ordered their men to charge, splashing across a narrow stream known as Plum Run and into the Devil's Den, later called the Valley of Death by survivors. A hail of Minie balls struck gray and butternut troopers around him. A nearby tree exploded, bark flying off in all directions; a piece of it nicked his cheek, but otherwise he remained unhurt.

Ahead loomed the three hundred foot high wooded slope of Big Round Top. Among the jumbled rocks and crags he spotted flashes of rifle fire, while atop the summit a semaphore flag waved excitedly. Morgan knew from history that Big Round

Top was lightly defended. "Come on!" he shouted to the men around him. "We can take this hill!" Wild Rebel Yells erupted as the Southerners pressed their attack. The Union sharpshooters who weren't killed quickly retreated. Morgan and his comrades continued climbing to the summit, sobbing for breath when they reached their goal.

Across a wooded defile rose Little Round Top, where more Yankee signal flags waved atop the summit. In less than an hour the Confederates would be ordered to charge up that hill, which Morgan knew was rapidly being reinforced by Union regiments including Joshua Lawrence Chamberlain's 20th Maine. But at the moment he was too tired to care as he wiped the blood trickling down his wounded cheek.

The game seemed deliberately designed to wear him down, perhaps to the point of nervous collapse, and he wondered who would want to do that. He had no real competitors, as most other VR producers offered their customers visits to pure fantasy worlds, usually sexual in nature. Ares was almost alone in offering realistic experiences taken from actual history. Perhaps a designer who once worked for him harbored a grudge. Leigh Roberts came immediately to mind, and he had to admit there might be more than one. But it was always his policy that differences of opinion or style could be worked out provided everyone acted like an adult. Morgan never went out of his way to screw over anyone.

He should have done a more thorough job of vetting the design team, but that would've involved a flight to their hometown. No serious businessperson had time for that. Conferences were done on the Web, though with modern technology there was no way to tell if the person you were talking to was real. Software was available for reading a heat signature from a living person, but other software could mimic that for a VR character.

"Hey, Corporal! Glad to see you're still among the living." He turned to see the young Cherokee with the solitary black feather in his hat.

Morgan grinned as he shook the character's hand; at the same time he felt there was something familiar about his new friend. "Good to see you, too. Never caught your name."

"Folks just call me Johnny, for Johnny Reb, mostly 'cause palefaces can't pronounce my real name."

"Let me try. I grew up around Native Amer—Indians."

Johnny ignored the request and pointed at the summit of Little Round Top. "Guess that's our destination," he said as officers and NCOs began mustering the exhausted men.

The sun was sinking in the west, but the air was still hot and muggy as with defiant Rebel Yells the Confederates charged across the defile. As more Minie balls rained down Morgan climbed the rocky slope. Gasping, he suddenly remembered another way to stop the Gettysburg Game.

Although death experiences could not be programmed into a battle game, as no one alive knew what that felt like, players always tried not to get killed because if one's character died the game would automatically end. But with this program attempting such a termination was risky. Anything less than a direct hit could cause him to linger in indescribable agony for hours or even days.

Nonetheless, this couldn't go on. His actual blood pressure was doubtless soaring through the roof; a heart attack or stroke was not far off.

He spotted a Union sharpshooter taking aim at him. A clean shot would hit him in the head or chest, both would be instantly fatal. So he stood perfectly still as the VR foeman took aim and saw the weapon flash.

Then something knocked him to the ground. Cursing, Morgan felt Johnny covering him. "Not yet, Mr. Hunt," he whispered. "Our bio-scans show your vital signs still haven't passed the point of recovery." Morgan froze. "Johnny" was not just a VR character but a player like himself.

The Cherokee's face suddenly became familiar. Age the features and he would resemble Martin Blackfeather, the founder of Reality First. "You said no deaths have ever been recorded due to VR use," Morgan said aloud. "So you arranged to initiate one?"

"Don't be muttering to yourself, boy; it sets a bad example for the men," a lieutenant told him just before he was hit and killed. Blackfeather's character disappeared. Pandemonium reigned as everyone from captains down to buck privates shouted commands to keep moving and shoot. The effect combined with endless deafening gunfire was dizzying. Experienced war gamer though he was, Morgan wanted nothing more than to curl into a fetal ball. *But that's exactly what Reality First hopes I'll do—lie down and die—so they can use my death to prove their point that my work is a goddamn menace!* He resolved not to give them the satisfaction.

Above him, near the summit, he saw a single Union officer raise his sword and yell, "Come on! Come on, boys!" before charging the Confederate host alone. "Lieutenant Holman Melcher, Company F, 20th Maine Regiment," Morgan gasped. Seconds later a few men followed, then more, then with an animal roar that rivaled the Rebel Yell's ferocity descended in a human flood. Union sharpshooters concealed in the surrounding woods maintained fire.

One by one the Confederates lost their nerve and began to bolt. Morgan suspected that Reality First intended him to be paralyzed with fear, but instead this accurate portrayal of Melcher's courage inspired him. It was the reason Morgan wanted to bring history alive for a modern audience. He threw down his weapon and attempted to surrender to the Maine Yankees. Just then something sharp and hot struck him at the base of his spine and, gasping, he collapsed on a jumble of rocks.

Unable to do anything but moan, he lay for hours as everything around him grew dark. At first he figured the game was trying to simulate death, then he realized that it was only night coming on. Through a haze of pain he heard someone say, "Here's another Reb. Looks like he's still breathin'." Rough hands lifted him onto the bed of a wagon which proceeded to bounce him about in agony.

As he drifted in and out of consciousness, the scent of whiskey brought him fully awake. A lamp hung overhead, revealing a man in a blood-spattered apron. "Bullet's lodged in his spine. He probably won't survive the operation."

"We have to try," another voice said as a recognizable face came out of the shadows. "If we let Reb prisoners die they'll do the same to our men."

"Ever heard of Andersonville Prison?" Morgan asked weakly. "But you really don't want me to survive this operation do you, Mr. Blackfeather?"

Blackfeather smiled back, seeing no point in remaining in character. "You're proving a lot harder to kill than we thought. It's nothing personal, Mr. Hunt. As this game demonstrates, virtual reality is a

threat to its users. Sadly no one will heed our warnings unless there is a death; a prominent one."

"You mean like a drug dealer dying from an overdose?" Morgan groaned. "Whatever helps you sleep at night."

"Look at it this way, your death will probably save thousands." The surgeon began sharpening his knives. Morgan began to panic, then spotted the pistol on Blackfeather's hip.

He reached out to snatch the gun from its holster while crying out, "This man is an Injun! He's gonna scalp us all!" Then he cocked and fired the pistol after aiming the barrel at Blackfeather's stomach.

The head of Reality First screamed and collapsed on the ground. "War is hell," Morgan gasped as a nearby nurse pounced on him and tried to wrestle the gun from his grasp. "Morgan!" she screamed. "What the hell are you doing?" The lamp-lit interior of the tent faded.

The nurse's rough face morphed into the far more pleasing features of Leigh Roberts as she threw his headset on the floor next to his couch. "Christ, you look like hell. How long have you been in VR?"

He sucked in a lungful of air, waiting for his heart rate to slow. "The game? Is it over?"

"Damn straight!" She tapped the phone on her wrist. "I'm calling the paramedics. Don't even think about arguing!"

"How…how did you know I needed help?"

"I didn't. After our last video chat I decided we needed to thrash things out in person."

"Thanks," he said behind a sigh. He sincerely hoped Martin Blackfeather had also survived the Gettysburg Game, so that he and his little group of crusaders could be prosecuted for attempted murder.

*Copyright © 2016 by Jeff Calhoun*

*Jack McDevitt is a Nebula winner (and sixteen-time Nebula nominee) as well as a multiple Hugo nominee. He is the author of twenty-two novels, five collections, and eighty short stories.*

# HENRY JAMES, THIS ONE'S FOR YOU

## by Jack McDevitt

It came in over the transom, like a couple hundred other manuscripts each week, memoirs of people nobody ever heard of, novels that start with weather reports and introduce thirty characters in the first two pages, massive collections of unreadable poetry from someone's grandmother.

They all go into a stack for the screeners, who look through them, attach our form rejection, and send them back.

Actually there's only one screener. Her name is Myra Crispee. She has one green eye and one blue eye, and a talent for going through the slush pile. She picks out the occasional possibility and gets rid of the rest. Every day. Love my job, she says. When I ask her why, she says it's because I pay her the big bucks.

Tempus Publishing isn't a major oufit, but we do okay. We don't specialize. Tempus will publish anything that looks as if it'll make money. But most of the manuscripts we see have already made the rounds at Random House, HarperCollins, and the other biggies. Some come in from an agent, but that has no effect on the way we treat them. Unless we know the author, they all go into the pile.

Sometimes we get lucky. We published a couple of self-help books last year that did extremely well, and a novel about Noah's ark that became a runaway bestseller.

Anyhow, the day it arrived was cold and wet. The heating system had gone down again so I was wrapped in a sweater. I'd just opened the office and had turned on the coffee when Myra came in, carrying an umbrella and a manuscript. That was unusual. She doesn't usually take these things home. "Hey, Jerry," she said, "I think we've got a winner."

"Really?"

She was beaming. "Yes. I was up half the night with it." She trooped over to her desk and sat down in front of what I thought was a second manuscript, but which turned out to be the rest of the submission.

"My God," I said, "that looks like a thousand pages."

She peeked at the end. "Twelve hundred and twelve. I've only read a few chapters, but if the rest of it is like what I've seen—."

"That good, huh?"

"I couldn't put it down." The magic words. We seldom saw anything that wasn't easy to walk away from. She leafed through the pages. "Incredible," she said. "Who *is* this guy?"

"What is it?" I asked.

"He calls it *The Long War*. It's about the war in the Middle East."

"Which one?"

"How many are we involved in? I didn't see the news this morning."

"It's been done," I said.

"Not like this, boss." She was still turning pages.

"Who's it by?"

"Guy named Patterson." She shook her head. "Edward Patterson. Ever hear of him?"

He was a stranger to me. "What's the cover letter say?"

She needed a minute to find it. "'Novel enclosed.'"

"That's all?"

"That's it."

We used to have a screener's box where she could deposit manuscripts that were potentially publishable. We dispensed with it because Myra rarely put anything in it. So she just brought the manuscript over and laid it on a side table. Then she walked back to her desk, pulled the next submission off the pile, and began turning pages. But I knew she was really waiting for me. Wanted me to pick up *The Long War*. "I'll look at it before I go home," I said.

She continued turning pages, sighed, and touched her keyboard. The printer kicked out a fresh rejection. "Okay," she said.

I was working on *Make Straight the Path*, an inspirational book by Adam Trent. It was pious and reassuring, loaded with anecdotes showing how the unbelievers get theirs. You wouldn't believe how his other books had sold. Penguin would have loved to have him.

I stayed with it, resisting the temptation to look at Patterson's epic. It *resembled* an epic. The manuscript obscured a coffee stain half a foot above the table. That made it official.

Now, lest you think I'm one of those editors who only cares how many copies can be moved, let me tell you that, while sales figures matter, it's always been my ambition to discover a new writer. Well, okay, all editors feel that way. But that's because we're generous and compassionate. So when Myra got up and headed for the washroom, I took a look.

Patterson lived in New Hampshire.

I lifted the cover page and glanced at the opening lines. That night I hauled it down in the elevator, the whole twelve hundred pages, and took it home.

☼

I read it on the train. Read during dinner at Milo's. Read through the evening and took it to bed. In the summer of 2001, I went to the Army recruiting office with the young college student hero and cringed while he joined the Reserves. I rode with the UN inspectors while they played tag with Iraqi 'escorts,' and tried to surprise their hosts at suspect facilities. I sat in the councils of the president while his aides urged an attack on Saddam and constructed arguments they hoped the UN and the voters would buy.

The night got away from me, and I finally closed my eyes when the first light of dawn was hitting the curtains. I called Myra's voicemail a couple hours later, letting her know I'd be late. Called again around nine to tell her I wouldn't be in at all.

It wasn't simply one more war novel. This one had that cliffhanging quality, yes. But it was vastly more. It *owned* the war. Through the eyes of its characters the reader saw how it had happened, came to grasp the inevitability of the conflict. He understood what it had meant to ride shotgun on the convoys or to go house to house in Fallujah. He experienced what it was to fight an enemy who wasn't afraid to die. Who imagined killing to be a divine imperative.

I spent time with a group of insurgents, and came to understand what drove them. I carried stretchers through the burn wards of an Iraqi hospital when shattered bystanders were brought in. And finally I was with mothers in Ohio when the dread news came.

It had perspective, passion, fear, the determination of obviously flawed men and women in authority to get things right, the mounting frustration as those who had been liberated refused to throw roses.

I was holed up with it for six days. The outside world simply stopped until the last shots had been fired, and the fallout had begun to take its political toll.

It was a *War and Peace* for our time.

I had done better than find one more professional writer who could sell a few thousand copies of whatever. I had found a new Herman Wouk.

I finished late on a drizzly, cold evening and sat staring out my apartment window at downtown Boston, thinking about Edward Patterson. On that night, only I, and Myra, knew who he was. Within a year, the whole world was going to know.

He lived in Laconia, at the foot of the White Mountains.

It was a quarter after ten. A bit late to be calling. On the other hand, this was a guy who, as far as I could determine, had never been published. I remembered my own reaction when the postcard had arrived from *Guns and Ammo* announcing my own first sale.

Myra, anticipating me, had gotten Patterson's number from information and printed it neatly above the title. I made myself a scotch and soda and reached for the phone.

☼

*"Wonderful,"* he said. *"Mr. Becker, that's great. You're actually going to publish it?"* He sounded younger than I'd expected.

"Yes, Mr. Patterson. Ed. Is it okay if I call you *Ed?*"

*"Sure. Yes. Absolutely. Can you hold a second?"*

"Okay."

He must have covered the phone. But I knew what was happening. He was passing the good news to his wife. Or girl friend. Or whomever.

*"I'm back,"* he said.

"Good."

*"Mr. Becker, you have no idea what this means to me."*

"I can guess," I said. "Ed, are you by any chance free to come into Boston tomorrow?"

He made a sound deep in his throat. *"I'm a teacher,"* he said. *"At the high school."*

"Okay. How about Saturday?" We don't usually open the office Saturday but in this case I was willing to make an exception.

*"I can do that,"* he said.

"Fine. I'll have a contract ready, and we'll celebrate by going to lunch." The truth was that I wanted him signed and delivered before he found out how good *The Long War* was. If he realized what he had, I'd wind up having to deal with an agent. Or possibly even get caught in a bidding war with MacMillan.

✿

He was maybe twenty-five. Tall, with a nervous smile. Light brown hair already beginning to thin. Sallow cheeks, pale skin, watery gray eyes behind bifocals. He wore a fatigue jacket and hauled a laptop in a stitched bag over one shoulder. Didn't look much like Hemingway.

He turned the pages of the contract with long, thin fingers, not examining it, I thought, so much as admiring it. When he got to the advance, he stopped. "Twenty thousand dollars?" he asked.

I was about to say I'd be willing to go higher because I liked the book. I'd expected to go higher. But it was always best to start out with a conservative figure. You can always move up.

"Seems like a lot," he added.

"Well," I said, trying to conceal my surprise, "Tempus believes in being generous." It didn't really matter. The book was going to make a ton, so there was no risk.

"It's certainly very kind of you." He smiled again. He looked like the kind of guy the other kids had picked on in the schoolyard. And I would never have believed him capable of the kind of rugged prose that informed *The Long War*.

I showed him where to sign, explained what we expected, that we'd want to be able to use his bio and likeness in promoting the book, that we might ask him to make a few guest appearances. I didn't mention that he was signing over all TV and movie rights, that he was giving Tempus a healthy share of any foreign sales, that we would also collect seventy-five percent of book club rights. And of course there was the option clause. "Normally, Ed," I told him, "we'd want to retain the right of first refusal on your next novel."

"But—?" he said, suddenly looking worried.

"I want to be up front with you, Ed. Is there going to be a sequel?"

"A sequel?" His eyes clouded. "There'll be another book."

"Okay. Good enough. Tempus is willing to forego the option. We'd like instead to sign you to a three-book deal. Beyond *The Long War*."

His eyes slid shut, and I was looking at the most beatific smile I'd ever seen. Paradise had arrived.

"We're offering a seventy-five thousand dollar advance for the three."

He put the glass down and stared at me. "I don't know what to say."

"Don't say anything," I said. "Just sign on the line." I showed him where.

I know what you're thinking. But we do not try to take advantage of our authors. We were providing a major service for Ed Patterson. We were giving him a chance to launch a new career, to break away from his teaching job, to fulfill a lifelong dream. When you've been in this business for a while, you discover that it takes a lifelong dream to drive someone to write a novel. Especially a big one.

He signed the contract. Four books in all. In triplicate. I put one in a manila envelope and handed it to him. "Your copy," I said.

He was glowing.

"Now let's go celebrate."

✿

We went across the street to Marco's. It's a quiet Italian restaurant just off the Common. It was still a little early for lunch, so hardly anyone was there. We ordered a decanter of red wine, and I filled both glasses. "To you, Ed," I said. "And to *The Long War*."

He wore a grin a mile wide. "Thanks, Jerry." He sipped the wine, made a face at it, put it down. "Strong stuff," he said.

I finished my own and refilled the glass. "I have to tell you, Ed, *The Long War* is pretty good. How long have you been working on it? Four years? Five?"

"I guess you could say ten or eleven. Somewhere in there."

"*Ten* years? You've been writing this since you were, what, fifteen? Do I have that right?"

"Oh, no, Jerry. I didn't *write* the novel. Max did."

"Max? Who's Max?"

"Ah," he said. "That's the *real* accomplishment. That's my surprise."

I finished the second glass in a swallow. "You didn't tell me there was going to be a surprise."

The waiter arrived. We ordered. When he was gone we picked up where we'd left off. "What surprise?" I demanded. "Who wrote the book? Are you his agent?"

"Hell, Jerry, anybody can sit down and write a novel. All you have to do is be willing to stay with it for, what, a year or so? Or five, I guess. Sit down and be willing to write every day. That's all it takes."

"What are you trying to tell me, Ed? Who's Max?"

He'd dropped the laptop onto the seat beside him. Now he set it on the table and opened it. Lights blinked on and the screen glowed cobalt blue. "This is Max," he said.

I stared at the computer, then at Ed. It was an ordinary HP model. Myra had one like it. Black case, the logo printed on the lid. "You said Max wrote the book."

"He did."

"Max is a computer."

"Actually, he's an artificial intelligence, Jerry." He leaned forward, breathless. "A *real* one."

"The computer wrote the book."

"He's an AI." He looked at me as if waiting for me to cheer. When I didn't a cloud crossed his face.

"I don't care what you call him," I said, "no machine could have written *The Long War*."

The big grin came back. "But he did."

"I don't believe it."

"A few years ago they were saying no computer would ever compete with a chess master. You look recently to see who's world champ?"

We sat staring at each other. The door opened and people came in. A family with a little boy. The boy had a pulltoy.

"It took four days," he said.

"What took four days?"

"To write the novel."

A chill settled into my bones. I drank down more of the wine. Two plates showed up. Pizza for Patterson. Spaghetti and meatballs for me. But my appetite had gone south. "Four days," I said.

"Yes. Well, maybe a bit more. But not much." He took a deep breath and smiled modestly. "It took me almost as long to tell him what kind of book I wanted."

"It's just not possible."

"That doesn't include printing time, though."

"You're signed to do three more novels."

"Yes."

"I was expecting world-class stuff."

"They'll be good. Max was years in the making and has spent a long time analyzing the great books."

"How long?" I asked.

"How long what?" He was chewing on the pizza, obviously enjoying himself. But he looked as if he couldn't understand why I was unhappy.

"How long will it take to deliver the other novels?"

"Probably two weeks. It takes a while to run them off."

"Two weeks for another novel like *The Long War*?"

"Two weeks for all three. But they won't be like *The Long War*, although they'll be of comparable quality." He pushed his chair back and tried to look upbeat. "We've already decided on the next book. It'll be about the power and the downside of religious belief. Along the order of *The Brothers Karamazov*. But different, of course. Original."

I sat frozen. Yep, no problem for Max. You want something to make people forget *The Winds of War*? Have it for you Tuesday.

"You all right, Jerry?"

"I need some fresh air." Or maybe we'd get a new *Huck Finn*. This time around we'd take a hard look at anti-gay prejudice. I threw money on the table and headed for the door.

"Jerry, wait." He was right behind me.

Maybe a new Dreiser novel. By Max.

Or something in the mode of Scott Fitzgerald.

Traffic outside was heavy. Buses, delivery trucks, crowded sidewalks. "If Max wrote the book, why's your name on it?"

"Legal reasons. He's not a person. Can't sign checks. Can't really do anything."

"Except write great novels."

"You got it."

He stood in front of me and flashed an enormous grin. He had no idea what he'd done. This *child*, who was obviously very good with electronics had canceled William Faulkner, Melville, Cather: What would their work be worth in the shadow of this *thing*? I assumed if he could do *Karamazov*, he could produce a new symbolic masterpiece in the spirit of

James Joyce. Call this one *Achilles*, in which a man's life is driven by a search for control. Or maybe something to push *Remembrance of Things Past* off the charts. In eight volumes, delivered over the course of a month.

"I couldn't be sure it had worked," Patterson said. "I don't read that much. Not fiction. I didn't know whether it was any good or not. What Max wrote. You were the test. We'll put *his* name on the cover though, if that's okay."

"What's Max's last name?" I asked.

A bus was coming up behind him. It was a local, headed for Massachusetts Avenue. It had just picked up passengers at the corner, seen an opening, and was accelerating. It had broken loose from the traffic.

"Winterhaven. Max Winterhaven."

"Sounds pretentious."

"I thought it sounded literary."

Max Winterhaven was slung over his shoulder. I looked up at the bus driver, and I swear he knew what I was going to do before I did. I saw it in his face the instant before I gave Patterson his quick shove. His eyes went wide and he toppled backward. People screamed, the brakes screeched, and I either said, or thought, "This one's for Henry James."

I got clean away. The descriptions that showed up on CNN a few hours later sounded nothing like me. They also reported that the dead man had been carrying a laptop, but it had been smashed. Police were trying to reconstruct it, but I never heard anything more.

There was no widow, I'm pleased to say. I don't know who had been with him the night I called. *The Long War*, as we all know, has become an international bestseller. We are sending the checks to the deceased's mother.

Literary authorities are on the tube almost weekly, decrying the loss of Edward Patterson, a man of incredible talent, who would have become a towering literary figure, had he only been given time.

*Copyright © 2005 by Jack McDevitt*

*Tina Gower is a winner of Writers of the Future, the 2013 Daphne du Maurier Award for Best Mystery/Suspense, and nominated for the RWA Golden Heart. This is her fifth appearance in* Galaxy's Edge. *In 2015 she collaborated with Mike Resnick on the Stellar Guild novel,* INCI, *and this year her first solo novel,* Romancing the Null, *was published.*

## THIS IS HOME. YOU ARE WELL.

### by Tina Gower

### AFTER

I'm meditating alone in the priestess' hut when Anya taps me awake.

"It is time," Anya says, carefully avoiding eye contact. She rubs her hand against the tree needles as though she'd like to get the feeling of my skin off her fingertips. Already the shunning has begun. My husband has blackened our family name because he has taken up arms and fought in war. It doesn't matter the circumstances, our people value peace, and we punish those who do not. Peace cannot be maintained if there are those who do not support it. He was sent to negotiate, to help find a compromise, and instead he chose a side and fought.

I thought I'd have more time to decide, but the villagers seem to already know my choice. I loved Amil. It's true. Our pairing was foreseen to fulfill a majestic destiny, a joining of two revered tribes. He kissed me shyly on the cheek and offered my father dried grains from his land that had been cut after the first triple full moon of our lifetimes. I had many suitors, but none as patient, or as peaceful as Amil. I chose him for his even temper and distaste for conflict. Qualities we respect in our village.

The scent of fermented roots and earth fills the tent. Anya leaves a bowl of soaked grain as a meal and a cup of tepid water. My stomach feels as though it has rocks grinding against one another. I can't eat. I part the waterfall of husks that block the suns and peer out, blinking into the sky. The shuttle is a small speck that grows like mold through the redwood tops. One moment the ship is so tiny I think I can brush it away. The next moment it's so large it's rotted the bread.

I crawl through the opening. Villagers part for me, turning their backs as I walk through the crowd. I haven't decided if I'll greet Amil with a kiss on the cheek, an acceptance for his behavior, or spit at his feet and turn away, showing alliance for my people.

A group of younger children gather and point at the shuttle. "Sky ship!"

It isn't often that we permit the shuttles to fly this close to our village. We prefer to live as though we're indigenous. No running water, no food but what we can grow. In touch with the planet and remaining as natural as possible, insures that we will stay pure. We won't allow outside influences to sway us. Our elders are wise, because this has also made our people grounded in a way that allows us to provide reliable mediation to the rest of our solar system.

The shuttle's thrusters engage when it's several hundred feet above our village. It must land in a small clearing by the lake. Close to where the elders have set up a temporary shelter for Amil, until he can leave. The wind kicks up dried plants, dust, and debris. The elders turn their backs. Denying my husband the sacred ritual of *Yawin*, a welcoming to his native home. I keep my eyes on the descending shuttle, for I'm to be the last to turn away, or by right, I can give up my place as priestess and join my husband's shame.

The doors are about to open and I still do not know what I'll do.

### BEFORE

My father eyes me from across the fire. He speaks with Gerrard, the eldest of the task council. It has been three of the largest moon's cycles since Amil and I have joined our families. We anticipated every problem in the adjustment. Our families make demands on our time and we must show how we work together to solve problems.

Both families pushed on us, giving us opportunities to negotiate, compromise, and show our skills as a couple. All the while the elders have watched to see if we're well matched, not just in feelings for each other but also in values. Only the strongest matches are permitted to continue.

Amil's shadow flickers from the firelight beside me. I glance up to see him grinning. "Do not watch too closely. I feel your anxiety from across the forest."

"They are discussing our future." I weave needles into a basket. "Should we not go and speak with them?"

He shakes his head. "No, I'd rather stay here and make a basket with you." He plops next to me and begins inspecting the tree needles, comparing thicknesses. "Here," he says, "These are the strongest for the sides around the base."

I eye them, disbelieving. "But they're too thin."

He weaves two needles together with expert precision. "Two together are stronger than a thick one alone. The thick ones do not weave and bend as easily." As he explains he weaves the next line together and I see what he means. It curves the basket up, making it flexible, yet stable.

I lean in and run my finger along his work. "That is remarkable."

He kisses me on the nose, and then with his fingers on my chin, he guides my lips to his.

My father clears his throat above us. I jerk away from Amil's embrace as though I were caught doing something I shouldn't have. Although, we're permitted to touch in public. My cheeks burn. A kiss is rather intimate even if it's allowed.

The elder raises his eyebrow, amused. My father's face is plain, hiding his disapproval.

"It is decided that you will be allowed to present your match to the task council once a replacement has been found for the peace council. Shepherding a match requires a lot of attention. We cannot spare the resources until both councils have been filled."

"But we have been waiting for our task as a couple for longer than normal. Is there a problem with our match? If there's a problem—"

Amil places a hand on my leg and a tingle runs straight to my hips. I forget what I was going to say.

Amil continues for me. "Lani and I are grateful for your efforts and we are eager to move to the next stage as a coupling. Our hut is ready. I'm overjoyed to be joining her tribe. I wish to do what is needed to speed up the process so we can live together."

My father's lips flicker, holding back a grin. He gives me an approving look. He has told me in private on more than one occasion that he is impressed with Amil's abilities to smooth out the tension in a situation.

Gerrord scratches his chin and leans on his walking stick. "You and Lani are an excellent match. We have no objections. It is just we do not wish to rush any pairing, good or bad. If your match is strong, you will withstand the wait. I assure you no pairing has suffered adverse effects from more time."

My father nods in his agreement. I'm disappointed, but these are wise points. The matter is settled.

Amil places his hands in his lap, watching me. I offer a weak smile. His forehead wrinkles in concern.

His gaze is steady on mine. "Those are wise words. I agree that my match with Lani is strong and we will withstand a longer than normal wait, but that still leaves the problem of your shortage on the peace council. I would like to volunteer. It will aid me in integrating into my new community."

The elder's eyes widen in surprise, my father is equally stunned they look to each other for objections and find none. Amil is from a village that has only three generations established since settlement on the planet. Our village boasts seven generations. Many of the surrounding villages send apprentices here. The younger establishments are often eager and ambitious and mirror the technology driven people in the other galaxies. Amil is like an old soul. He is ambitious only in his desire to bring positivity and peace. He fits.

Gerrord taps his stick against the ground, deciding. "It's a heavy responsibility to take on as a new member of the community, but since you'll be learning our ways and joining a committee soon, it makes sense to start that process now. And we do need to keep the councils filled. Without them we risk falling into problems and disagreements among other tribes. Maintaining peace is our highest priority and that requires constant effort."

Amil bows his head. "I am honored to be a member of a tribe that holds its values so close to my own."

The two older men leave. Amil continues to weave our basket.

I whisper to keep my voice low, so no one else can overhear. "The peace council is a lot of responsibility for someone just beginning their negotiation studies. I didn't know that you were so ambitious."

"I've no desire to be on the council." I give him a disbelieving look and he grins and nuzzles my ear. "However, I have a desire to be with you and that empty council seat was spoiling that wish. Besides, I'll suggest that they move me to a council with less responsibility and move someone up who is better suited. The most important thing is that we will not have to wait to start our lives together.

"This is home." He grips my hand in his. "We are well."

These are the words of my people. We believe that it binds our souls together.

We kiss and this time I don't care if father sees.

## AFTER

The shuttle doors open and my heart beats against my ribs like it is a prisoner begging for escape. My mouth is dry.

No matter, since the spitting is only a symbol that I acknowledge Amil has crossed a line that should never be crossed. There is always an alternative to violence and he chose to fight. I don't understand it and I burn with the wish to know. It is my right to know why he chose that life over his life with me.

He appears in the door carried on either side by medics. His feet weakly touch the ground, his arms are slung around the backs of the men and his bruised head is covered in mud and grime. His clothing is torn. His robes that once fit his muscular body hang loose. When he looks up, there is no light or humor in his eyes. This is not Amil, this is a shell.

My hands ball into fists. I turn to Anya who faces away from the shuttle. "I can't. I must go to him. He is hurt." And I must have answers. My eyes water and my throat swells.

Anya doesn't acknowledge me; she steps away, which shows my choice. Although after speaking with Amil I may change my mind at any time.

I run to my husband and help the guards to the hut.

Amil chokes, his voice rasps words I do not understand. I look to the medic for some answers.

The medic doesn't meet my eyes. "You are Lani?" I nod yes. "He has been calling out to you."

I lay a hand on Amil's chest. He turns to me as though he cannot believe it is really me.

"I'm here. This is home."

He shakes his head and swallows as though it is the most painful thing he's had to do. "No. Lani, you will leave. You must go."

And then he falls into a deep sleep before I can get my answers.

## BEFORE

"Do not fret, Lani." Amil grinds the umpa seeds into fine flour. "You're descendent of four generations of priestesses. They will not cast your nomination aside."

"But what if they wish to give another family a chance?" I wring my hands together, wishing for the dye to set faster, so I can get back to my work. I envy Amil's work, but we only have one stone. "My father says he doesn't wish for it to appear we've had a monopoly on the position."

"Then let the committee decide. It's not a decision your father can make for them." He sets the stone next to him and shifts the flour through a mesh grate. The larger pieces will not fall through and he can grind them again.

I pick up the stone. He backs away as I take over his task. "Since I missed the trade ships this morning, what is the news from above?"

He doesn't answer right away. Instead he scratches his chin and stares into the distance.

"Amil?"

"There is some tension between one of the villages and the ship of settlers. A disagreement on land and how the supplies are gathered and divided."

"Then they must send for one of the mediators. This is what we've been trained for. Our village will keep the peace between the groups."

He nods, crossing his arms.

"Well?" I wave my elbow as though to prod him even though he's too far to touch. "Who will they send?"

"They will send me."

I laugh at his joke. "Very funny, Amil. Who will they send?"

He doesn't laugh.

"But you're newly trained. You only joined to fill an empty seat. You asked to be removed a few nights ago. You're a farmer and your skills are much better working the land or on the trade committee than to be sent to a ship a thousand miles into the sky.

Didn't Ustof want your position? I thought it was settled." My thoughts race.

"The peace counsel thought it was best to send the most neutral party. My home village is very far removed from the disagreement. We sent a list to the concerned parties and they had to mutually agree on a name. That name was mine. It seems I'm the only neutral party in their eyes. Or both sides think they can manipulate me." He does let out a mirthless laugh now. "I don't know."

"Then you're the only one." My fingers are numb on the grinding stone.

I'd never expected his position in our community to change from being anything but my partner. He's quiet, soft-spoken. He didn't want to be a part of the peace committee, but they were in need of volunteers. Our people were raised and trained in negotiation tactics from an early age. Avoid conflict. Find compromise. We valued our abilities to keep calm and level reasoning. When the settlers moved in, we saw they had a different value system. They fought more often. Our services were needed more in recent years, but we always helped them to find a peaceful solution.

But Amil is skilled. I've seen it. My parents have seen it. The council must have seen it. "You will do well. You will honor our tribe."

"I will honor you." He kisses me. "Everything I do is for you, my priestess."

"Not yet," I correct.

"I don't leave for three nightfalls, we will know if that is true by then. And I'll never forget this is my home. You are well."

Then he leads me to the pallet on the floor and we make love as though everything will work out fine, because we had no reason to believe it wouldn't. But I don't sleep.

## AFTER

I wash the grime and bits of leaves that have been shoved against his field dressing. "What is this? They didn't have the supplies to clean the wound?"

He slides his arm toward the injury, his fingers tremble as he gets closer, and stops short. His eyelids crack open, too swollen to open all the way.

"The medic had herbs from his home village to prevent infection."

"It is still very red."

"My unit was kept from proper medical facilities for a week, trapped between two battles that blocked the group."

His talk of war makes my jaw clench shut. "It's fine." I clean the area as best I can and grind garlic into a paste for an antibiotic ointment.

"Please, do not bother with this. It will be easier if you leave me and turn your back as the rest have done. I'm broken. My soul is broken. I'm not long in this body."

"To leave a man suffering, even a disgraced one, is against our ways. I will heal you."

"No." He jerks to sit up and I startle, holding his bandage in place. I fear he will injure himself more. "That is cruel. To fix me and then leave me. I won't have it. I want you to leave. I don't want you this way, or your pity."

"My pity?" I speak, lowering my voice at an even tempo, and fail. My hands firmly hold his mid-section together. "Do you think I haven't suffered?"

"I knew you would be ashamed that I fought. I knew you'd be forced to shun me if I were ever to return. It must have made your position as a priestess difficult—"

"I don't care about any of that!" I press his wound for emphasis and he cringes, as though he's now feeling the stabs of pain he didn't before. "Do you not think the first thought in my mind when I woke up was if you were in danger and the last thought before I'd sleep was if you were dead? No, I didn't know why you chose to fight. We didn't know why. It is against our ways and you knew the consequences. You knew it would be a choice between me and our people, and that it would then force me to choose the same."

His eyes lower. His body shakes. He gradually lies back onto the pallet. "That isn't what I want."

"Not what you want." I mutter to myself as I smear the garlic paste into his cut and cover him with a clean cloth. "It is what I want. Leave our community or leave you? That is not a choice for me." I move to the edge of the hut, as far from him as I can go without leaving. If I leave, I will not be permitted to return. It means that I have declared Amil dangerous and someone will be sent in to care for him. It will only be the minimum requirement to keep him alive for as long as he chooses or until he is well enough to leave.

"You still haven't decided." He stares at the ceiling, his eyelids close slowly. He is fighting to stay awake, but won't last long.

I turn away from him and busy myself with taking stalk of our supplies. We will be given a small ration each day until my choice is made. I can take as long as I wish. But once I choose I cannot go back. "I'm here aren't I?"

"For now." His eyes close and soon his breathing becomes ragged even though he sleeps.

## BEFORE

Anya comes to us with the news. The priestesses are gathered in a meditation circle. We search for an answer to the turmoil between our allies. The candles dance when the hut flaps open. Our candle that was lit as a symbol of peace blows out again. It has not stayed lit since we started the ritual. The furs below my robes make my thighs sweat. Anya hooks the flap of the hut to the wall to allow for more air, but the hot moisture outside brings us little relief.

"They have three new ships. It is said that the villagers fear that they will send down soldiers to raid. They threaten to take what is rightfully theirs."

My heart beats quickly, my peaceful meditation disrupted. To be truthful, it never stopped rattling against my ribs like a trapped animal after my husband announced he would be the mediator between the two groups.

Anya and the eldest priestess whisper between one another, I strain to hear until I can't take it anymore and interrupt. "What word of Amil? Has he been permitted to negotiate?"

The women all turn to me. Each of their thirty expressions holds a different emotion. Some shake their heads in disbelief at my outburst, others show concern for my situation, and others blink away when my eyes meet theirs.

"If he hasn't been allowed to negotiate he hasn't technically failed. It was a trap to adhere to the treaty. They know they cannot raise arms without consequence from the Universal Alliance. It has been stated they will allow negotiation before force."

One of the younger priestesses, Shyla, leans toward me. "Hush. It is not polite to speak out of turn. We understand your distress. We know you wish to defend your husband—"

"I'm not defending him. If he hasn't been able to perform his task it is not an issue of our counsel. We must send more mediators to plead with the *Aurora*."

"The *Aurora* is not the only ship in orbit now. We have received reports of another."

There is a collective gasp. The women burst into discussion. Two ships? But what would the *Aurora*, a trade ship, need of another ship? The *Aurora* alone could carry twice the agreed supplies.

The eldest priestess rings the bell. Its tone is low and deep, too calm compared to the turmoil in the room. "I call for peace in this moment."

We all obey. Our hands return to prayer position, our backs straighten.

"You will return to meditation. I will travel to the next village this afternoon to gather the details. I have contacts on a carrier ship that may know details of the dispute. I will return in the morning." Anya helps her to rise from her seated position on the hut floor and she leaves.

Three ladies in training enter to line the sidewall with bread and roots. When our meditations are done we will be permitted a meal. I search the room for friendly assurances. None of the women return my gaze, but I keep searching. Resigned, I train my gaze straight ahead and attempt to concentrate. Out of the corner of my eye I see Shylo's gaze wander to me. I flick my focus to her, but she straightens and brings her attention to center quickly.

I do not meditate. My thoughts are with Amil. Is he well? Did he reach the ship? Have negotiations begun? I put my faith in Amil. Our people have trained for thousands of years to keep the peace. This is what Amil was born to do. He will not fail.

It isn't until the head priestess returns that my hopes are dashed.

She gathers us all together. I'm not granted a private meeting.

"News of the *Aurora* has come. The villages surrounding the dispute have observed that the talks have turned to violence. Those who wished to leave have done so, those who wished to fight stayed."

"And what of Amil?" I ask. "If he was permitted to leave—"

"Amil has chosen to stay. He has chosen to fight."

She looks each of us in the eye. Everyone but me.

## AFTER

Amil struggles in his sleep. Although he is flat on his back, his legs slide up as though he wishes to curl up into himself, but his stomach injury will not allow the position. He shivers. I watch him from my corner of the room, hugging my legs. He has changed. His features are sharper, his smooth lines and easy smile are gone. This is why our people advocate against violence. It destroys the soul and tears families apart. There is no disagreement worth it. To participate in any behavior that encourages distrust, jealousy, or turmoil is forbidden.

We are taught from an early age to recognize the traps. It is nature, some say. That anger and violence are normal. But they're not. Anger is an emotion that can be trained. Violence is a choice and there are a thousand choices. War is failed negotiation or failure to understand.

I crawl to Amil and cover him. I smooth his hair with the palm of my hand, massaging the lines of distress along his forehead. He eases.

I glance around the room, searching for some task, but there is nothing. The elders have removed any burden. Our only goal is to work out the arrangement. As a priestess, I'm expected to do what is for the greater good for our people. I cannot be allowed to condone an act of violence. My husband has no recourse to atone his decision due to the nature of his offense.

He didn't hesitate, the elders said. He admitted to believing his side was justified in their complaint. No remorse over the tactics he chose. No restraint.

His movements start up again. His legs saw and kick as though the blanket is holding him down. He claws at the air.

I sigh and place my hand on his cheek. He wakes with a rush of air into his lungs and his eyes go wide. He blinks and fixes his gaze on the drying herbs above his head, before coming to this reality.

"Shh," I comfort him. "This is home. You are well." These are the words of my people.

It is said that when a soul is wrestling with great remorse it will wander from the body during sleep. If it does not return this means the person is lost. We beckon its return by reminding it of its rightful place. We encourage it to stay with us. I fear my husband's soul may have long ago left him and this is why he wishes me to leave him. If that is the case, then my presence here is no longer necessary. I must find the strength to leave him. *When he is healed*, I tell myself.

"You are still here," he says when his eyes open.

"Where else would I be?"

"Gone."

There is silence and I think he has fallen asleep again, but his even breaths mean he hasn't.

"I must know." I whirl to face him and his hollow eyes meet mine. "Why did you stay? Tell me it was not to fight. Tell me it was to continue to attempt to negotiate and you didn't give in. Tell me you advocated for peace and then I will plea with the elders for you—"

"I wasn't the only negotiator." He threads his fingers together over his chest and closes his eyes. "There was someone from Distil, he was far more skilled than I. The villagers insisted that the settlement wouldn't negotiate. That they had been forcefully taking supplies and killing those who stood in their way. We didn't believe that there was nothing to be done, so we marched into the settlement with our hands held high and asked to speak with the captain. He met with us. He had a patient ear. He nodded as we detailed the complaints and our suggestions for allowing everyone something that they wanted.

"He smiled. Thanked us for meeting with him. Then he took out a gun and shot the negotiator from Distil in the head then he turned to me and said his people had desperate need of the supplies. He was doing this to save many from starvation. He told me he spared me to return to the village and negotiate with them to not resist if we wanted a peaceful outcome, or there wouldn't be anyone left to harvest. I explained that there was another way. We could help his people if he chose a peaceful path. His men surrounded me with guns and marched me from the settlement."

"You could have worked out another negotiation. Sent for help. Why start a war?"

"Yes, we tried, but no one could get through. We had more negotiations and all that passed was time. It wasn't long before the village stopped producing. The harvest had been decimated. The land had been reaped, the soil overworked. The captain gathered the villagers and asked for details of the surrounding villages. He wanted details of their crops, the supplies. He promised to pay them for their service and asked them to dig a large hole and he would fill it with fertilizer for the next year's crops, but instead he filled it with their bodies. I escaped because the host family I'd been staying with had grown distrustful of the captain's promises. We began to gather tools to use as weapons; we traveled to the surrounding villages to warn others. We told them to leave if they wished to avoid conflict, harvest and hide their crops."

"You tried to find a peaceful way to end the conflict."

"Yes. We thought that once the crop ran out and the people became useless to him he would leave. But instead he had plans to raid the surrounding villages. He would have eventually come here. You would have had no protection, no one to fight for you. Our village is the most peaceful on this land. He chose this side of our planet because we wouldn't struggle. He killed those who resisted so they wouldn't send for help."

Amil coughs and sputters. I bring him a cup of water and he sips. When he is ready he continues. "We gathered villagers to hide in the next village he planned to raid. We had sharpened tools and planks against guns, but we had the element of surprise and a plan. It wasn't long before we had some guns, too. And we fought them, so that the next village wouldn't die as the ones before them."

"But many died. Why not continue to hide?"

"Because we didn't want to take the risk that they wouldn't stop. Yes, many died so that more could live, so we could preserve our way of life. We sent word to the Universal Alliance. They are gone. The captain is dead. The ships have retreated."

When he says those last words it is not with relief. I know that Amil doesn't believe that the settlers will stay away. Over the next nights I care for his injuries and wipe the sweat from his brow when he cries in his sleep. I hold his hand as his grip becomes weaker. He repeats the stories of war and the men who fought with him. Amil tells me more details of the fight and more about the settlers. Then he speaks very little. He is only awake for small amounts of time.

"This is home." I whisper to him. "You are well."

They are the last words he hears.

The elders come for his body and Gerrard offers me his hand. "Return to the meditation hut, Lani, they will aid you in mourning. It was a generous and peaceful thing to aid Amil as he left this world. It is shameful that he chose violence in the end. The council will not hold it against you if you choose to continue your training as a priestess."

He doesn't turn his back to me. He assumes that Amil's death has solved the disgrace. My stomach burns. The sacrifice Amil has made, that others have made will go unnoticed. It will be seen as a failure and never be thought of again. They do not realize the horrible things they have been spared. The bloodshed. The violence.

I turn my back to him. I turn my back to all of them.

I march to the shuttles. I will return to the village where my husband fought. If the settlers return, I will be there, waiting.

*Copyright © 2016 by Tina Gower*

*Jean-Claude Dunyach is one of the leading science fiction writers in France. He is the author of seven novels and eight collections, and has won the Prix Ozone, the Priz Rosny-Aine, the Prix de l'Imaginaire, and the Eiffel Tower Award. He also writes lyrics for a number of French singers. This is his second appearance in Galaxy's Edge.*

## LOVE YOUR ENEMY

### by Jean-Claude Dunyach

The helicopter approached the island after a tight turn over the bay. The Tyrrhenian Sea rolled out its usual carpet of sun-crushed greens and violets. It took Cayre's practiced eye to make out the iridescent trace left by a ship in the middle of the proliferating algae. Sighing in exasperation, he took out his tablet and coded a short report.

"Stop that!" (Although the cockpit was soundproofed, the pilot had spoken over the general communication system so that the intervention would be recorded by the black boxes.) "No interference during landing."

Cayre shrugged. There were no other passengers; flight security was the least of his concerns.

"We'll fly another circle over the seaweed strip. I want to plot the pollution trace. Can you take photos?"

"We have fifteen minutes of fuel left. And we're already behind schedule."

"It won't take more than five minutes."

"It's your dime…"

The colorful blanket measured only two hundred meters long. Not a true degassing, rather a fuel leak. What intrigued Cayre, though, was the course chosen by the polluting boat. Right in the middle of the algae, where the long stems threatened to wrap around the propellers. A smuggler? The Center's surveillance system would have spotted it. He scrawled his questions on the tablet and set it to sleep mode.

With a grumble, the helicopter dove for the island.

Without waiting for the composite blades to come to a stop, Cayre stepped out of the cockpit, back hunched. It was fine and all knowing that there was no risk of decapitation; he still tucked his head down into his shoulders out of reflex. He forced himself to stand straight and walked over to the end of the concrete field where an electric cart with an immense sunshade was waiting for him. The driver saluted and opened the door.

The Center's buildings covered half the slope of a hill in the middle of the Island. At the peak, windmills stretched their skeletal silhouettes, waving their articulated arms, to make the most of the ocean breeze. Plastic greenhouses, separated from the road by honeycombed brick walls, stood in tight rows. As they drove farther from the sea, the few rare access points were covered with kabalistic prohibitions and symbols that Cayre was unable to decipher. Overwhelmed by an impulse, he motioned at the driver to stop, shaking his digital tablet.

Grudgingly, the other man parked the vehicle on the dust shoulder. Cayre climbed out and walked to the closest greenhouse to examine it. The heat stuck to him like glue.

The plastic shutters were locked by a double security system: code and handprint. The system remained inert under his fingers. Through a tiny slit next to a support beam, he saw rows of plants supported by carbon stakes. No way to determine what they were. He pretended to scribble on his tablet. Drops of sweat trickled down between his shoulder plates as he walked back along the short wall to the cart.

From the corner of his eye, he noticed a brown spot in the narrow tunnel between two greenhouses. The driver glanced at him, exasperated. Grimacing, Cayre climbed over the small wall and walked into the passageway.

He blinked in the heavy shadows that reigned there. After walking a few meters, he saw a couple of naked children huddling together, their puny buttocks facing him. No more than five years old, he thought as he came to a stop. He coughed. The little girl turned halfway around and stared at him. Then she tore a flower out of the ground and waved it at him like a talisman.

Cayre had never seen that type of plant before. The fleshy petals formed an irregular corolla, with an unhealthy color: a mixture of chrome and flesh, with iridescent streaks, like garbage oil that has been

recycled too often. The flower seemed to twist in the dirt-covered fingers that caressed it. Cayre approached and the sweet odor of rot grabbed him by the throat. Just before he turned, he saw the child tear off a piece of the corolla and chew it with an earnest expression. Her pupils dilated and she turned her back to him, her body shuddering.

The day was already well underway when Cayre entered the meeting room at the Center. He kept the pleasantries to a minimum. (Yes, he'd eaten at the previous stopover, no coffee thank you, yes he would greet the boss later.) They had him wear oversized sterile overalls, and he submitted to the decontamination ritual before entering a series of white-tiled laboratories. The flat screens hanging on the wall displayed segments of genetic code or single-cell colonies magnified thousands of times. However, the DNA sequencers were resting, their control panels turned off. Cayre supposed that they had interrupted all of the experiments in progress before his arrival. The usual scientific paranoia.

Close-ups of *Caulerpa Taxifolia* were scattered about the desks, particularly the most recent mutations that grew more than a meter per day and whose toxins attacked everything that moved. The spectacle was familiar to him. At this very moment, hundreds of laboratories around the world were working on cleaning up the planet's pollution and he, Cayre, was responsible for making sure that the taxpayer money was spent wisely.

He listened to the spiel carefully prepared by the two team leads. The Center had two specializations: treating oil derivatives—a remnant from the time when oil was particularly inexpensive in Greece—and controlling the flora in the Mediterranean depths. The situational analyses were detailed, obviously based on data that was updated in real time. The results, on the other hand, seemed fuzzy to him. And the medium-term research strategy could be summed up in a handful of empty sentences, heard thousands of times elsewhere.

Cayre forced himself to listen to the presentations until the very end, without interrupting the speakers. He asked a few routine questions and requested the budget evolution graphs and the hiring curve for each team. The Center was operating at full capacity; the researchers—with impressive pedigrees—seemed both motivated and conscientious. But nothing was coming out of their labs. No revolutionary articles, no original technical solutions. Barely more than a few routine announcements on scientific sites. That was what had caught Cayre's attention and convinced him to come and inspect the island.

He leaned back in the articulated chair in the conference room and opened his tablet with a flick. Despite the air conditioning, he felt damp. Opposite him, the two team leads sat shoulder to shoulder, flanked by a handful of scientists who had joined them.

"Before I forget," Cayre said, "I flew over the alga carpet surrounding the island on my way in and I saw something curious."

A reedy but perfectly audible whistle rose from the group of researchers. One of the leaders turned around, frowning, and silence fell.

Cayre allowed the discomfort to grow, then added, "There were traces of oil in the water. A polluting trail that the satellites should have detected."

"No doubt from a fishing boat. The area isn't really off limits even if we try to discourage the curious."

"I understand. However… (Cayre smiled ironically) the wake was heading straight for the algae. I believe that the invasive strains of *Taxifolia* produce toxins that prevent them from being nibbled at by the submarine fauna. Not exactly the kind of place where one would expect to find miraculous catches. More likely a place people would avoid, if they don't want to twist a propeller. Am I mistaken?"

The oldest scientist shrugged ostensibly and said, "There are always a few imbeciles who go places they shouldn't. If that's all you saw, I'll send a report to the surveillance department."

"That's all I saw in fact. But I plan to spend a few days on the island and glance here and there. It is possible that I may complete your report with my own observations."

Cayre was assigned a tiny studio apartment in the housing complex next to the Center. In principle, he should have left the same evening, as no arrangements had been made for his stay. The bed was barely large enough for him. But the view from the balcony redeemed everything: beyond the greenhouse zone, the sea sparkled. The water looked unusually clean, as blue and transparent as during the time of Ulysses, despite the presence of algae.

Cayre considered asking them to loan him a swimsuit, then thought better of it. He'd wait for the night to swim. He knew he was a good swimmer, even though he wasn't used to saltwater. In France, the pools and certain mountain lakes were the last places people could paddle about without fearing skin rashes.

Overhead, a jet streaked the sky with twin furrows. The effect was disturbing. Cayre recalled what his father said to him shortly before his death, "We constantly draw the lines of our own destruction and no one knows how to read them!"

He pulled on a T-shirt with the Center's logo and set out to explore the island.

Behind the wheel of a mini-cart, he turned to the landing zone. A narrow road circled the island, bordered on one side by the sea and on the other by the greenhouses. From time to time, an olive tree stood out on the horizon. Cayre was starting to feel hungry. He had seen no one outside the Center. The island was inhabited only by the scientists and the few rare seasonal workers who took turns at harvest time. For a long time, European agriculture had been so mechanized that the peasants had been replaced by agricultural machine programmers or by artificial intelligences that analyzed the satellite data to adjust watering sessions in real time. But most of the arable land of the old continent had been polluted by industrial waste that overflowed in wild discharges, impossible to treat. For the time being, the oceans served as garbage cans for the entire world.

Cayre noticed a cloud of dust above the greenhouses, on the other side of the promontory he drove along. Instinctively, he slowed. The sun was low on the horizon; work must have stopped. As soon as he could, he parked on the shoulder.

Behind the greenhouses, there was an enormous compost hole filled with dry algae, sand, and dirt. A small mechanical shovel buzzed all around it, biting into the soil and spitting out enormous mouthfuls. A man, bare-chested, mouth hidden beneath an enormous mustache, operated the machine by remote control from on top of the rock where he was seated. Another rolled a large can toward the hole, using a motorized dolly. Then, to Cayre's surprise, he simply removed the plug and allowed a thick, black, oily liquid, which smelled all too familiar, to trickle onto the compost.

"What are you doing? Are you crazy?" Cayre sprung out into the light without thinking. The two men looked up at him and watched him approach, gesticulating, without interrupting their work.

"That's oil! You're polluting the entire zone."

"Ne?"

The man operating the machine glanced at him, eyes questioning, and uttered a long sentence in Greek. Cayre shook his head. The man shrugged, placed the remote control on the ground at his feet and pulled a folded piece of paper with the Center's logo on it from the back pocket of his jeans. It was a list of instructions, in Greek and English. One sentence caught Cayre's eye: *spraying on Zone 4, oil and garbage waste, Tanks 1 to 6.* The current date.

The Greek held out his hand for the paper. Dumbfounded, Cayre folded it back up and returned it. The mechanical shovel went back to work as a second tank was emptied over the hole, its contents mixed with the dirt. The stench of oil and crushed algae rose from the compost but the laborers seemed unconcerned.

When Cayre headed back to his vehicle, the Greek saluted him nonchalantly. As he opened the door, the investigator saw his reflection in the rear-view mirror. The logo on his T-shirt identified him as a Center scientist. That made him a big enchilada on the island.

His mind filled with questions, he headed back toward the sea.

He had to leave the car under a pine tree at the end of a road that was barely passable. After ten minutes on foot, he reached a tiny beach enclosed by two rocky outcroppings covered with algae. The water was incredibly clear, barely hemmed by foam. He undressed, placed a stone on his clothing to keep it from blowing away, and raced over the burning sand to the fringe of the waves.

All too soon, the water irritated his feet and calves, which were covered with reddish blisters. Swearing, he covered them with sand to relieve the pain. He heard the echo of laughter behind him. A half dozen children, as naked as he was, were pointing at him from the end of the promontory. One after

another, they jumped into the water and raced toward the open sea, shrieking in excitement. When they reached the edge of the algae fields, they dove together, disappearing under the surface, their brown bodies wrapped in filaments like obscene mermaids.

Cayre dressed quickly before limping over to the rocks. *Caulerpa* runners, dried by the sun, cracked under his shoes. He knelt to examine them, taking care not to touch them.

Most were covered with teeth marks.

He wrapped a few specimens in his T-shirt and headed back to his car.

Lying on the balcony, his legs coated with a fishy-smelling cream the Center's nurse had prescribed, Cayre finished reading the most recent scientific articles published by the island researchers. He had long realized that the convoluted phrases of the official reports were hiding more information than they provided. Laboratories around the world were fighting a fierce war, through espionage and sophisticated data mining techniques. Each patent was a victory, each publication a potential breach that the enemy could exploit. To a certain extent, he understood the phenomena, even though he wasn't sure he approved of it. But the Center's publications were decidedly empty of useful content, as if anything that could provide a trail had been painstakingly peeled away.

Cayre smiled inside. His specialty was filling in the missing zones in the reports, based on clues as tenuous as the absence of a crucial reference in a bibliographic list. When that wasn't enough, he investigated, guided solely by his intuition. And he never gave up without obtaining results.

An iced coffee and the *Taxifolia* runners he picked up on the beach stood on the plastic table next to him. He hastily scribbled on his tablet and shook his head. All of the elements he had gathered were organized in keeping with the missing zones, like a cloud of stars orbiting black holes.

He glanced at his watch. It was getting late, but the Center operated on Greek time. No doubt the researchers were staying behind in the labs. It would cost nothing to check.

The research block was locked. The retinal scanner ignored all of Cayre's attempts to be recognized. He settled for banging on the wall until someone came to open up for him.

Once he was decontaminated, a guard took him directly to the meeting room. He was not surprised to find the two team leads who had met with him in the late morning there. With a nod, he took a seat in the first free chair and turned his tablet on with a flick.

"Let's save a little time," he started. "My purpose in coming here is to understand what the enormous budget that has been allocated to you is really being used for. (He raised his hand to forestall any interruptions.) I also suspect that additional funding has been given to you by various industries. What we give you is not enough for you to obtain your results. I'm talking, among other things, about new the varieties of *Caulerpa* that you've developed, while your mission was specifically to find a means to eradicate those algae."

"You don't understand…" said the youngest of the team leaders.

"I'm all ears. A word of warning, however, I know enough to be able to tell when you're trying to lie to me."

"You've only been here since this morning and you think you understand everything that's going on here?"

"I have a few ideas. I've seen your greenhouses and your compost pit. I've picked up various unusual specimens here and there. In short, I have more than enough evidence to bring a battalion of experts here. If that's what you want, of course."

"How much?"

The hostility in the researcher's voice was so strong that Cayre felt like throwing out a figure, just to watch his reaction.

"Sorry, you're off track. All of the information contained in my tablet is transmitted to my department in real time. I'm under surveillance as well."

"Show him the bins, Franz," murmured the older of the two men. "As soon as you've signed a confidentiality agreement, we'll give you the owner's tour. That should convince our patrons that the money they're sending us is being put to good use. You'll leave your tablet in this room."

A half dozen scientists in rumpled overalls were gathered in front of their workstations or their microscopes. They never even looked up as the group walked past. For the first time since arriving, Cayre felt that the Center was something more than a fake window for visitors. Whatever research work was going on here, those taking part in it considered it crucial.

"We think we've made a fundamental breakthrough," echoed the oldest of the researchers, pressing his eye against the security scanner. "We came at the problem from the other side, with a new look."

"The *Caulerpa*?"

"The pollution of the planet, and particularly the oceans." (The wall slid open with a well-oiled hiss.) "The *Caulerpa* is a means, not a problem. You'll see."

In the middle of a room lit by horticultural neons stood a transparent bin, measuring several cubic meters, filled with water. A mass of algae with clearly recognizable fronds grew on the sandy bottom. The stems were a disgusting color; they shone as if coated in grease.

"Our latest baby," the scientist murmured proudly. "Created through bio-engineering in seventeen months, despite insane specifications. It's still growing a little too slowly, but we should be able to solve that problem soon. After all, the original strain grows several meters per day, when the conditions are favorable."

Cayre walked over to the bin. The network of clues he had gathered pointed in that direction, but he still found it hard to believe. He could not imagine what had driven an entire team to develop an improved version of the enemy.

As if reading his thoughts, the young scientist opened a metal locker, revealing a row of flasks.

"Choose your poison." (He picked up a bottle randomly and looked at the label.) "Mercury sludge. We also have crude oil, concentrated manure, motor oil… Everything that has been poisoning our planet for decades."

He climbed a step ladder and tilted the flask over the surface of the bin.

"Are you timing this, Georges?"

As Cayre watched, dumbfounded, the scientist poured the content of the flask into the bin. A brown cloud spread over the algae. The water grew so murky that it was almost opaque. An unpleasant odor swept over the room.

"We have about ten minutes to wait. Would you like a coffee? There's a distributer in the lab."

"Black, no sugar." (Cayre had replied automatically.) "But I'll wait until this is over."

He walked over to the transparent wall and looked through it. The dirty water was gradually clearing. He looked for a pump or some sort of filtering device, but found nothing.

"It's the *Caulerpa* that do the work. This strain feeds off all the substances we consider pollutants. It proliferates in the most affected sites and restores the purity of the water in a few months. We've conducted full scale tests around the island. The results are spectacular."

"The trail of oil I noticed when I arrived," murmured Cayre.

"An hour later and you wouldn't have been able to locate it."

The water in the tank was almost clear. Seized by an impulse, Cayre climbed the ladder and bent over the surface.

"Be careful! The *Caulerpa* gives off rather aggressive toxins," warned Georges. "Don't dip your fingers in the water!"

"I know…"

The sludge had disappeared, gobbled up by the reddish fronds. The sand at the bottom was once again visible.

"Franz has created another variety of garbage plants, as we call them. These one are for on land. A poppy mutation, halfway between the common poppy and the Afghan variety. It grows without any problem on public landfills or along highways. In the long run, it will cover all abandoned industrial zones.

"I think I've seen a specimen. It looks rather repulsive."

"To us perhaps. But our descendants will get used to it without any problems. Do you want us to show you how the *Caulerpa* processes the oil slicks?

"I've seen enough, thank you. I suppose everything you have here is protected by patents?"

"Not yet. Our experts have drafted the applications but we're waiting for the green light from our other sponsors to submit them." The scientist shrugged. "Personally, I don't really care. We're working for all of humanity, to clean up the mess our species has left behind itself. Thanks to what we've done, pollution will soon be nothing but a bad memory."

Franz and Georges accompanied Cayre back to his room, after making a detour to the cafeteria which served frozen dishes sprinkled with Retzina. Now that the veil of silence had been lifted, the two researchers seemed to be delighted to talk about their results. The three men settled on the balcony with a bottle of wine and plastic glasses. Under the star-studded sky, the sea was as calm as a bed sheet.

"I'll leave at dawn tomorrow," Cayre said. "What you've accomplished here will change the world."

As he put his glass down on the plastic table, he felt the *Caulerpa* runners he had picked up crumble under his fingers. The image of the chewed stems, teeth marks clearly visible, leaped into his mind.

In a voice that barely changed, he asked, "Your creations, these garbage plants as you call them… It would surprise me if they were a good mix for the human species. Apart from the fact that they're hideous, they must also be toxic for current herbivores. How do you plan to get rid of them, or at least limit their proliferation?"

There was a heavy silence and then Georges cleared his throat. "We've already solved that problem. I think you know that."

Cayre recalled the little girl's look, eyes dilated as she chewed the petals of the obscene flower, the color of used oil. Once again he heard the joyful cries of the flock of naked children setting out to graze the algae fields along the coast.

"I guessed it, in fact," he said while pouring another glass of wine.

*Copyright © 2005 by Jean-Claude Dunyach*

*Paul Di Filippo is the author of nine novels, fifteen collections, and more than seventy-five short stories, and is an omnipresent reviewer in the prozines. This is his second appearance in Galaxy's Edge.*

# THE MIRROR CRACK'D FROM SIDE TO SIDE

## by Paul Di Filippo

Dr. David Vitrine had no harm in mind when he perfected the tailored retroviral agent soon to be dubbed the "Love Bug." In fact, his honorable intentions were just the opposite of malign—although they were, admittedly, grandiose. He simply wanted to end all violence, whether by individuals or groups or nations; to foster understanding and empathy between people; and to bring peace and a spirit of altruistic cooperation to the entire Earth, ushering in a new Golden Age of amity and concord.

He could never have foreseen that his invention would succeed beyond his wildest hopes. Nor that it would subsequently result in the near-extinction of the human race. Nor that the only path back to survival would be to undo, at least in part, his dreams of harmony.

David Vitrine had been physically abused as a child. But he had overcome this bad start with a combination of resilience and native intelligence, and had gone on to become a leading authority in his field of neurochemistry. Yet as a mature and successful and respected adult, he still cringed at any hint of physical or even emotional violence in his personal life, or in events falling under his scrutiny. Headlines about murders and riots, wars and massacres, and ethnic cleansings left him shattered and despairing for hours or days.

Despite the arguments of experts like Steven Pinker, who had convincingly charted a decline in global violence from past centuries, Dr. Vitrine had the sense that the world was growing more and more belligerent, perhaps as a result of too many people competing for dwindling resources, with violence often the first recourse to "solving" any practical problem or ideological debate or territorial competition.

Feeling this way, Dr. Vitrine sought a "cure" for the innate brutality of the species.

His initial researches caused him to focus on two aspects of human biology, one neuro anatomical and one hormonal.

"Mirror neurons," those specialized structures in the brain that played a large part in empathy and emulation and resonant understanding, were half of his anti-violence equation.

Oxytocin, the hormone produced by the hypothalamus which stimulated affection and bonding and tranquility, constituted the other half.

After laborious trials, Dr. Vitrine succeeded in learning how to do two things simultaneously.

Enhance the number of mirror neurons and amplify their activity; and increase the production of oxytocin by an order of magnitude.

These changes could be installed in the brains of humans by an otherwise benign carrier virus that would also write the changes permanently into the eggs and sperm of the "victims."

The virus was transmittable by mere aerosol contagion: a sneeze, a touch.

In isolation, Dr. Vitrine tested the virus on himself. He had no cure for his virus, but was quite prepared with a dead man switch to incinerate himself and all his stock of the Love Bug should he deem it necessary.

But he liked the resulting changes in his mental and emotional apparatus. So he loosed the Love Bug on the general population.

Within less than a year, the world was transformed beyond recognition.

Anyone infected by the Love Bug protocols found they simply could no longer countenance hurting another being in any way.

There was no more war, no more terrorism, no more theft, no more assaults. So far so good, thought Dr. Vitrine.

But there were unanticipated results as well.

All sports and games ceased to be played. Winners could no longer stand seeing losers in any kind of distress.

All artistic representations of violence were banished. Even reading about or viewing fictitious pain proved intolerable, and no one could write such scenes.

Profit-seeking commercial activities suddenly felt horribly wrong, too much akin to theft, and so all trade, investments, banking, and retailing ceased.

Of course, in one of the biggest shifts, slaughter of animals for food now triggered utter revulsion in all Love Bug hosts, and so the whole world went vegetarian. Animals, however, were immune to the Love Bug, and so instances of tribesmen voluntarily letting themselves be eaten by hungry tigers, or watching peaceably as their villages were trampled by rogue elephants, proliferated. Likewise, even a practice as beneficial as killing malaria-carrying mosquitos required a certain bracing up of the spine, and could only be carried out by rationalizing that more good than bad resulted from such slaughters.

Even many small social rituals had to be modified. For instance, four-way stop signs at traffic intersections produced only immovable stasis, since no driver wanted even mildly to annoy any other driver by arrogating the right to go first.

But none of these challenges were, in the end, insurmountable. With immense resources and energies freed up from investment in violence, the human race could adapt without too much stress.

At the end of five years' time, Earth had indeed entered the Utopia envisioned by Dr. Vitrine. Alas, the liberator himself was not around to witness his triumph. He had been walking down a Manhattan street one day when an air-conditioner fell from a dozen stories above. Several people other than Vitrine witnessed the event in time to intervene and save him, but none of them could bring themselves to shove him roughly out of danger.

Humanity was tooling along nicely when the aliens arrived. Resembling Cthulhu crossed with a mythological griffin, they hailed from the habitable exoplanet around the star known as Tau Ceti, a mere twelve lightyears from Earth. Having learned from our broadcasts that we were now utterly non-belligerent, they had come to claim our real estate.

After an initial submission, seeing that the "Tee Cees" intended to exterminate homo-sapiens, human scientists frantically sought to produce some warriors. The only solution they could devise was to take human embryos and wipe out their fetal mirror neurons and hypothalamuses completely, then raise the morally crippled children as soldiers.

The resulting adolescent sociopaths, utterly without compassion, quickly slaughtered the unsuspecting invaders.

And then the children tried to subjugate their makers, whom they viewed as sheep.

This treachery had been anticipated. A special army of brainwashed and drugged adult Love Buggers proved capable of putting down their savage progeny. But the offense to their buried empathetic psyches still proved traumatic enough to cause them to commit mass suicide once their bloody work was done.

Humanity paused then to reassess Dr. Vitrine's legacy. Ways were found to prune mirror neuron networks and dial down oxytocin production.

So nowadays the world is still much kinder and more peaceful than it was when Dr. Vitrine unleashed his plague.

But noisy car horns, hamburgers, touch football, and the occasional shout of "Go to hell, you moron!" are part of the landscape once again.

*Sheila Finch won the Nebula for her "Reading the Bones," and is the author of close to a dozen novels. This is her first appearance in* Galaxy's Edge.

# FORK POINTS

## by Sheila Finch

The backstage maze at the New Globe InterAct PlayHouse reeked of cannabis when Cass arrived, in spite of the director's recent lecture about what smoke did to the delicate Sonytronic rig. The head gaffer had an Aiwa negative ion pulsar going over by the mainboard in the control room. Someone had draped a plastic Christmas wreath over the fire extinguisher next to the board.

The gaffer looked up at Cass. "How's it going?"

"Not my favorite time of year."

"And Jamie?"

She shrugged.

The PlayHouse, a large, rambling, done-over art deco mansion just off Hollywood Boulevard, was almost freezing. Computers needed it cold; Inter-Actors didn't count for much. Amazing somebody hadn't already tried to replace them with machines. Cassandra Romano, she thought, an incredibly realistic simulation of a human being. Maybe not so realistic this time of year.

She headed down a dark corridor to Wardrobe. The costumes in this show were her immediate problem. The third decade of the previous century had glorified flat, skinny women, and Cass was neither any more. Wardrobe had wanted her in a chunky tweed suit for the first act, huge padded shoulders, ugly fur collar, the jacket belted army-style over a skirt with inverted pleats, and a sort of black fur helmet on top. She'd yelled so much they settled on an ankle length maxi coat and more fur trim.

Then Myron had added insult to damage by lecturing her on her slipping audience appeal, measured each week in the box office receipts by the number of people willing to pay to help her character make decisions in the interactive drama.

This morning the insect-squeaking voice of the scale had announced the addition of another two pounds to stuff into the costume.

Fork point. Why not quit now?

Because of Jamie, that was why not.

It started with the parade down Colorado Boulevard in Pasadena, a sunny, rose-scented December day ten years into a new century. A hero's welcome home, the last of a dozen similar cavalcades across the country. Johnny in the back seat of the convertible, bronzed and athletic as she remembered him from high school playing fields, champagne glass in one hand. Later she'd learn how much NASA hated that champagne glass, and how they would come to hide behind it.

But for now, Johnny Romano was the first astronaut to set foot on an asteroid, and that counted for something. She could never remember which one it had been.

Seeing her face in the crowd, he stopped his driver and pulled her aboard. "Marry me!" he shouted in her ear over the roar of the crowd as the parade passed the Norton Simon Museum. His fingers tangled in her long dark hair. He was so drunk. "Sure," she said, because his face had been on all the nets for days and hadn't she just about always known him?

Minor actresses never had too many options. Yet there had been choices, a show in Cincinnati, a little theater production in Des Moines. They glimmered at the back of her mind, shut out by the glamour spotlight of Johnny's triumphal tour, and were abandoned in that moment under the flags, the scent of rose petals and the deafening cheers. She was an actress; she lived for attention.

They were a media creation: space hero weds sexy actress, high school sweethearts. They married in Hollywood and honeymooned in Las Vegas.

Where she sat up all night for the first time, cradling him in her arms while he writhed in silent nightmares. The headaches and nausea started six months after that.

*By then she was already pregnant with Jamie.*

"All right!" Myron shouted. "Theme One, Scene Three people. Take your places, please!" She took the east backstage maze—actually a staircase off-limits to the audience—down to the "parlor" of the house in London where she did the scene in *V Stands for Victory*. Cameron Gordon, male lead, winked as she came through the cast door; he fiddled with his headset, adjusting reception. For rehearsal they all wore larger versions of the two-channel Maxon earplugs employed for the actual performance. The large versions had tiny mikes attached so the cast could talk back.

Cass snugged her headset in place. A stagetech eased past, checking out the electronics for the special effects. The New Globe was state of the art. First of its kind. Revolutionizing the field. Her agent's words. It had imitators now, but it was still the best. For now. She was very lucky to be working here after allowing the media to forget about her for so long— the agent's words again. There'd been an entire revolution in acting while she'd been gone. She'd caught up, made the best of it.

She'd been an InterActor for almost five years, but she still got the shivers walking the mazes behind the rooms the audience saw. That vanished the day Myron introduced her to Noreen Vincenza, pouty, redheaded and ten-years-younger. Cass's understudy.

Miss Pouty-Lips was standing by a mahogany occasional table, tea tray in hand, ready for her walk-on part. She had to be at least twenty pounds lighter than Cass but still managed to look as if she was about to split the seams of the skimpy parlor-maid's outfit. Noreen was supposed to be a one-liner with very limited fork point options, but judging by the number of moves she managed to squeeze out of the peanut gallery's cheapie say-sos, she thought she was the star.

*"Cassandra?"* Myron's voice sounded as if it was coming over a child's tin can telephone. *"Darling, are you on this planet or orbiting? For the third time— Patch in!"*

Cam Gordon ran a comb through graying hair. He was sitting in the big wingback chair beside the fireplace, watching Noreen. Cass sat down opposite him on the red and gray striped sofa. The lights came on.

*"Curtain,"* Myron's voice said in her ear.

Funny how the old terms persisted. Pretty soon the younger generation of InterActors wouldn't even know what "curtain" and "backstage" used to refer to.

Cam, as Winston Churchill, accepted a cup of tea from Noreen. "Thank you, Alice. That'll be all."

Noreen/Alice gave a whimsical half-curtsey that the dramatist had yelled about a couple of times, but Myron had defended on the grounds that what the audiences didn't know about English manners in 1938 would fill a book. She tucked the empty tea tray under her arm.

Cass's dummy-line came next. "Mr Churchill, I must say that I fail to understand—"

"Miss Faversham." Cam groped for a second, didn't find what he was seeking, then mimed picking up and lighting a cigar. "I have already done all the explaining I intend to do."

Once a week, the cast went over the skeleplay to make sure they hadn't wandered too far from the original hardline. It wasn't just the casual changes, the little bits of improve—action or dialogue, spontaneous one night but gradually solidifying—that tugged the skele off course. Sometimes the real cognoscenti, saying-so for a few crucial roles that they bought into several nights in a row, could wreck the cast's attempts to follow the hardline. Theatrical dilettantes swapped notes and prepared strategy, making a point of working through the most bizarre choices. This was tough on an InterActor, but exhilarating if they were good at blending dummy-lines with improv.

Noreen/Alice was supposed to leave the room— this wasn't a fork point—but she was dawdling around today trailing a faint, musky perfume. It put Cass off a fraction of a second.

"You are truly an arrogant man!"

The scene coach scolded in her ear. *"You're picking up late, Cass!"*

A play had a life of its own, and it changed over a period of several performances. Once an InterActor really got into improvving to fit a good say-so, he or she tended to unconsciously add those possibilities in the next time, as if they were part of the hardline, And when that happened, the writers' union squawked if they didn't track it back on inside contract limits. Eventually the cast might get to a point where there was no way out.

"London is full of well-bred, sensitive young ladies, Miss Faversham," Cam delivered Churchill's lines. "Any one of them would seize this chance."

Cass stood up, careful to turn her face toward the north wall where the audience who'd chosen to say-so for Myra Faversham would be later. Miss Faversham was indecisive, adjusting the abominable fur hat.

"Well, Miss Faversham? What is your decision?"

Fork point.

☼

NASA specialists couldn't find anything. "Stress of re-entry," one suggested. "Psychological effect," another wrote. It had been a rough trip home—but that was classified. Nobody could blame Johnny for feeling a little less than his normal self for a while. This too shall pass.

The prospect of fatherhood seemed to rally him; the headaches and the nausea receded. But not the nightmares. He refused to talk about them, even to her, and certainly not to the NASA shrinks.

Then the amnio sent up warning flares and the ultrasound was indecisive, and the doctor had been frowning when he spoke to her.

She brought Johnny the news one day at sunset. He was sitting on the balcony of their condo in Santa Monica where the scent of roses in the courtyard below was as heady as champagne. He'd taken to sitting for hours like this, staring into the distance.

NASA wondered weekly when he was coming back to work. They spoke of choices: implants, desk jobs, virtual orbiting, the best way to use his experience and skill. He ignored them.

"The doc thinks I should abort." All the way home she'd practiced how to say this, finally deciding on cold words that cut cleanest.

He didn't turn his head to look at her. She hadn't expected him to. She studied the black curls lying unkempt on the back of his neck.

"No."

"There's something wrong with it, Johnny."

"No!"

He did turn to her then, his face full of nightmares, and she dropped to her knees beside him, her hands raised to cradle his face. In that moment, perhaps, she truly loved him.

"We could try again later—"

In answer, his hands made an obscene gesture at his crotch. "Before this falls off, you think?"

His voice was high, bordering on hysteria. She'd seen his hands move that way in his sleep, a pathetic warding off of things with no name, dark things with no shape that inhabited the lonely sweep of outer space. Things that he believed had destroyed his manhood. She didn't believe in them because she didn't understand anything about his life in space. But she believed in him.

"All right. We'll take the chance. It'll mean a lot of monitoring—drugs. We'll have to be careful."

"I won't touch you, if that's what you mean," he said, anger darkening his tone. "I couldn't if I wanted to."

Jamie was born five months later, premature, underweight, a tiny white pearl of a child with eyes the black of deep space. He was so beautiful it took her breath away.

He never cried, even at the moment of first breath.

☼

*In an actual performance, the say-sos who'd paid to influence the Myra Faversham character would signal their choice of two alternatives by pressing a button on their little handheld transmitters. Option A meant Myra stayed; Option B meant she valued her dignity (and her chastity) and walked. The winning decision would light up on the main board in the control room, and then the tracker's job was to relay it as fast as possible to the cast so there was no delay in the scene.*

"Option A," Myron instructed, today picking one for practice.

Cass sat down again. Now she went into Myra's dummy-lines that would lead to her becoming Churchill's secretary, and the scene played out until the next fork. If he'd said "B," she would have delivered a speech about the purity of English womanhood and stalked off stage. And then she'd have been in line for several scenes where she actively worked against Churchill becoming prime minister. Ultimately, the play would have finished very nearly in the same place, but it would have arrived there by different routes.

"Very well, Mr. Churchill," Cass's option A lines went. "Tell me what it is you expect of me."

She ran through her scene without giving it much thought today. She always found it harder to get into her part in these dry run-throughs. Improvving was what gave the play fire, the excitement of trying to outfox some particularly cunning say-sos and get where she was supposed to be going in the hardline without detracking the entire play. Without the life breathed into it by real interactive performance, the skele, the play as it was written, seemed dead.

At regular intervals the scene coach updated them on what had been happening in the two major scenes that played at the same time as theirs but in other rooms of the house, as well as the little bits of business that went on in the pantry and the upstairs hall. Even a walk-on could skew this play if he gave it half a try. InterActors needed to be prepared if some off-brand kink in the skele was zooming down the wire from some other scene. One night, some little bastard playing a delivery boy from the local baker had a cheering section from his former high-school drama class primed to twist his one say-so into a major disaster, and—

*"Cassandra!"* Myron screeched in her ear. *"What's the matter with you today, darling? Are you having your period? Pick up the tempo for Chrissakes!"*

She imagined him squatting like a spider in the middle of his control room web, peering at three screens in turn and listening to multi-tracks of dialogue.

She took a breath. "IdotypingMrChurchillbutId on'tmaketea—"

*"Don't overdo it, Cass, there's a good girl,"* the scene coach said mildly. He wasn't fond of Myron either.

Somehow she got through the rest of the rehearsal without incurring Myron's wrath again. Afterwards, the cast stood around drinking java, telling plans for the upcoming holidays. The Fabulous Miss Noreen was cooing at Myron, flattering the old goat.

"Saw your ex on the trivid last night, Cass," Cam said, passing her with aromatic mug in hand. "What's he doing taking a space job again, after all these years?"

✧

The midnight eyes saw only darkness. That was the first thing they learned. The seashell ears were sealed against them.

Weeks of doctor visits turned into months, a year, two years. A long line of specialists pronounced themselves baffled. NASA, fearing some unimaginable liability, blamed it on alcohol. She knew the champagne had been something special to the day.

Jamie grew, flawless in every way except one. The pale, beautiful body seemed quite empty like an anencephalic clone grown in a transplant tank.

They fought every night now. He wanted her to put Jamie in an institution.

"He's more than you can handle. Maybe they'll find a cure. And even if they don't, you'd be helping science."

She knew it was Johnny who ought to be helping science, but she didn't say it. She never told him half what she thought or knew. His nightmares had faded, but they slept in separate bedrooms. He became enraged if she accidentally interrupted him in the bathroom they shared, covering his genitals like an adolescent boy in a locker room. What was left of his genitals.

"Life isn't a set script in one of your damn theaters," he said. "Sometimes you have to make hard choices."

"I'll manage," she said, stubborn in the face of his rigid opposition.

"I can't take this much longer. You have to make a decision."

She lifted the sleeping child from his crib and held him close to her breast that he'd never learned to suck. "I'm keeping Jamie."

He went out the door without replying, leaving the closet full of his clothes and his wedding ring on the bed.

✧

Skeleplays weren't that much different from the old idea of interactive books Cass's mother had played with. *If you want Captain Kirk to beam down to the planet, turn to page 38. If You want him to stay on the Enterprise, page 51*—the difference was the InterActors, and their ability to improv. Cynical Cameron had a different view. InterAct theater was popular in inverse proportion to the amount of governmental control its fans experienced in their lives. In that case, she'd said, we'll be in business a long time! Cam had shaken his head. "Always something new," he'd said. "Always fork points."

The setting sun smeared the sky with dull red as she changed into her costume for the evening performance. Christmas three days away, another visit to Jamie—

She crammed the ugly hat on her head. Wardrobe found it in a thrift shop. It gave off a faint odor of mildew.

They ran three interlocked themes at once, subplots: Churchill's battle to save England from the Axis powers, the problems he had with rivals in Parliament, and Churchill's romance with his secretary. A small change in only one theme—for instance, Miss Faversham stalks offstage and on the way out passes a committee of MPs who've just been "say-so'd" into braving the bulldog in his den—meant another theme would have to change course to accommodate. Or she could pass one of her rivals for Churchill's favor, and that might send a jealous Myra back into his arms.

InterActors couldn't memorize every possibility, because the plot never followed the same course two performances in a row. Some things had to be improvved. They had to be fast thinkers and good with clever dialogue. She'd never been one of the best, coming to it late in her career, but she'd managed to keep up until now.

She adjusted the tiny Maxon plug that would let her hear the tracker, allowing herself to ease into the character. The theater came alive when the audience took its place. In the backstage maze, the rustle of programs and murmur of voices were muted. Cass glanced through a peephole onto the parlor set where Cam was playing a scene with two members of the Liberal party. Behind him, she saw the audience, thumbs on the buttons of their transmitters, intent on taking part in the play by making their say-so's. She recognized several of the regulars. Behind the row of seats stood the "cruisers" who wandered from scene to scene rather than stay with one character throughout.

She heard her cue and entered the scene through the cast door. Improvving was what gave the play fire, the excitement of trying to outfox some particularly cunning say-sos and get where she was supposed to be going in the hardline without detracking the entire play. The familiar scene between Churchill and Miss Faversham began to play.

She'd done this particular play four times a week for two years now. Sometimes a rowdy audience could get carried away by their sense of taking part in the action, but not tonight. They sat hunched forward in their seats, paying close attention.

"Well," Winston Churchill said. "What is your decision?"

The scene had arrived at Myra Faversham's fork point.

She was aware of the flutter of fingers on transmitters in the hands of the group who'd paid to influence Myra's actions. A fraction of a second passed and the tracker's voice murmured in her ear.

*"Option B."*

"I very much regret to say that I value my honor, Mr. Churchill, more than I value financial reward," Cass said haughtily, drawing on gloves that seemed too tight. "England's womanhood cannot be bought by promises—"

Under her words, she heard the tracker again, warning of a kink in the skele. *"Lord North on his way with dispatches."*

No problem. She'd just have to cut her lines to fit the revised scene when Churchill's colleague arrived, working the crucial parts around their dialogue. Cam caught her eye meaningfully; he'd been advised of the kink. The trick was to make it seamless, and not to add too much that might cause problems somewhere else or further on.

Lord North burst into the room, a new InterActor, given to tripping over his lines if he got flustered. Cass wove her lines in around their exchange and got off the set credibly.

Myron was in the maze, frowning as usual. She squeezed past him, heading for her next scene, a confrontation with two members of the opposition party that Option B had set her up for.

"Cass. Wait up." Myron caught her by the sleeve. "You had a net call. Your ex. Said he's at Lunar Base Two."

"Johnny?" She hadn't heard from him in three years. She'd learned from a buddy in the corps that he'd gone back to NASA as a desk pilot. "Why'd he call? What's he doing on the moon?"

"You know I don't like the cast conducting personal business during a performance," Myron said. "I terminated the transmission."

✿

Sometimes life resembles a play with a bozo skele, all the fork points leading down to absurdity or despair.

Johnny was half right. It wasn't that she couldn't take care of Jamie, his needs were minimal, food, clean diapers. But he continued to lie unmoving in his crib, his small body almost bloodless in its white perfection, past his first and then his second birthday. He never cried out or made gestures she could understand. He never learned to ask for anything.

It was a question of why.

Like Johnny, the doctors urged her to put the baby away. A home they said, excellent care, and success with puzzling cases like this—well, not quite like this.

NASA sent her half Johnny's pay check. More might have been an admission of liability.

At three, Jamie learned to walk.

Then one day a pop-vid show that hyped its revelations of celebrity secrets found out about Jamie and sent a remote cam to hover a foot above her head for months. It even followed her into the bathroom where Johnny had been ashamed to let her see his ravaged manhood.

The home the doctors recommended would cost more than the NASA payments allowed. If she put Jamie away—and what difference would it make to the child who didn't know she was his mother?—she would have to go back to the theater. Older. Heavier. Life drained out of her in the service of Jamie who couldn't use it.

It truly was a bozo skele. All anyone could do was hope it didn't go down to disaster.

✿

Myron called a meeting after the performance. Cass sipped thick java a scene coach pressed into her hands and watched him gesticulating. He was in a bad mood. They'd had a string of real InterActive aficionados recently, some of them bright kids from Cal Tech who liked to cause mischief. The cast had to work hard to keep the play tracking. They'd been using a lot of special effects to get out of impossible kinks and deadends that these say-sos forced. All that high tech was expensive.

Noreen made some comment that Cass missed. Everybody laughed, including Myron.

"All right, folks. Listen up." Myron banged a mug against a steel strut. "I've got business to share. Stuff I want you to keep to yourselves."

*Several of the InterActors, the younger ones including Noreen, sat cross-legged on the floor. Cass dragged out a folding chair. A tall man wearing glasses and a dark suit stood beside Myron, a nuleather folder in his hand. The stranger spoke about innovations in InterActive equipment that she didn't understand. Then he tucked the folder under his arm and held something out on the palm of his right hand. The InterActors leaned forward, doing a crowd scene around him. Noreen made ooh and aah noises.*

"What is it?" Cass asked one of the scene coaches.

"Bio-chip," the coach said. "Space agency has 'em, but I didn't know we'd managed to rip the technology off yet."

Myron gazed across the bent heads at her. "Lightspeed communication, darling. It'll eliminate that delay that's been killing us. Multi channels for InterActors, director, techs. Everybody! This will revolutionize the field."

"Give it to us in English," Cam said.

"You haven't seen InterActive drama till you see how this little chip is going to work. The InterActors will be able to monitor all the say-sos at every single fork point, not just their own. And they'll receive my instructions for all scenes simultaneously. Without bulky headphones."

"Why would we want to hear everybody's say-sos?" a young man asked. "It's tough enough dealing with our own."

Myron stared thoughtfully at him. "Think what it'll do to a drama if you know what everybody's doing and can incorporate their decisions into your own."

"Sounds like we're going to need a Ph.D. just to be able to do it," she said.

"That's what's wrong with you, Cassandra," Myron said. "You're not flexible any more. This is a young field, darling. InterActive drama's changing. You need to grow with it. Nobody's indispensable." He turned away from her. "This is the future, folks! And we're going to be the first company to get it."

The thought of surgeons cutting her head open and burying a piece of metal in her brain scared her no less than it had once scared Johnny. And that wasn't all. She could imagine what it'd be like, stuck with the thing in her skull, never able to turn it off. Like being on-stage all the time, even when she was home.

They would've known at NASA when Johnny tried to hide his genitals from her in the bathroom.

"Of course, according to contract, we can't actually force you to have the implant," Myron said. "But we're going to be awfully appreciative of those who volunteer."

Now they were all asking questions.

"Disability pay for the six weeks while you recuperate, and for the retraining period that'll be necessary after that."

"Do we have a choice of hospitals?" someone wanted to know.

"Well—" Myron's face had that fixed smile it got when he was trying to weasel some particularly low clause past them into the contract. "We've made arrangements with a clinic in New Delhi."

"You mean the procedure's not licensed in the States?" Cam asked.

Myron said smoothly, "The risks are negligible. Theater's going to be dark for a couple of months, starting now. We're just extending the normal end-of-year break a little bit. Then we're starting rehearsal on a brand new version of this play."

And of course, there she rose: Miss Pouty-Lips herself, standing so close to Myron he could hardly look at her without staring down the low-cut front of her costume.

"Myron," she said, "I want to be first to volunteer."

She reminded Cass of herself a billion years ago, before she'd made other choices.

"Fabulous, baby! Anyone else?"

Several hands went up, including Cam's. But Cameron's went up more slowly.

"Cassandra?" Myron asked when he'd finished noting the volunteers, almost the entire cast.

*She was tired of it all. Tired of making decisions that never changed anything for the better. Tired of living her life day after day with the knowledge of her strange child, her lost marriage and her failing career.*

"Won't last long," one of the scene coaches muttered. "Same chip technology supports VR. And then where'll we be?"

Myron bit his fingernail. "It's your decision, Cassandra. But you should know your audience ratings have been diving."

Fork point.

✧

Anonymous, red-tiled communities jamming the San Fernando Valley flashed by outside the maglev window. The hillsides were choked from valley floor to hill crest with apartment buildings, motels, shopping malls, high-rise office blocks, swimming pools and health clubs, like 3-D photocopies of one community stacked endlessly side by side.

At Woodland Hills Cass got off the train and transferred to the slow electric tram winding down Topanga Canyon Road. Oak Grove House, private residential home for developmentally disturbed children, stood behind a brick wall. The brief winter afternoon was already fading as she reached the path to the main building. Rosebushes lining the path, shriveled and dry, were empty of perfume. The green Christmas wreath on the front door enveloped her in its scent of snowy forest.

The director came outside to meet her. "He's in the garden."

"How is he?" She asked the same question, month after month, year after year.

And she always got the same answer: "As well as we can expect. We mustn't look for miracles, must we?"

She didn't know why not.

She walked across the sloping lawn to the play area under the trees. From the distance the children climbing the jungle gym, the toddlers shrieking on the teeter-totter and the slide, all looked healthy and very normal.

Eight-year-old Jamie was all by himself, safety-belted into the swing. She stood a few feet away and looked at him. His cheeks glowed, translucent as if light moved under his skin. His hair had been freshly cut, the white curls brushed back from his forehead. He wore the spaceship sweatshirt she'd brought him six months ago. It was still too big.

"Hello, Jamie."

She knew he couldn't hear her, but it helped her to speak.

He swung back and forth, back and forth, his blind gaze fixed on trees at the dark edge of the lawn. If I didn't know, she thought, I'd think he was normal.

Normal. There it was. In Johnny and Cass's bozo skele they'd chosen a fork that led to poor, abnormal Jamie.

But that wasn't quite right either. Normal was a word for other children. Jamie had been touched by something that couldn't be measured by human standards of normal.

"How have you been, Jamie? Are they treating you well here?"

Jamie continued to swing.

One of the therapists came up beside her, a young black man. He flashed her a quick smile, then stopped the swing and unbuckled her child.

"Time to stop swinging, Jamie. Mom's here."

"You talk to him too," she said. "But he can't hear."

"There may be other ways of hearing," he said.

Startled, she stared at the dark young man with the unresponsive boy in his arms. "His father went into space."

"I was in high school, but I followed his news."

"It ate him up. Whatever it was."

"No," he said. "It gave you a gift."

He set Jamie down on the lawn at her feet.

*Jamie seemed preoccupied with his delicate hands, the long fingers weaving like ghosts through the air. Almost like he was trying sign language, she thought.*

"Look. Have you tried to teach him to sign? I mean, Helen Keller made it. Perhaps he could...."

She broke off. Of course they'd tried. Dozens of doctors, scientists of all the new disciplines of space medicine. But nobody here would know the language if Jamie had one in his brain. Nobody on Earth.

The therapist touched her hand gently. "Love him as he is, Miz Romano. He isn't like the rest of us."

He put the boy's hand in hers and walked away, leaving her with Jamie. She bent to lean her cheek against the boy's, her nose brushing his pale, snow-scented hair. Jamie stared sightlessly at the darkening trees.

They walked back across the lawn in the gathering dusk. She began to talk to the child about his father on the moon. Overhead, a satellite winked its way across the sky and she pointed it out.

Fork points, she thought. Life was full of them.

---

*Jody Lynn Nye is the author of forty novels and more than one hundred stories, and has at various times collaborated with Anne McCaffrey and Robert Asprin. Her husband, Bill Fawcett, is a prolific author, editor, and packager, and is also active in the gaming field.*

## BOOK REVIEWS

## by Bill Fawcett and Jody Lynn Nye

***Gentleman Jole and the Red Queen***
by Lois McMaster Bujold
Baen Books
February, 2016
ISBN-13: 978-1476781228

Ever since reading *The Warrior's Apprentice*, I've loved Ms. Bujold's writing. Her characters are so unexpected but so well-drawn that you get to feel you know them. Her plots never go in the way you think they will, and that just adds to the pleasure of anticipation. I was thrilled to have another chance to visit the Vor saga. Her prose is beautiful, with lyrical, romantic moments of tingling delight, sly humor, and wrenching pathos.

It's been a long time since there was a story devoted to Cordelia, Miles Vorkosigan's brave, free-spirited Betan mother who brought so many changes to moribund Barrayar. The book begins some three years after the death of her husband, Count Aral. Cordelia has taken over as solo Vicereine, handling the office with deft intelligence. She seems diminished and still grieving, but she's determined to move on and find happiness again.

Cordelia and the handsome and charming Admiral Oliver Jole, who was Aral Vorkosigan's lover, have been in a trine relationship over the past decades. Now that third point of the triangle is gone, and the survivors have time to determine how they will cope with that loss. Cordelia has also decided to fulfil a long-deferred dream. The brutal circumstances of Miles' birth prevented her from wanting to try to have more children. She's ready now. Seventy-six years of age is by no means too old to have a bevy of daughters, thanks to the incubator technology and advanced genetic techniques. She also has a rare and precious gift for Jole, a memento from Aral, a gift for his own future. But all is not perfect in Cordelia's second chance at life. Miles, now an inquiry agent for the Emperor, arrives to investigate his own mother.

Unlike the action-packed novels that are typical of the series, this one moves at a gentle, measured pace. Although Bujold offers plenty of background information to keep a new reader from getting lost, Gentleman Jole isn't a good introduction to the series. It feels more like a prequel for future novels, which one hopes are forthcoming. If you loved *Shards of Honor*, you'll enjoy *Gentleman Jole and the Red Queen*.

✿

***City of Angels***
by Todd McCaffrey
WordFire Press

Spring, 2016
ISBN-13: 978-1-61475-416-9

McCaffrey is well-known as the son of Anne and her collaborator in her last years on the bestselling Dragonriders of Pern books. *City of Angels* is his first solo novel outside that series.

A number of seemingly unrelated events begin to occur, each with a time-code heading identifying them as beginning 271 days before an unnamed catastrophe. What a brilliant scientist obsessed with nanotechnology and traffic patterns, CalTech's seismology department, a homeless veteran who can hear abandoned babies, the CEO of a nearly impoverished satellite technology company, programmers at the Vatican, and the mayor of Los Angeles have in common is revealed slowly but irresistibly in this compelling, intricately plotted high-tech novel.

A mysterious little girl who claims to be the spirit of Los Angeles is trying to cope with her sudden birth into consciousness. She can save the world, or at least the southwest corner of the United States—if only politics, fear and distrust don't get in her way. If the ending seems expected or too pat in having every loose end tied up, it doesn't detract from its appeal.

An easy and intriguing read, fast moving right from the beginning. This book is written in such a filmic style that it seems destined to make the transition to a movie one day. Todd McCaffrey shows some impressive chops. Anyone who likes a high-tech thriller with a heart will enjoy *City of Angels*.

✿

## The Rogue Retrieval
by Dan Koboldt
Harper Voyager Impulse
March, 2016
ISBN-13: 978-0062451910

One of the real rewards in doing book reviews is after sixty years of reading SF, I'm still finding exciting new writers. Based on his first novel, *The Rogue Retrieval*, Dan Koboldt is certainly one of those new talents we should all watch.

The story is based on the premise of a modern man suddenly plunged into a world of magic. In this case, it concerns a multi-national (er multi-dimensional?) powerful corporation that sees the world through bottom line glasses. The new world is full of resources and other exploitable assets, but it is also populated by humans, some of whom actually use magic. In fact, magicians are highly regarded and belong to a powerful and jealous guild. What sets this story apart from others in the genre featuring strangers coming into a new realm is that the hero does not suddenly find himself able to cast spells, nor is he a former Navy SEAL or other military hero. Instead, Quinn Bradley is a stage magician/illusionist recruited from the Las Vegas theater scene by the corporation to fake performing magic. It is only after he gets to the world of Alissia that Quinn finds out just how jealous the real magicians are, and that the penalty for claiming falsely to be one is death.

Quinn, a competent illusionist, has to track down another company agent who had gone native, or perhaps rogue, with a backpack full of tech items and weapons. He and the other pursuers have to blend in, as the last thing the corporation wants is for Alissia's magicians to become aware of them. Then, things really get complicated.

The writing is crisp, the story moves quickly, and the characters are well drawn. Quinn also keeps his sense of wonder, even as he is nearly eaten by a wyvern. This is a more than impressive first novel; it is a rollicking good read, and I look forward to more. If you enjoy humor or contemporary fantasy, add this one to your list.

## Ramadi Declassified
by Colonel Anthony E. Deane (ret.) and Douglas Niles
Praetorian Books
May, 2016
ISBN-13: 978-1943052073

Warning, this is not Science Fiction book. Instead, it is a resource that anyone who reads military or action SF, and particularly those of us who write it, should read and will also enjoy.

In May 2006 the war in Iraq was "over" but many parts of the country were still war zones. Colonel Deane and his armored Task Force "Conquerors" were given the job of subduing the worst thorn in the Allies' side: the almost totally hostile city of Ramadi and surrounding Anbar province. When they arrived, the best anyone had been able to do was try to keep the lid on. In the next year the Conquerors and attached engineer and National Guard units successfully evolved a way to effectively deal with the terrorists, Islamist Extremists, and the religious tensions that had turned the province into a free-fire zone. It was not a simple answer, though clearly explained, and was reached only after a lot of painful mistakes and casualties.

The story is compelling, more so because it is true. Colonel Deane and noted SF author Doug Niles (*Fox on the Rhine*, numerous Dragonlance novels, *Watershed, Chaos War*, and *Seven Circles* series) tell us about what and how all this real history happened. You cannot make up fiction to match what happened in Ramadi. The narrative follows Deane and his soldiers as they evolve ways to deal with the IEDs and other constant threats, reach out to potential allies, and eventually bring about a complete change in the situation. This is also the Colonel's highly personal tale, and he holds nothing back emotionally as he loses soldiers and allies. He shares the real wrenching tragedy of having men under his command die following his orders and how battle forever changed the men and their commander. Actions are described in detail. I particularly like Deane's maxim that if you are an armored commander crouching under fire behind your car with just a pistol, something has gone wrong. Things do go wrong, but successes are achieved. We see from the inside how it affects the men who are fighting an enemy they can only identify after the shooting starts. It could be said that his book is to modern urban warfare what Hans Guderian's book *Panzer Leader* was for open field armored combat.

If you ever want to write about or just understand being a soldier, the reality of combat, or the complexity of modern armored warfare, then reading this book is a must. It is well written and a great read. It is also can give any reader insights into what is happening in Iraq yet again today. If this were a fiction book, I would be recommending it as an exciting, suspenseful, and occasionally tragic read.

✿

*Starship Troopers*
by Robert A. Heinlein

ACE
May, 1987
ISBN-13: 978-0441783588

If you are asked to pick THE classic military SF novel, it has to be *Starship Troopers*. To handle the dirty laundry first, forget the movie. Generously, the title was the same, but not much else remained of the original besides the bugs. Granted, the movie was pretty good on its own, but was more inspired by Heinlein's brilliant novel than portraying it. The book begins with the graduation from high school of Rico, the son of a wealthy businessman. In Heinlein's future, only those who have given two years federal service are really citizens and can vote or hold office. This service can range from sweeping streets to being a soldier. Rico is nudged, rather than really chooses, to join the military. His first choice is to be a space pilot (whose isn't?), but reality slides him past all of his choices to the last one on his list: Armored Infantry.

The book opens and ends with two really excellent combat scenes, one early in the war and another, a pivotal victory, years later. What *Starship Troopers* really tells is Rico's coming of age story from reluctant grunt to veteran commander. It is not just a book about the military, but about the mind and attitudes of those who serve, relevant then or today. The story deals much more with why men fight and how they feel than with the really excellent hardware and battle scenes. It does this in a powerful way, one that any reader, even if you don't generally read military SF will enjoy.

After Rico joins up, a number of doses of reality jar him out of his complacent civilian attitudes. The training is rough and aggressively tries to weed out the losers. Over chapters, we see how Rico changes and his priorities shift. We see how the *espirit de corps* of a combat unit develops and how it changes those in it. The common experiences in war can turn men into that band of brothers so vital for mutual support and survival. If you want to see for yourself what Heinlein is talking about, introduce two old marines to each other in a bar, then sit back and listen.

The training is still going on when the enemy, an insectoid hive-mentality, hits the Earth and wipes out a good part of Argentina, killing Rico's mom. Earth fights back, but victory is hardly guaranteed when fighting a race that can simply hatch tens of thousands of new soldiers in a few months. Rico is a CAP, a powered armor trooper. Heinlein's was the first, and is still among the best, powered armors ever portrayed. He served in the Navy in WWII. The author later admitted on panels the real inspiration for his missile-throwing, heavy-weapon carrying powered suits was naval destroyers. He even tends to show his soldiers deployed in lines separated by miles, fighting in the same way that each warship dominates the area immediately around it. The suits are great wish fulfilment for any infantryman; any CAP trooper in his power suit would easily beat Iron Man. If you ever doubted that science fiction inspires real life, check out the Army's Talos project, among others.

So why read this classic? First, because the writing is as powerful today as when it was written. WWII vet Heinlein also gives some real insights into the military mind of that war and battlegrounds of today. Students of history may find the social attitudes from fifty years ago interesting, including why Heinlein felt the need to explain in detail why there are women flying combat aircraft. Anyone who enjoys books by Dickson, Anderson, Weber, Pournelle, or Ringo should read Starship Troopers. If you have yet to read this book you have a real treat coming. It is not only among the first, but remains one of the best military reads ever written. Other readers will find this book a fast reading coming-of-age tale set in a dangerous and war-torn future.

*Copyright © 2016 by Bill Fawcett and Jody Lynn Nye*

*Gregory Benford is a Nebula winner and a former Worldcon Guest of Honor. He is the author of more than thirty novels, six books of non-fiction, and has edited ten anthologies.*

# THE FOURTH DIMENSION

## by Gregory Benford

Suppose that next to you, right now, a pale gray sphere appeared. It grew from baseball-sized to a diameter as big as you—grainy, gray, cool to the touch—then shrank to a point...and disappeared.

You would probably interpret it as a balloon blown up, then deflated. But where did the flat balloon go?

Or you could realize that you had been visited by a denizen of a higher dimension—a four dimensional sphere, or hypersphere. In three dimensions, it looks like a sphere, the most perfect of figures, just as a sphere projected in two dimensions makes a circle. The fact that this isn't an everyday occurrence implies that travel between dimensions is uncommon, but not that it is illogical.

Probably you would not have thought of such ideas before 1884. That is due to the Reverend Edwin Abbott Abbott, M.A., D.D., headmaster of the City of London School.

Respected, well liked, he led a strictly regular life, as proper as a parallelogram. He had published quite a few conventional books with titles like *Through Nature to Christ, Parables for Children* and *How to Tell the Parts of Speech*. These did not prepare the world for his sudden excursion into the fantastic in 1884. Beneath his exterior he was a bit odd, and his short novel, *Flatland* has proved his only hedge against oblivion, an astonishingly prescient fantasy of mathematics.

Abbott's oddity began with his repeated name, which a mathematical wit might see as A times A or A Squared, $A^2$. Abbott's protagonist is A Square, a much troubled spirit. Liberated into another character, Abbott seems to have broken out of his cover as a prim reverend, and poured out his feelings.

The book has a curiously obsessive quality, which perhaps accounts for its uneasy reception. Reviewers termed it "soporific," "prolix," mortally tedious," "desperately facetious," while others found it "clever," "fascinating," "never been equaled for clarity of thought," "mind broadening," and even likened it to *Gulliver's Travels*. This last comparison is just, because beneath the math drolleries lurks a penetrating satire of Victorian society.

A Square's society is as constrained as were the prim Victorians. Women are not full figures but mere lines. Soldiers are triangles with sharp points, adept at stabbing. The more sides, the higher the status, so hexagons outrank squares, and the high priests are perfect circles.

In a delicious irony, the upper classes are polygons with equal sides—but their views certainly do not embrace equality. Mathematicians term equal-sided figures "regular," and in nineteenth century terms, proper upper class polygons are of the regular sort.

A Square learns that his view of the world is too narrow. There is a third dimension, grander and exciting, but his hidebound fellows cannot see it. This opening-out is the central imaginative event of the novel, Abbott echoing an emergent idea.

In the late nineteenth century higher dimensions were fashionable. Mathematicians had laid the foundations for rigorous work in higher-dimensional space, and physicists were about to begin using four-dimensional spacetime. Twenty centuries after Euclid, the mathematician Bernhard Riemann took a great leap in 1854, liberating the idea of dimensions from our spatial senses. He argued that ever since Renee Descartes had described spaces with algebra, the path to discussing higher dimensions had been clear, but unwalked.

Descartes' analytic geometry defined lines as things described by one set of coordinates, distances along one axis. A plane needed two independent coordinate sets, a solid took three. With coordinates one could map an object, defining it quantitatively: not "Chicago is over that hill." but "Chicago is fifteen miles that way." This appealed more to our logical capacity, and less to our sensory experience.

Riemann described worlds of equal logical possibility, with dimensions ranging from one to infinity. They were not spatial in the ordinary sense. Instead, Riemann took dimension to refer to conceptual spaces, which he named manifolds.

This wasn't merely a semantic change. Weather, for example, depends on several variables—say, $n$—like temperature, pressure, wind velocity, time of day, etc. One could represent the weather as a moving point in an $n$-dimensional space. A plausible model of everyday weather needs about a dozen variables, so to visualize it means seeing curves and surfaces in a twelve-dimensional world. No wonder we understand the motions of planets (which even Einstein only needed four dimensions to describe), but not the weather.

Riemann revolutionized mathematics and his general ideas diffused into our culture. By 1880, C.H. Hinton had pressed the issue by building elaborate models, to further his extra-dimensional intuition; he tried to explain ghosts as higher-dimensional apparitions. Pursuing the analogy, he wrote of a fourth-dimensional God from whom nothing could be hidden. The afterlife, then, allowed spirits to move along the time dimension, reliving and reassessing moments of life. Spirits from hyperspace were the subject of J.K.F. Zollner's 1878 *Transcendental Physics*, which envisioned them moving everywhere by short-cut loops through the fourth dimension.

Mystics responded to the fashion by imagining that God, souls, angels and any other theological beings resided as literal beings of mass ("hypermatter") in four-space. This neatly explains why they can appear anywhere they like, and God can be everywhere simultaneously, the way we can look down on a Flatland and perceive it as a whole. Some found such transports of the imagination inspiring, while others thought them crass and far too literal. I am unaware of Abbott himself ever subscribing to such beliefs.

Still, Abbott and his adventuresome Square longed for the strange. More than any other writer, Abbott coined the literary currency of dimensional metaphor. By having a point of view which is literally above it all, surveying the follies of a two-dimensional plane, Abbott can adroitly satirize the staid rigidities of his Victorian world. (Perhaps this is why he first published *Flatland* under a pseudonym.)

"Irregulars" are cruelly executed, for example. Do they stand for foreigners? Gypsies? Cripples? We are left to fill in some blanks, but the overall shape of the plot is clear—flights of fancy are punished, and A Square does not finish happily.

At a deeper level, the book harks toward scientific issues, and the difficulty of comprehending a physical reality beyond our immediate senses. This is the great theme of modern physics. The worlds of relativity and the quantum are beyond the rough-and-ready ideas we chimpanzees have built into us, from our distant ancestors' experience at throwing stones and poking sticks on African plains.

Still deeper, in this fanciful narrative the good Reverend tries to speak indirectly of intense spiritual experience. The trip into the higher realm of three dimensions is a fine metaphor for a mystical encounter.

The thrust of the deceptively simple narrative is to make us examine our basic assumptions. After all, our visual perceptions of the world are two-dimensional patterns, yet we somehow know how to see three-dimensionality. One knows instantly the difference between a ball and a flat disk by their shading in available light. Objects move in front of each other, like a woman walking by a wall. We automatically discount a possible interpretation—that the woman has somehow dissolved the wall for an instant as she passes. Instead, we see her in her three-dimensionality. The eye has learned the world's geometry and discards any other scheme.

A Square learns this lesson early as he first visits Lineland in a dream. The only distinction the natives can have is in their length. They see each other as points, since they move along the same universal straight line. They estimate how far away others are by their acute sense of hearing, picking up the difference between a bass left voice and a tenor right; the time lag in arrival tells the distance. The king is longest, men next, then boys are stubby lines. Women are mere points, of lower status. Their views of each other are partial and instinctive. They never dream of how narrowly they see their world.

This sets the stage for A Square's conceptual blowout when a Sphere visits him and yanks him up into the hallucinogenic universe of three dimensions. Its realities are surrealistic. A Square struggles to fathom what for us is instinctive.

The reality of three dimensions we take for granted, but for us, what is the reality of two dimensions? Would flatlanders have physical presence in our world—that is, could we perceive a two-dimensional universe embedded in our own? Could we yank them up into our world?

Flatlanders could be as immaterial as shadows, mere patterns in our view. If an isosceles triangle soldier cut your throat it would not hurt. Abbott did not consider this in his first edition, but in the second he says that A Square eventually believes that flatlanders have a small but real height in our universe. A Square discusses this with the ruler of Flatland:

> I tried to prove to him that he was "high," as well as long and broad, although he did not know it. But what was his reply? "You say I am 'high,' measure my 'high-ness' and I will believe you." What could I do? I met his challenge!

If flatlanders were even quite thick, they would not be able to tell, if in that direction they had no ability to move or did not vary. Height *as a concept* would lie beyond their knowable range. Or if they did vary in height, but could not directly see this, they might ascribe the differences to qualitative features like charisma or character or "presence." There would be rather mysterious forces at work in their world, the Platonic shadows of a higher, finer reality.

If a flatlander soldier of genuine physical thickness attacked, it would cut us like a knife. Otherwise, it could not impinge upon us. We would remain oblivious to all events in the lesser dimensions.

In a sense, a truly two-dimensional flatlander faces a similar problem if it tries to digest food. A simple alimentary canal from stem to stern of, say, a circle would bisect it. To keep itself intact, a circle would have to digest by enclosing whatever it used for food in pockets, opening one and passing food to the next like a series of locks in a canal, until eventually it excreted at the far end.

This is typical of the problems engaged by thinking in another dimension. Not until 1910 did artists respond to non-Euclidean spaces, with Cubism and its theories. Mute image and poetic metaphor, they said, were ways of perceiving what scientists could only describe in abstractions and analogies.

They were right, and many, including Picasso and Braque, struggled with the problem. Looking downward at lower dimensions is easy. Looking up strains us.

Visualizing the fourth dimension preoccupied both artists and geometers. A cube in 4D is called a tesseract. One way to think of it is to open a cubical cardboard box and look in. By perspective, you see the far end as a square. Diagonals (the cube edges) lead to the outer "corners" of a larger square--the cube face you're looking through. Now go to a 4D analogy. A hypercube is one small cube, sitting in the middle of a large cube, connected to it by diagonals. Or rather, that is how it would look to us, lowly 3D folk.

Cutting a hypercube in the right way allows one to unfold it and reform it into a 3D pattern of eight cubes, just as a 3D cube can be made up of six squares. One choice looks like a sort of 3D cross. Salvador Dali used this as a crucifix in his 1954 painting *Christus Hypercubus*. Not only does the hypercube suggest the presence of a higher reality; Dali deals with the problem of projecting into lower dimensions. On the floor beneath the suspended hypercube, and the crucified Christ, is a checkerboard pattern—except directly below the hypercube. There, the hypercube's shadow forms a square cross. (Shadows are the only 2D things in our world; they have no thickness.) Comparing this simple cross with the reality of the hypercube which casts the shadow, we contemplate that our world is perhaps a pallid shadow of a higher reality, an implicit mystical message.

Robert Heinlein gave this a twist with "And He Built a Crooked House," in which a house built to this pattern folds back up, during an earthquake, into a true hypercube, trapping the inhabitants in four dimensions. Much panic ensues.

Rudy Rucker, mathematician and science fiction author, has taken A Square and Flatland into myriad fresh adventures. I met Rucker in the 1980s and found him much like his fictional narrators, inventive and wild, with a cerebral spin on the world, a place he found only apparently commonplace. His *The Sex Sphere* (1983) satirizes dimensional intrusions, many short stories develop ideas only latent in *Flatland*, and his short story "Message found in a Copy of Flatland" details how a figure much like Rucker himself returns to Abbott's old haunts and finds the actual portal into that world, in the basement of a Pakistani restaurant. He finds that the triangular soldiers can indeed cut intruders from higher dimensions, and flatlanders are tasty when he gets hungry. As a sendup of the original it is pointed and funny.

In science fiction there have been many stories about creatures from the fourth dimension invading ours, generally with horrific results. Greg Bear's "Tangents" describes luring 4D beings into our space using sound. While we puzzle over whether an unseen fourth dimension exists, modern physics has used the idea in the Riemannian manner, to expand our conceptual underpinnings. Riemann saw a mathematical theme of conceptual spaces, not merely geometrical ones. Physics has taken this idea and run with it.

Abbott's solving the problem of flatlander physical reality by adding a tiny height to them was strikingly prescient. Some of the latest quantum field theories of cosmology begin with extra dimensions beyond three, and then "roll up" the extras so that they are unobservably small—perhaps a billion billion billion times more tiny than an atom. Thus we are living in a universe only apparently spatially three-dimensional; infinitesimal but real dimensions lurk all about us. In some models there actually are eighteen dimensions in all!

Even worse, this rolling up occurs by what I call "wantum mechanics"—we want it, so it must happen. We know no mechanism which could achieve this, but without it we would end up with unworkable universes which could not support life. For example, in such field theories with more than three dimensions, which do not roll up, there could be no stable atoms, and thus no matter more complex than particles. Further, only in odd-numbered dimensions can waves propagate sharply, so 3D is favored over 2D. In this view, we live not only in the best of all possible worlds, but the only possible one.

How did this surrealistically bizarre idea come about? From considering the form and symmetries of abstruse equations. In such chilly realms, beauty is often our only guide. The embarrassment of dimensions in some theories arises from a clarity in starting with a theory which looks appealing, then hiding the extra dimensions from actually acting in our physical world. This may seem an odd way to proceed, but it has a history.

The greatest fundamental problem of physics in our time has been to unite the two great fundamental theories of the century, general relativity and quantum mechanics, into a whole, unified view of the world. In cosmology, where gravity dominates all forces, general relativity rules. In the realm of the atom, quantum processes call the tune.

They do not blend. General relativity is a "classical" theory in that it views matter as particles, with no quantum uncertainties built in. Similarly, quantum mechanics cannot include gravity in a "natural" way.

Here "natural" means in a fashion which does not violate our sense of how equations should look, their beauty. Aesthetic considerations are very important in science, not just in physics, and they are the kernel of many theories. The quantum theorist Paul Dirac was asked at Moscow University his philosophy of physics, and after a moment's thought wrote on the blackboard, "Physical laws should have mathematical beauty." The sentence has been preserved on the board to this day.

One can capture a theorist's imagination better with a "pretty" idea than with a practical one. There have even been quite attractive mathematical cosmologies which begin with a two-dimensional, expanding universe, and later jump to 3D, for unexplained reasons.

Einstein wove space and time together to produce the first true theory of the entire cosmos. He had first examined a spacetime which is "flat," that is, untroubled by curves and twists in the axes which determine coordinates. This was his 1905 special theory of relativity. He drew upon ideas which Abbott had already used.

The eminent British journal *Nature* published in 1920 a comparison of Abbott's prophetic theme:

> (Dr. Abbott) asks the reader, who has consciousness of the third dimension, to imagine a sphere descending upon the plane of Flatland and passing through it. How will the inhabitants regard this phenomenon? ... Their experience will be that of a circular obstacle gradually expanding or growing, and then contracting, and they will attribute to *growth in time* what the external observer in three dimensions assigns to motion in

the third dimension. Transfer this analogy to a movement of the fourth dimension through three-dimensional space. Assume the past and future of the universe to be all depicted in four-dimensional space and visible to any being who has consciousness of the fourth dimension. If there is motion of our three-dimensional space relative to the fourth dimension, all the changes we experience and assign to the flow of time will be due simply to this movement, the whole of the future as well as the part always existing in the fourth dimension.

In special relativity, distance in spacetime is not the simple result we know from rectangular geometry. In the ordinary Euclidean geometry everyone learns in school, if "d" means a small change and the coordinates of space are called x, y and z, then we find a small length (ds) in our space by adding the squares of each length, so that

$$(ds)^2 = (dx)^2 + (dy)^2 + (dz)^2$$

The symbol "d" really stands for differential, so this is a differential equation.

Contrast special relativity, in which a small distance in space-time adds a length given by dt, a small change in time, multiplied by the speed of light, c:

$$(ds)^2 = (dx)^2 + (dy)^2 + (dz)^2 - (cdt)^2$$

The trick is that the extra length (cdt) is subtracted, not added. This simple difference leads to a whole restructuring of the basic geometry. The mathematician Minkowski showed this some years after Einstein formulated special relativity.

A thicket of confusions lurks here. Reflect that the total small (or differential, in mathematical language) length is (ds), found by taking the square root of the above equation. But if (cdt) is greater than the positive (first three) terms, then (ds) is an imaginary number! What can this mean? Physically, it means the rules for moving in this four-dimensional (4D) space are complex and contrary to our 3D intuitions. Different kinds of curves are called "spacelike" and "timelike," because they have very different physical properties.

Einstein was fond of saying that he viewed the world as 4D, with people existing in it simultaneously. This meant that in 4D the whole life of a person (their "world-line") was on view. Life was eternal, in a sense—a cosmic distancing available mostly to mathematicians and lovers of abstraction.

Einstein's was the first major scientific use of time as an added dimension, though literature had gotten there first. By 1895 the widespread use of dimensional imagery led H.G. Wells to depict time as just another axis of a space-like cosmos, so that one could move forward and back along it. In a sense Wells's use domesticated the fourth dimension, relieving it of genuinely jarring strangeness, and ignoring the possibility of time paradox, too.

Einstein's theory contrasts strongly with visions such as Wells' in *The Time Machine*, which treats motion along the (dt) axis as very much like taking a train to the future, then back. In Einstein's geometry, only portions of the space can be reached at all without violating causality (the "light cone" within which two points can be connected by a single beam of light). Paradoxes can abound.

Logical twists have inspired many science fiction stories. The issues are quite real; we have no solid theory which includes time in a satisfying manner, along with quantum mechanics, as a truly integrated fourth dimension. I spent a great deal of space in my novel *Timescape* wrestling with how to make this intuitively clear, but the struggle to think in four dimensions is perhaps beyond realistic fiction; perhaps it is more properly the ground of metaphor.

Physicists began envisioning higher dimensions because they got a simpler dynamic picture, at the price of apparent complication. More dimensions to deal with certainly strains the imagination, and is at first glance an unintuitive way to think. But they can lead to beauties which only a mathematician can love, abstruse elegances. Thus Einstein, in his 1916 theory of general relativity, invoked the simplicity that objects move in "geodesics"—undisturbed paths, the equivalent of a straight line in Euclidean, rectangular geometry, or a great circle on a sphere—in a four-dimensional space-time. The clarity of a single type of curve, in return for the complication of a higher dimension.

Einstein's general relativity said that matter curved the four-dimensional spacetime, an effect we see as gravity. Thus he replaced a classical idea, force, with a modern geometrical view, curvature of a 4D world. This led to a cosmology of the entire universe which was expanding, and therefore pointed implicitly backward to an origin.

Einstein did not in fact like this feature of his theory, and in his first investigations of his own marvelously beautiful equations fixed up the solution until it was static, without beginning or end. His authority was so profound that his bias might have held for ages, but Edmund Hubble showed within a decade that the universe was expanding.

Even so, the concept of a beginning (and perhaps an end) may be an artifact of our persistent 3D views. Implicitly, space and time separate in the Einstein universe. They are connected, but can be defined as ideas that stand alone.

The essence of talking about dimensions is that they can be separately described. But this may not be so. At least, not in the beginning.

Even Edwin Abbott did not foretell that in the hands of cosmologists like Stephen Hawking and James Hartle, time and space would blend. Though the universe remains 4D, definitions blur.

Following the universe back to its origins leads inevitably to an early instant when intense energies led to the breakdown of the very ideas of space and time. Quantum mechanics tells us that as we proceed to earlier and earlier instants, something peculiar begins to happen. Time begins to turn into space. The origin of everything is in spacetime, and the "quantum foam" of that primordial event is not separable into our familiar distances and seconds.

What is the shape of this spacetime? Theory permits a promiscuously infinite choice. Our usual view would be that space is one set of coordinates, and time another. But quantum uncertainty erupts through these intuitive definitions.

Begin with an image of a remorselessly shrinking space governed by a backward marching time, like a cone racing downward to a sharp point. Time is the length along the axis, space the circular area of a sidewise slice. Customarily, we think of the apex as the beginning of things, where time starts and space is of zero extent.

Now round off the cone's apex to a curve. There, length and duration smear. This rounded end permits no special time when things began. To see this, imagine the cone tilted. This model universe could be conceptually tilted this way or that, with no unique inclination of the cone seems preferred. Now the "earliest" event is not at the center of the rounded end. It is some spot elsewhere on the rounded nub, a place where space and time blend. No particular spot is special.

Another way to say this is that in 4D, time and space emerge gradually from an earlier essence for which we have no name. They are ideas we now find quite handy, but they were not forever fundamental.

In the primordial Big Bang, there is no clear boundary between space and time. Rather than an image of an explosion, perhaps we should call this event the Great Emergence. There we are outside the conceptual space of precisely known space and well defined time. Yet there are still only four dimensions—just not sharp ones.

Einstein's cosmology thus begins with a time that is limited in the past, but has no boundary as such. Neither does space. As Stephen Hawking remarked, "The boundary condition of the universe is that it has no boundary."

Perhaps Edwin Abbott would not like the theological ramifications of these ideas. He was of the straitlaced Church of England. (The American version is the Episcopal faith, which happens to be my own. As an boy I was an acolyte, charged with lighting candles and carrying forth the sacraments of holy communion, in red and white robes. The robes were intolerably hot in our Atlanta church, and once I fainted and collapsed in service—overcome by the heat, not the ideas. I'm told it provoked a stir.) However, it is notable that members of that faith had a decided dimensionally imaginative bent, at least in the nineteenth century; Lewis Carrol and H.G. Wells come to mind.

No doubt, psychologically the sharp-cone cosmological picture, with its initial singular point suggests the idea of a unique Creator who sets the whole thing going. How? Physics has no mechanism. For now, it merely describes.

Here lurks a conceptual gap, for we have no model which tells us a mechanism for making universes, much less one in which such basics as space and time are illusions. We need a "God of the gaps" to explain how the original, defining event happened. These new theories seem to bridge this gap in a fashion, but at the price of abandoning still more of our basic intuitions.

Much of God's essence comes from our perceived necessity for a creator, since there was a creation. But if there is no sharp beginning, perhaps we need no sharp, clear creator. Without a singular origin in time, or in space for that matter, is there any need to appeal to a supernatural act of creation?

But does this mean we can regard the universe as entirely self-consistent, its 4D nature emerging with time, from an event which lies a finite time in our past but does not need any sort of infinite Creator? Can the universe be a closed system, containing the reason for its very existence within itself?

Perhaps—to put it mildly. Theory stands mute. Yet this latest outcome of our wrestling with dimensions assumes that there are laws to this universe, mathematically expressed in a stew of coordinates and algebra and natural beauties.

But whence come the laws themselves? Is that where a Creator resides, making not merely space-time but the laws? Of this mathematics can say nothing—so far.

Edwin Abbott would no doubt be astonished at the twists and turns his Lewis Carroll-like narrative has taken us to, only a bit more than a century beyond his initial penning of *Flatland*. The questions still loom large.

So such matters progress, sharpening the questions without answering them in final fashion. We can only be sure that the future holds ideas which he, and we, would find stranger still.

*Copyright © 1995 by Gregory Benford*

*Barry N. Malzberg is the winner of the very first Campbell Memorial Award, a multiple Hugo and Nebula nominee, twice the winner of the Locus Award for Best Non-fiction Book, and the author of more than ninety books.*

# FROM THE HEART'S BASEMENT

## by Barry N. Malzberg

### There is No Defense

Judith Merril (1920-1997) had big ideas in the 1950s: she was going to take down all of the barriers between what she called the science fiction "ghetto" and the "mainstream." She was going to prove that the barriers were artificially constructed and made no sense.

We were living in a science fiction world: Frederik Pohl and Cyril M. Kornbluth had proved that on the social register. And Hiroshima, Nagasaki, and Sputnik demonstrated that this was not a sick little genre for (what Isaac Asimov called) "crazy kids."

She embarked upon her campaign, writing book reviews (she eventually became *Fantasy & Science Fiction's* regular reviewer) and inaugurating her Annual *Best SF* series in 1957, which was taken on by Dell for mass market and which became immediately the most significant and influential of all the annuals. She wrote pandering introductions to stories by Russell Baker and Jorge Luis Borges reprinted in her annuals, arguing that they proved that literary figures and *New York Times* columnists were writing the stuff just as well or better as the hacks in *Astounding* and *Galaxy*.

She persuaded Anthony Boucher (who had his own shaky and ambivalent fix on the field) that everything was science fiction. And Boucher hired Arthur Jean Cox to write an ongoing movie column in which he noted that the musical *Li'l Abner* was hard-core science fiction. Her columns in *Fantasy & Science Fiction* disdained or ignored category publications as largely hackwork, and she used the space to dismiss almost all of it and surely to propagate the British New Wave writers who were really shaking the earth and changing everything. That led to her commercially disastrous Doubleday

anthology *England Swings! SF*, which Donald A. Wollheim, who published the paperback, told me was the worst-selling Ace paperback in history. This is just part of what the former Josephine Grossman was doing in the critical period 1955-1968 after she had essentially written *finis* to her career as a fiction writer; but it was quite enough to get the job done. A decent writer and a highly intelligent person, she did the field more damage than Raymond Palmer or Roger Corman, Ed Earl Repp or Ed Wood. The field certainly survived, it had demonstrated the pre-Lucas capacity to survive anything, but it was irreversibly damaged.

It was irreversibly damaged because Merril's influence in those years was great, and she was on a methodical, hardly understated campaign to tear down the walls and destroy the category. As a failed mainstream writer who had essentially been rescued by her friends Theodore Sturgeon and Philip J. Klass, and pointed toward commercial writing, Merril was determined to find another way into the mainstream. And if that involved rupturing or destroying science fiction, well, that would be collateral damage.

I had a little of this syndrome myself—like Merril I came to science fiction in my mid-twenties as a failed angry quality lit writer. But I never forgot that science fiction had essentially rescued me, that *Final War* which had been deemed "too grimly realistic" for *The Hudson Review* and condescendingly bounced had been taken by Edward L. Ferman, and in that simple act he had saved my creative life, and I was grateful. I was not contemptuous of science fiction or anxious to pummel the misshapen but occasionally beautiful field of literature because it was a means of default. Rather, I was grateful and having read a great deal in the genre at a formative time (so had Merril) I knew that it was a legitimate brand of literature which was being screwed mercilessly by the academy and the quality lit gatekeepers and spirits. Their casual contempt (like the contempt of the *Hudson Review*) infuriated me and still does. But I never blamed science fiction for what the larger culture had done to it. Merril did. Merril was the kind of liberal who in different circumstances would blame James Baldwin and Cassius Clay for bad manners, for giving their people a bad name.

Merril ignored or elided or just did not give a damn about a truism expressed mockingly in W.S. Gilbert's lyric in *The Gondoliers* for Arthur Sullivan's music. There lived a King in days of old of whom a story was told: he made royalty of the entire Kingdom. Merril made science fiction of the entire compass of drama and literature, from *Don Quixote* to Sophie Treadwell's *Machinal*. Earls and dukes and ladies of court were a dime a dozen, but the King forgot "That if everyone is somebody, then no one's anybody." His subjects, rather than wallowing in their promotion, were angry, felt cheated. And if everything was science fiction—well, then, *nothing* was science fiction.

Merril, before she gave up anthologies, criticism, and citizenship to expatriate herself to Canada in 1968, was made desperate by the unending, irretrievable, uncorrectable stupidity and murderousness of Vietnam. She had been on an increasingly evident, now unapologetic campaign to destroy science fiction.

She knew it: the campaign was purposeful. In her story introduction to Bob Shaw's "Light of Other Days" in her final volume, she conceded that the excellence and rigor of the story called her back to an earlier time when she had been entranced by such work and her own desire to replicate. But that story introduction was half or three-quarters an apology: its appearance in *Best SF*, its very quality, were an implicit rebuke to the scattered, unfocused, false literary emptiness which had come to occupy most of the anthology. Meanwhile, she was writing savage reviews in *Fantasy & Science Fiction*, reviews as savage as those of Alfred Bester's half a decade earlier which had created a good deal of foul karma and eventually got him fired.

Algis Budrys observed from a distance in his *Galaxy* reviews Merril's convulsions in the late 60s. He wished her well in her efforts to depart, but added that he could not imagine what otherwise Merril could do, and therefore found those efforts misguided. Budrys had his own problems—one of my earliest columns here commented at length on his deterioration—but attachment to the field and respect for rigor had never been among them. And his offhand sentence pretty well adumbrated the dislocation, the wandering of Merril's final quarter century. She was the Queen of Canadian Science Fiction, maybe, and she had a good many acolytes, more for her feminism than philosophy. But she was as lost as Bester, who had lost his ear and sense. It is a hard concession, but I am not in a merciful mode—as I have become both the perpetrator of a body of work now close to unknown, and yet still clutched by the passion to believe that Science Fiction which changed the world in its inception and gave us the world in which we however unwillingly dwell...science fiction still matters. It will always matter, and in all the worlds in all of time its light will never be lost.

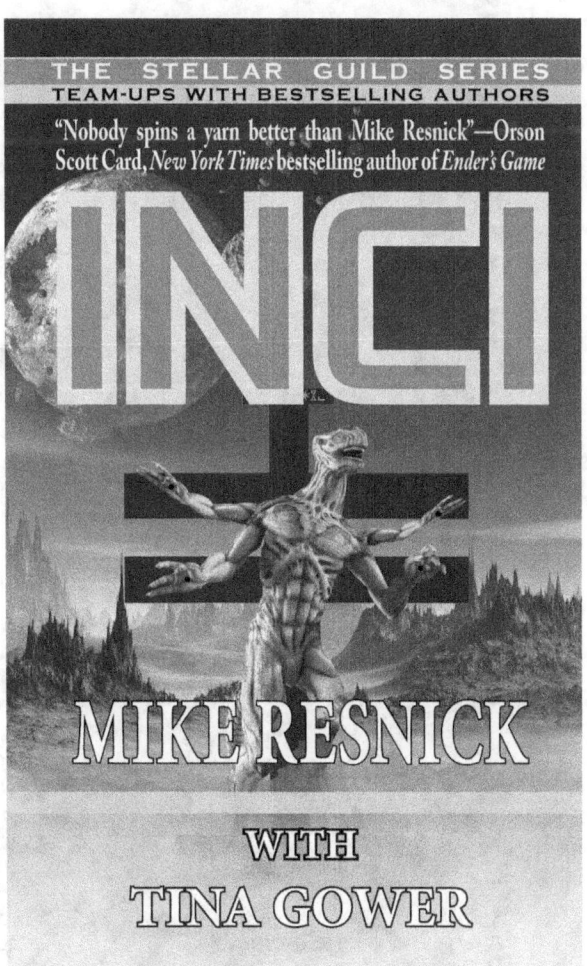

# The BEST OF GALAXY'S EDGE 2013-2014

Larry Niven
C. L. Moore
Nick DiChario
Robert T. Jeschonek
Tina Gower
Mercedes Lackey
Ralph Roberts
Ken Liu
Marina J. Lostetter
Andrea G. Stewart
Eric Cline
Tom Gerencer
Nancy Kress
Sabina Theo
Gio Clairval
Steve Cameron
Brad R. Torgersen
Eric Leif Davin
Kary English
Lou J. Berger
Brian Trent
K. C. Norton
Leena Likitalo
James Aquilone

*Edited by*
*Mike Resnick*

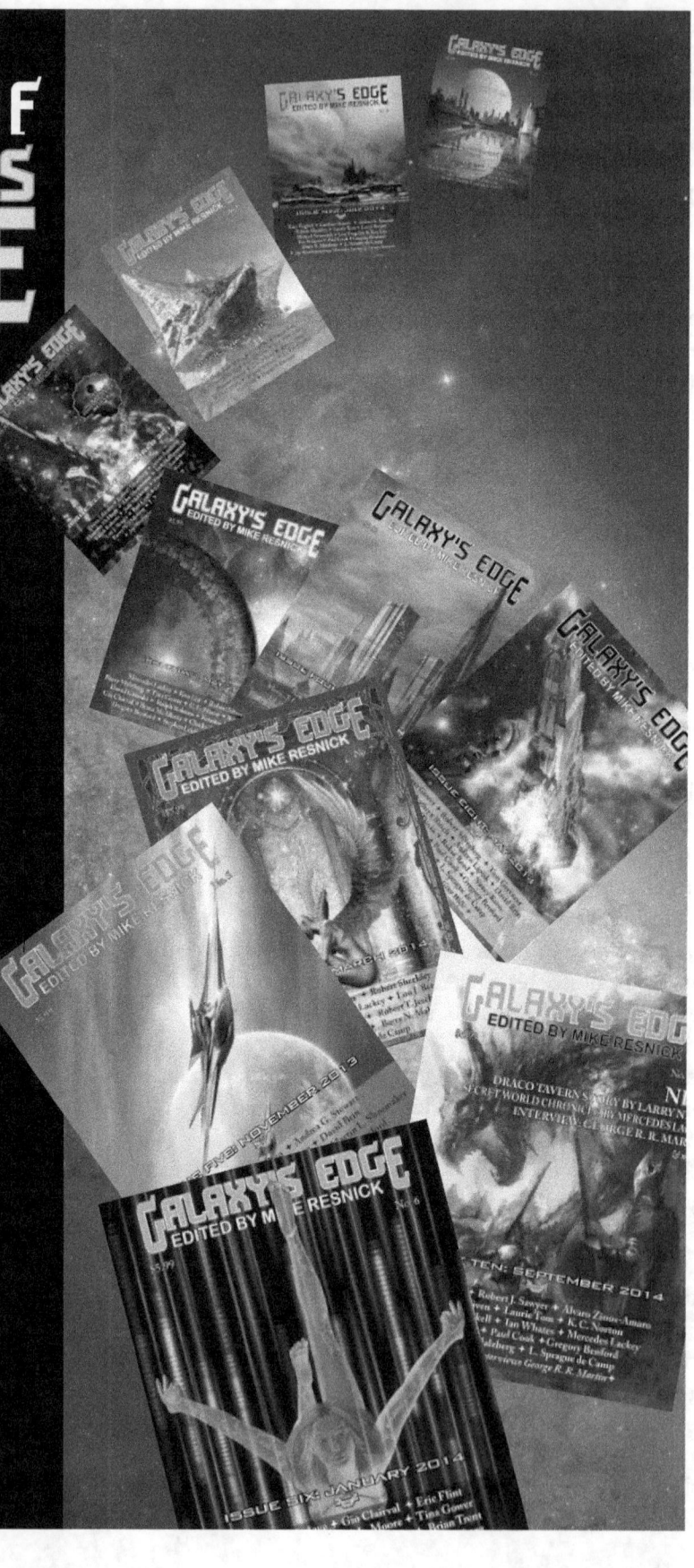

# SUBSCRIBE NOW!

# www.GalaxysEdge.com

*Joy Ward is the author of one novel. She has several stories in print, at magazines and in anthologies, and has also done interviews, both written and video, for other publications.*

*George R. R. Martin, one of the most prolific writers of our time and a man who is considered by many to be one of our greatest living writers, was kind enough let Joy visit with him in his den, overseen by a full-size functional replica of Robby the Robot and numerous other fascinating models and collectible space toys, including his first set of spacemen.*

## THE *GALAXY'S EDGE* INTERVIEW

### Joy Ward interviews
### George R. R. Martin

**Joy Ward:** *How did you get started writing?*

**Martin:** I've always written. As far back as I can remember. When I was a little kid I used to make up stories about my toys and write them down. Give them all names. I had a collection of space men. I learned later they are called Miller Aliens. On the basis of where they were from like being from Mars or the dark side of the moon, but that was enough for me. I gave them all names and I decided they were a gang of space pirates. This guy was the brains of the operation and here was this lieutenant. This guy was in charge of torture. There's a little guy there who's holding a weird weapon that looked to me like a drill so I said "Oh, this guy must be in charge of torture," because he drills people with that little drill. They had weird guns and all that so I invented personalities for the whole thing and adventures of them, this gang of space pirates. I couldn't have been more than nine or ten at that time.

I would also write monster stories that I would sell to the other kids in the projects for a nickel and I could buy a Milky Way bar. Usually, the stories were two pages long handwritten. They had a werewolf and I would howl for them. I liked to frighten the other kids.

It was a short-lived career though, because one of the other kids was having nightmares. His mother came to my mother and said, "Stop frightening the other kids. You can't tell them these monster stories anymore." So it dried up my source of extra Milky Ways and comic books.

**JW:** *What did you do then?*

**Martin:** I just went back to not scaring the other kids for a few years. I read a lot. Books were my comic books.

At a certain formative age one of my mother's friends gave me a Scribner's hardcover copy of *Have Space Suit—Will Travel* by Robert A. Heinlein. That, of course, is still one of my favorite science fiction books; one of the great science fiction books of all time. Up there with the best of Heinlein, I think, even though it was part of his juvenile series. It works for adults too. I can still read that book with pleasure.

That got me into reading science fiction. I had my dollar a week allowance so I had to decide, because paper books were 35 cents, did I want to take the equivalent of 3 comic books and spend it on one paperback? It was a hard decision to make sometimes. You had to figure out these budgets here. Well, there's a new Spiderman and Fantastic Four but oh, look at this here's a Robert A. Heinlein I haven't seen or an Andre Norton or A. E. van Vogt. The Ace Doubles. I liked the Ace Doubles because you got, for thirty-five cents you got two stories. The Heinlein of *Have Space Suit—Will Travel*, which was actually a beautiful first edition Scribner's hardcover, I read that to pieces but for a decade it was the only hardcover book I owned because we didn't have much money.

**JW:** *What other writers did you read?*

**Martin:** Well, I mentioned a few of them. Andre Norton was the other big writer that was part of the Ace Doubles. I loved her stuff.

I liked Jerry Sohl. He wrote some good Ace Doubles. I read A. E. van Vogt but I didn't quite get into him. It was interesting but his stories were kind of confusing in some ways and they're still confusing. But he was certainly an original. Münster, Isaac Asimov, Jack Williamson, all of the people who were writing back then and from previous decades.

I discovered Doc Smith at one point and devoured the Skylark series, *The Skylark of Space* and its sequels.

Then at a certain point I discovered fantasy. The first discovery was a little book called *Swords and Sorcery* by L. Sprague de Camp and I picked that up off a spinner rack and it had a Conan story. I was hooked, particularly by Conan.

I got into horror, which I didn't call horror; I just called them monster stories. The same way, there was an anthology that I found on a spinner rack, Boris Karloff's favorite horror stories or something. In that book I encountered "The Whisperer in Darkness," my first H. P. Lovecraft story. I'd never read anything so terrifying as what Lovecraft did.

**JW:** *What's the first thing you sold?*

**Martin:** Before pro, I was a published fan. I wrote for fanzines initially.

I've been outspoken on the Internet and other places in not being in favor of fan fiction. Sometimes I get criticized by fans who don't understand and say, "You say you wrote fan fiction and now you're against fan fiction." What I wrote was not fan fiction like that term is used today. Today when people say fan fiction, they talk about taking my characters or Robin Hobb's characters or Robert Jordan's characters or Kirk or Spock or any characters from a television show or movie and writing stories about them. Writing stories about someone else's characters. I never did that and I never approved of that.

I did write what we called fan fiction. In the sixties it was simply fiction written by fans and published in fanzines. They were original stories about original characters. Yeah, some of them were pretty derivative. You could sort of look through the thin layer of cloth there and see, wow, this is Batman, even though they've changed his name to Kookaburraman.

I wrote stories about Manta Ray and Powerman and Doctor Weird and numerous other characters, some created by me, some created by other writers who then solicited me to write about their characters. They were published in the fanzines and I became

pretty popular. I got a lot of praise, which encouraged me.

I was a very shy and introverted kid. I think the life of the imagination was a refuge for me; daydreams and books and comic books.

I was always a little hesitant to put myself out there. I don't know, fear of rejection or whatever. But actually having these things published in fanzines and having editors say, "This is great, one of the best stories we've ever gotten here," readers writing in and saying, "This George Martin is terrific," was really encouraging to me. I think it was a crucial step in my development.

**JW:** *What did that say to you, that people were writing in saying you were a great writer?*

**Martin:** It says to me they were high school kids who didn't know any better. So was I. I mean, comic fandom in those early days was 90% high school kids and younger. There was a 10% college kids and adults that were sort of in the leadership position that got things rolling but the guys I was dealing with were all high school kids. So you were in the little leagues. You weren't in the major leagues. You were a star in the little leagues. But that didn't mean you were able to play in the majors. I always dreamed of playing in the majors.

I knew that eventually I wanted to write comic books professionally. I wanted to write stories professionally. But I was hesitant even then to make that leap. What if they didn't like it? What if they rejected me? What if they said, "You're no good?" So I always wanted to save it until I got better. A few years I'll be a little older, I'll be a little better.

By this time I was in college. In college at every opportunity I took courses that would allow me to write fiction. I took creative writing and short story writing.

Even in other courses I would say, "Instead of a term paper can I do fiction?" I made that offer, it was my sophomore year at Northwestern University in Evanston, Illinois, and I was taking a course in Scandinavian history of all things. History was my minor. We were supposed to do a term paper for a big part of our grade and I approached the professor and said, "Could I write, instead of a term paper, historical fiction?" He had never had this offer before but he was intrigued by it. He said, "Sure. See what you can do with the history that we've taught you."

So I wrote a story about the Russo-Finnish War of 1808 and the surrender of the Great Fortress of Sveaborg, the Gibraltar of the North. It's a great mystery of history in that part of the world. I wrote a story where I explained it. It was called "The Fortress." It got an "A," which was great. But not only did it get an "A," the professor liked it so much that he sent it to a professional magazine called *American-Scandinavian Review*. They liked it too but they didn't publish fiction. They sent a very nice rejection letter to the professor, which he passed on to me. That was my first professional rejection. I said, "Okay, this is a professional editor and he said it was good. Maybe I don't have to be afraid."

So the next year I took a creative writing course and I wrote some science fiction stories and some mainstream stories. For the first time I started sending them out myself to professional magazines. The mainstream stories I never got anything but straight rejection slips on those. But the two science fiction stories I wrote, both of them eventually sold, though one of them took a decade. But the other one sold within a couple of years. That was "The Hero."

That was my first professional sale. I wrote it, I think, in my junior year at Northwestern for the creative writing course. I started sending it out and I got a rejection letter from John W. Campbell Jr., which was quite a feather in my cap. He wrote personal letters, too. Then I got an acceptance from *Galaxy Magazine*. It appeared in *Galaxy* in early 1971. I got $94 for it, which was real money back in those days.

I remember when it came out in February 1971. I was with my friends scouring all of Chicago to look for copies of it. Buying two copies at this news stand and two more at that news stand and oh, this doesn't have it and carrying it home. They didn't send you authors' copies in those days. You had to go out and hunt it down yourself.

It was pretty exciting. Your first time is always pretty exciting, whether it's publishing or sex. And you always remember it. Opening that envelope and seeing that check in there. It was pretty amazing seeing it on the news stand, seeing my name in print. This was my name in print attached to a story and that was pretty amazing.

I was very lucky. I know many people who have struggled for years, have collected a lot of rejection and certainly I did collect a lot of rejection. I wrote four stories in that creative writing course and the other three of them all got more than forty rejection slips. Some of them never sold.

Having had one story that broke through made the others not seem so bad. If all of the stories had gotten forty rejections I may have been so discouraged I might have stopped but instead it encouraged me to persevere. Then I wrote more stories and those started selling, too. Science fiction, fantasy. So all through the '70s I was publishing everywhere. There was one month in '73 I had three stories come out simultaneously in three different magazines—one in *Analog*, one in *Amazing* and one in *F&SF*.

It felt great. It felt like I was conquering the world.

I wrote short stories and published short stories all through the early and mid '70s. I was nominated for the Campbell Award. I didn't win. I was nominated for Hugos and Nebulas, although I didn't win. Finally I was nominated for a Hugo and I did win. "A Song for Lya" in 1975. Best Novella.

At that point I thought it was time for me to do my first novel. *Dying of the Light* was published in 1977. Once again, I was very, very lucky. All through the '70s new writers that I knew who breaking in were getting three thousand dollars for their first novel.

In 1977, just as I was completing my novel, and I had no confidence I could work in something that long because I had only worked in short ones so far. During the time that I was writing the book, the great science fiction boom of the late '70s hit. Science fiction books were beginning to hit the best-seller list for the first time. The great writers of the Golden Age and the '50s, Asimov and Heinlein, were having best sellers for the first time in their lives. The publishers that had them were happy but there were more publishers in those days. It wasn't the Big Five; it was the Big Thirty. The others were all looking around. Maybe that's the next Heinlein, the next Asimov. There were auctions going on, crazy auctions where people were bidding for a lot of money on first novels and second novels by younger writers.

I was in the right place at the right time. I got four publishers bidding on *Dying of the Light* so it went for a lot more money than I could have gotten even in a year. That made it possible for me to contemplate actually being a full-time writer.

Up to that point in my career I always worked other jobs. I'd been a chess tournament director. I'd done some journalism. I worked as a VISTA volunteer for two years. I'd done public relations. I was looking at the careers of other writers and saying there's Heinlein who has been a professional writer since the beginning. But there is also Clifford Simak, who was never a full-time writer. He always wrote his fiction on the side and I thought that's the kind of life I was heading toward until *Dying of the Light* sold for so much money.

After *Dying of the Light* I wrote *Windhaven* with Lisa Tuttle and *Fevre Dream*. It kind of brought me out from straight science fiction.

Then I wrote a novel called *The Armageddon Rag*. It provoked great enthusiasm among the people who had read it and it got me my first really big advance. Up to that point in my life I had led a charmed career really. Unfortunately, nobody bought it. It was commercially a huge failure. I quickly discovered that a world like publishing is not a world with a lot of security. You're as hot as your latest book or your latest movie or TV show.

**JW:** *How do you see that progression in yourself from probably television's best love story ever,* Beauty and the Beast, *to* Game of Thrones, *which is very different?*

**Martin:** For me it was not that different. I've always been different. As a kid I fell in love with science fiction, with fantasy, with horror, and I wrote all three. You look at my earlier stuff, "The Hero," that story

I sold to *Galaxy*. That was a hard-core science fiction story. The second story I sold to *Fantastic* was a ghost story set when people have stopped driving automobiles. That was a fantasy, a little bit of horror story and ghosts. Even in my first three stories I was hitting all three bases. I kept moving around. I never like to repeat myself. I always like to move around and change things and what should I do next?

I was a child of the spinner rack. We didn't have any bookstores in Bayonne, New Jersey, when I was growing up. I bought my paperbacks off the spinner rack next to comic books. There was no sorting there. Dumas was next to Vance and Norman Vincent Peale was on a shelf below. All the books were together. I've always read a lot of things and I like to write a lot of different things.

**JW:** *How do you use death in your writing?*

**Martin:** I don't think of it in those terms, that I'm using death for any purpose. I think a writer, even a fantasy writer, has an obligation to tell the truth and the truth is, as we say in *Game of Thrones*, all men must die. Particularly if you're writing about war, which is certainly a central subject in *Game of Thrones*. It has been in a lot of my fiction, not all of it by any means but certainly a lot of it, going all the way back to "The Hero," which was a story about a warrior. You can't write about war and violence without having death. If you want to be honest it should affect your main characters. We've all read this story a million times when a bunch of heroes set out on adventure and it's the hero and his best friend and his girlfriend and they go through amazing hair-raising adventures and none of them die. The only ones who die are extras.

That's such a cheat. It doesn't happen that way. They go into battle and their best friend dies or they get horribly wounded. They lose their leg or death comes at them unexpectedly.

Death is so arbitrary. It's always there. It's coming for all of us. We're all going to die. I'm going to die. You're going to die. Mortality is at the soul of all this stuff. You have to write about it if you're going to be honest, especially if you're writing a story high in conflict. Once you've accepted that you have to include death then you should be honest about death and indicate it can strike down anybody at any time. You don't get to live forever just because you are a cute kid or the hero's best friend or the hero. Sometimes the hero dies, at least in my books.

I love all my characters so it's always hard to kill them but I know it has to be done. I tend to think I don't kill them. The other characters kill 'em. I shift off all blame from myself.

**JW:** *What kind of advice would you give the young George Martin?*

**Martin:** Writing is a terrible career if you're looking at it as a way to have a career.

You should not choose writing as a way to make money, to make a name for yourself or any of these other external things. If you have to write, if the stories are in you, if you made up names and stories for your toy spacemen when you were little, if the stories come to you, ask yourself the question What if no one ever gives me a penny for my stories? Will I still write them? And if the answer is yes, then you're a writer. Then you have to be a writer. It's the only thing you can do. If the answer is No, I'm going to quit after a few years because I'm not selling, then maybe you should quit right now and learn computer science. I hear there's a real future in these computer things.

Everybody looks at the writer's lifestyle. There are a lot of cool things about it. The reason to write is you have stories to tell. You have people inside you clamoring to get out. That's what I'd tell the young kid.

**JW:** *What do you want to do that you haven't done?*

**Martin:** I want to be thirty years old again. I want to travel around the world. I want to keep going to amazing places and having adventures there. But I do want to work on that being thirty years old again.

*Copyright © 2014 by Joy Ward*

## SERIALIZATION
## THE LONG TOMORROW

### Part 3

by Leigh Brackett
Phoenix Pick, 2012
Trade Paperback: 202 pages.
ISBN: 978-1-61242-013-4

*Leigh Brackett was one of the greats. She began writing in the pulps, where her Martian tales rivaled those of Edgar Rice Burroughs. Hollywood called, and she wrote major screenplays for Humphrey Bogart* (The Big Sleep) *and John Wayne* (Rio Bravo). *Hollywood paid better, but science fiction was her first love and she kept coming back to it, resurrecting her hero, Eric John Stark, for three novels in the 1970s. She also wrote the initial screenplay for* The Empire Strikes Back. *Leigh and her husband, science fiction writer Edmond Hamilton, were co-Guests of Honor at the 1964 Worldcon. We are thrilled to bring you the serialization of Leigh's* The Long Tomorrow.

## THE LONG TOMORROW

### Part Three

### by Leigh Brackett

### EIGHT

The narrow brown waters of the Pymatuning fatten the Shenango. The Shenango flows down to meet the Mahoning, and the two of them together make the Beaver. The Beaver fattens the Ohio, and the Ohio runs grandly westward to help make mighty the Father of Waters.

Time flows, too. Little units grow into big ones, minutes into months and months into years. Boys become men, and the milestones of a long search multiply and are left behind. But the legend remains a legend, and the dream a dream, glimmering, fading, ever somewhere farther on toward the sunset.

There was a town called Refuge, and a yellow-haired girl, and they were real.

Refuge was not at all like Piper's Run. It was bigger, so much bigger that its boundaries were already straining against the lawful limits, but size was not the chief difference. It was a matter of feeling. Len and Esau had noticed that same feeling in a number of places as they worked their way along the river valleys, particularly where, as in Refuge, highway and waterway conjoined. Piper's Run lived and breathed with the slow calm rhythm of the seasons, and the thoughts of the folk who lived there were calm too. Refuge bustled. The people moved faster, and thought faster, and talked louder, and the streets were noisier at night, with a passing of drays and wagons and the voices of stevedores along the wharves.

Refuge stood on the north bank of the Ohio. It had come by its name, Len understood, because people from a city farther along the river had taken refuge there during the Destruction. It was the terminus now for two main trading routes stretching as far as the Great Lakes, and the wagons rolled day and night while the roads were passable, bringing down baled furs and iron and woolen cloth, flour and cheeses. From east and west along the river came other traffic, bearing other things, copper and hides and tallow and salt beef from the plains, coal and scrap metal from Pennsylvania, salt fish from the Atlantic, kegs of nails, fine guns, paper. The river traffic moved around the clock, too, from spring to early winter, flatboats and launches and tugs towing long strings of loaded barges, going with a fine brave smoke and clatter from their steam engines. These were the first engines Len and Esau had ever seen, and at first they were frightened out of their wits by the noise, but they soon got used to them. They had, one winter, worked in a little foundry near the mouth of the Beaver, making boilers and feeling as though they were already helping to mechanize the world. The New Mennonites frowned on the use of any artificial power, but the river-boat men belonged to different sects and had different problems. They had to get cargoes upriver against the current, and if they could harness steam in a simple and easily handmade engine to help them, they were going to do it, cutting the ethic to fit the need.

On the Kentucky side of the river, just opposite, there was a place called Shadwell. Shadwell was much smaller than Refuge and much newer, but it was swelling out so fast that even Len and Esau could see the difference in the year or so they had been there. The people of Refuge did not care much for Shadwell, which had only happened because traders had begun to come up out of the South with sugar and blackstrap and cotton and tobacco, drawn by the commerce of the Refuge markets. A couple of temporary sheds had gone up, and a ferry dock, and a cabin or two, and before anybody realized it there was a village, with wharves and warehouses of its own, and a name, and a growing population. And Refuge, already as large as a town was permitted by law to be, sat sourly by and watched the overplus of trade it could not handle flow into Shadwell.

There were few Amish or Mennonites in Refuge. The people mostly belonged to the Church of Holy Thankfulness, and were called Kellerites after the James P. Keller who founded the sect. Len and Esau had found that there were few Mennonites anywhere in the settlements that lived by commerce rather than by agriculture. And since they were excommunicated themselves, with no wish to be traced back to Piper's Run, they had long ago discarded the distinctive dress of their childhood faith for the nondescript homespuns of the river towns. They wore their hair short and their chins naked, because it was the custom among the Kellerites for a man to remain clean-shaven until he married, when he was expected to grow the beard that distinguished him more plainly than any removable ring. They went every Sunday to the Church of Holy Thankfulness, and joined in the regular daily devotions of the family they boarded with, and sometimes they forgot that they had ever been anything but Kellerites.

Sometimes, Len thought, they even forgot why they were here and what they were looking for. And he would make himself remember the night when he had waited for Esau on the point above the Pymatuning, and everything that had gone before to bring him there, and it was easy enough to remember the physical things, the chill air and the smell of leaves, the beating, and the way Pa's face had looked as he lifted the strap and brought it whistling down. But the other part of it, the way he had felt inside, was harder to call to mind. Sometimes he could do it only with a real effort. Other times he could not do it at all. And at still other times—and these were the worst—the way he had felt about leaving home and finding Bartorstown seemed to him childish and absurd. He would see home and family so clearly that it was a physical pain in him, and he would think, I threw them all away for a name, a voice in the air, and here I am, a wanderer, and where is Bartorstown? He had found out that time can be a traitor and that thoughts are like mountaintops, a different shape on every side, changing as you move away.

Time had played him another trick, too. It had made him grow up and given him a lot of brand-new things to worry about.

Including the yellow-haired girl.

It was an evening in mid-June, hot and sultry, with the sunset swallowed up in the blackness of an oncoming storm. The two candles on the table burned straight up, with no quiver of air from the open windows to trouble them. Len sat with his hands folded and his head bent, looking down into the remains of a milk pudding. Esau sat on his right, in the same attitude. The yellow-haired girl sat across from them. Her name was Amity Taylor. Her father was saying grace after meat, sitting at the head of the table, and at the foot, her mother listened reverently.

"—didst stretch out the garment of Thy mercy to shelter us in the day of Destruction—"

Amity glanced up from under the shadows of her brows in the candlelight, looking first at Len and then at Esau.

"—our thanks for the limitless abundance of Thy blessing—"

Len felt the girl's eyes on him. His skin was thin and sensitive to that touch, so that without even looking up he knew what she was doing. His heart began to thump. He felt hot. Esau's hands were in his line of vision, folded between Esau's knees. He saw them move and tighten, and he knew that Amity had looked at Esau too, and he got even hotter, thinking about the garden and the shadowy place under the rose arbor.

Wouldn't Judge Taylor ever shut up?

The Amen came at last, muffled in the louder voice of thunder. Hurry, thought Len. Hurry with the dishes or there won't be any walking in the garden. Not for anybody. He jumped up, scraping his chair back over the bare floor. Esau jumped up too, and he and Len went to picking up plates off the table so fast they jostled each other. On the other side of the candlelight, Amity slowly stacked the cups, and smiled.

Mrs. Taylor went out, carrying two serving dishes into the kitchen. At the hall door, the judge seemed on the point of going to his study, as he always did immediately after the final grace. Esau turned suddenly and gave Len a covert glare of anger, and whispered, "Stay out of this."

Amity walked toward the kitchen door, balancing the stack of cups in her two hands. Her yellow hair hung down her back in a thick braid. She wore a dress of gray cotton, high in the neck and long in the skirt, but it did not look on her at all the way a similar dress did on her mother. She had a wonderful way of walking. It made Len's heart come up in his throat every time he saw it. He glared back at Esau and started after her with his own load of plates, making long strides to get ahead. And Judge Taylor said quietly from the hall door, "Len—come into the study when you've put those down. They can get along without you for one washing."

Len stopped. He gave Taylor a startled and apprehensive look, and said, "Yes, sir." Taylor nodded and left the room. Len glanced briefly at Esau, who was openly upset.

"What does he want?" asked Esau.

"How should I know?"

"Listen. Listen, have you been up to anything?"

Amity went slowly through the swinging door, with her skirt moving gracefully around her ankles. Len flushed.

"No more'n you have, Esau," he said angrily. He went after Amity and put his pile of dishes down on the sink board. Amity began to roll her sleeves up. She said to her mother, "Len can't help tonight. Daddy wants him."

Reba Taylor turned from the stove, where a pot of wash water simmered over the coals. She had a mild, pleasant, rather vacuous face, and Len had marked her long ago as one of the incurious ones. Life had passed over her so easily.

"Dear, dear," she said. "Surely you haven't done anything wrong, Len?"

"I hope not, ma'am."

"I'll bet you," said Amity, "that it's about Mike Dulinsky and his warehouse."

"Mr. Dulinsky," said Reba Taylor sharply, "and get about your dishes, young lady. They're your concern. Run along, Len. Very likely the judge only wants to give you some advice, and you could do worse than listen to it."

"Yes, ma'am," said Len, and went out, across the dining room and into the hall and along that to the study, wondering all the way whether he had been seen kissing Amity in the garden, or whether it was about the Dulinsky business, or what. He had often gone to the judge's study, and he had often talked with him, about books and the past and the future and sometimes even the present, but he had never been called in before.

The study door was open. Taylor said, "Come in, Len." He was sitting behind his big desk in the angle of the windows. They faced the west, and the sky beyond them was a dull black as though it had been wiped all over with soot. The trees looked sickly and colorless, and the river lay at one side like a strip of lead. Taylor had been sitting there looking out, with an unlighted candle and an unopened book beside him. He was rather a small man, with smooth cheeks and a high forehead. His hair and beard were always neatly trimmed, his linen was fresh every day, and his dark plain suit was cut from the finest cloth that came into the Refuge market. Len liked him. He had books and read them and encouraged other people to read them, and he was not afraid of knowledge, though he never made a parade of having any more than he needed in his profession. "Don't call undue attention to yourself," he often told Len, "and you will avoid a great deal of trouble."

Now he told Len to come in and shut the door. "I'm afraid we're going to have a really serious talk, and I wanted you here alone because I want you to be free to think and make your decisions without any—well, any other influences."

"You don't think much of Esau, do you?" asked Len, sitting down where the judge had set a chair for him.

"No," said Taylor, "but that is neither here nor there. Except that I'll say further that I do think a great deal of you. And now we'll leave personalities alone. Len, you work for Mike Dulinsky."

"Yes, sir," said Len, and began to bristle up a bit, defensively. So that was it.

"Are you going to continue working for him?"

Len hesitated only a short second before he said again, "Yes, sir."

Taylor thought, looking out at the black sky and the ugly dusk. A beautiful forked blaze ran down the clouds. Len counted slowly, and when he reached seven there was a roll of thunder. "It's still quite a ways off," he said.

"Yes, but we'll catch it. When they come from that direction, we always do. You've done a lot of reading this last year, Len. Have you learned anything from it?"

Len ran his eye lovingly over the shelves. It was too dark to see titles, but he knew the books by their size and place and he had read an awful lot of them.

"I hope so," he said.

"Then apply what you've learned. It isn't any good to you shut up inside your head in a separate cupboard. Do you remember Socrates?"

"Yes."

"He was a greater and a wiser man than you or I will ever be, but that didn't save him when he ran too hard against the whole body of law and public belief."

Lightning flashed again, and this time the interval was shorter. The wind began to blow, tossing the branches of the trees around and riffling the blank surface of the river. Distant figures labored on the wharves to make fast the moorings of the barges, or to hustle bales and sacks under cover. Landward, between the trees, the whitewashed or weathered-silver houses of Refuge glimmered in the last wan light from overhead.

"Why do you want to hasten the day?" asked Taylor quietly. "You'll never live to see it, and neither will your children, nor your grandchildren. Why, Len?"

"Why what?" asked Len, now blankly confused, and then he gasped as Taylor answered him, "Why do you want to bring back the cities?"

Len was silent, peering into the gloom that had suddenly deepened until Taylor was no more than a shadow four feet away.

"They were dying even before the Destruction," said Taylor. "Megalopolis, drowned in its own sewage, choked with its own waste gases, smothered and crushed by its own population. 'City' sounds like a musical word to your ear, but what do you really know about them?"

They had been over this ground before. "Gran used to say—"

"That she was a little girl then, and little girls would hardly see the dirt, the ugliness, the crowded poverty, the vice. The cities were sucking all the life of the country into themselves and destroying it. Men were no longer individuals, but units in a vast machine, all cut to one pattern, with the same tastes and ideas, the same mass-produced education that did not educate but only pasted a veneer of catch-words over ignorance. Why do you want to bring that back?"

An old argument, but applied in a totally unexpected way. Len stammered, "I haven't been thinking about cities one way or the other. And I don't see what Mr. Dulinsky's new warehouse has to do with them."

"Len, if you're not honest with yourself, life will never be honest with you. A stupid man could say that he didn't see and be honest, but not you. Unless you're still too much of a child to think beyond the immediate fact."

"I'm old enough to get married," said Len hotly, "and that ought to be old enough for anything."

"Quite," said Taylor. "Quite. Here comes the rain, Len. Help me with the windows." They shut them, and Taylor lit the candle. The room was now unbearably close and hot. "What a pity," he said, "that the windows always have to be closed just when the cool wind starts to blow. Yes, you're old enough to get married, and I think Amity has a thought or two in that direction herself. It's a possibility I want you to consider."

Len's heart began to pound, the way it always did when Amity was involved. He felt wildly excited, and at the same time it was as though a trap had been set before his feet. He sat down again, and the rain thrashed on the windows like hail.

Taylor said slowly, "Refuge is a good town just the way it stands. You could have a good life here. I can take you off the docks and make a lawyer out of you, and in time you'd be an important man. You would have leisure for study, and all the wisdom of the world is there in those books. And there's Amity. Those are the things I can give you. What does Dulinsky offer?"

Len shook his head. "I do my work, and he pays me. That's all."

"You know he's breaking the law."

"It's a silly law. One warehouse more or less—"

"One warehouse more, in this case, violates the Thirtieth Amendment, which is the most basic law of this land. It won't be overlooked."

"But it isn't fair. Nobody here in Refuge wants to see Shadwell spring up and take a lot of business away because there aren't enough warehouses and wharves and shelters on this side to take care of all the trade."

"One more warehouse," said Taylor, pointedly repeating Len's words, "and then more wharves to serve it, and more housing for the traders, and pretty soon you'll need another warehouse still, and that is the way in which cities are born. Len, has Dulinsky ever mentioned Bartorstown to you?"

Len's heart, which had been beating so hard for Amity, now stopped in sudden fear. He shivered and said, with perfect truthfulness, "No, sir. Never."

"I just wondered. It seems the kind of a thing a Bartorstown man might do. But then I've known Mike since we were boys together, and I can't remember any possible influence—no, I suppose not. But that may not save him, Len, and it may not save you."

Len said carefully, "I don't think I understand."

"You and Esau are strangers. People will accept you as long as you don't run counter to their ways, but if you do, look out." He leaned his elbows on the desk and looked at Len. "You haven't been altogether truthful about yourself."

"I haven't told any lies."

"That isn't always necessary. Anyway, I can pretty well guess. You're a country boy. I would lay odds that you were New Mennonite. And you ran away from home. Why?"

"I guess," said Len, choosing his words as a man on the edge of a pitfall chooses his steps, "that it was because Pa and me couldn't agree on how much was right for me to know."

"Thus far," said Taylor thoughtfully, "and no farther. That has always been a difficult line to draw. Each sect must decide for itself, and to a certain degree, so must every man. Have you found your limit, Len?"

"Not yet."

"Find it," Taylor said, "before you go too far."

They sat for a moment in silence. The rain poured and a lightning bolt came down so close that it made an audible hissing before it hit. The resultant thunder shook the house like an explosion.

"Do you understand," asked Taylor, "why the Thirtieth Amendment was passed?"

"So there wouldn't be any more cities."

"Yes, but do you comprehend the reasoning behind that interdiction? I was brought up in a certain body of belief, and in public I wouldn't dream of contradicting any part of it, but here in private I can say that I do not believe that God directed the cities to be destroyed because they were sinful. I've read too much history. The enemy bombed the big key cities because they were excellent targets, cen-

ters of population, centers of manufacture and distribution, without which the country would be like a man with his head cut off. And it worked out just that way. The enormously complex system of supply broke down, the cities that were not bombed had to be abandoned because they were not only dangerous but useless, and everyone was thrown back on the simple basics of survival, chiefly the search for food.

"The men who framed the new laws were determined that that should not happen again. They had the people dispersed now, and they were going to keep them that way, close to their source of supply and offering no more easy targets to a potential enemy. So they passed the Thirtieth Amendment. It was a wise law. It suited the people. They had just had a fearful object lesson in what kind of deathtraps the cities could be. They didn't want any more of them, and gradually that became an article of faith. The country has been healthy and prosperous under the Thirtieth Amendment, Len. Leave it alone."

"Maybe you're right," said Len, scowling at the candle flame. "But when Mr. Dulinsky says how the country has really started to grow again and shouldn't be stopped by outgrown laws, I think he's right, too."

"Don't let him fool you. He's not worried about the country. He's a man who owns four warehouses and wants to own five and is sore because the law says he can't do it."

The judge stood up.

"You'll have to decide what's right in your own mind. But I want to make one thing clear to you. I have my wife and my daughter and myself to think about. If you go on with Dulinsky you'll have to leave my house. No more walks with Amity. No more books. And I warn you, if I am called upon to judge you, judge you I will."

Len stood up too. "Yes, sir."

Taylor dropped a hand on his shoulder. "Don't be a fool, Len. Think it over."

"I will." He went out, feeling sullen and resentful and at the same time convinced that the judge was talking sense. Amity, marriage, a place in the community, a future, roots, no more Dulinsky, no more doubt. No more Bartorstown. No more dreaming. No more seeking and never finding.

He thought about being married to Amity, and what it would be like. It frightened him so that he sweated like a colt seeing harness for the first time. No more dreaming for fair. He thought of Brother James, who by now must be the father of several small Mennonites, and he wondered whether, on the whole, Refuge was very different from Piper's Run, and if Amity was worth having come all this way for. Amity, or Plato. He had not read Plato in Piper's Run, and he had read him in Refuge, but Plato did not seem like the whole answer, either.

No more Bartorstown. But would he ever find it, anyway? Was he crazy to think of exchanging a girl for a phantom?

The hall was dark, except for the intermittent flashes of lightning. There was one of these as he passed the foot of the stairs, and in its brief glare he saw Esau and Amity in the triangular alcove under the treads. They were pressed close together and Esau was kissing her hard, and Amity was not protesting.

## NINE

It was the Sabbath afternoon. They were standing in the shadow of the rose arbor, and Amity was glaring at him.

"You did not see me doing any such thing, and if you tell anybody you did I'll say you're lying!"

"I know what I saw," said Len, "and so do you."

She made her thick braid switch back and forth, in a way she had of tossing her head. "I'm not promised to you."

"Would you like to be, Amity?"

"Maybe. I don't know."

"Then why were you kissing Esau?"

"Well, because," she said very reasonably, "how would I know which one of you I like the best, if I didn't?"

"All right," said Len. "All right, then." He reached out and pulled her to him, and because he was thinking of how Esau had done it he was rather rough about it. For the first time he held her really tight and felt how soft and firm she was and how her body curved amazingly. Her eyes were close to his, so close that they became only a blue color without any shape, and he felt dizzy and shut his own, and found her mouth just by touch alone.

After a while he pushed her away a little and said, "Now which is it?" He was shaking all over, but there was only the faintest flush in Amity's cheeks and the look she gave him was quite cool. She smiled.

"I don't know," she said. "You'll have to try again."

"Is that what you told Esau?"

"What do you care what I told Esau?" Again the yellow braid went swish-swish across the back of her dress. "You mind your own business, Len Colter."

"I could make it my business."

"Who said?"

"Your father said, that's who."

"Oh," said Amity. "He did." Suddenly it was as though a curtain had dropped between them. She drew away, and the line of her mouth got hard.

"Amity," he said. "Listen, Amity, I—"

"You leave me alone. You hear, Len?"

"What's so different now? You were anxious enough a minute ago."

"Anxious! That's all you know. And if you think because you've been sneaking around to my father behind my back—"

"I didn't sneak. Amity, listen." He caught her again and pulled her toward him, and she hissed at him between her teeth. "Let me go, I don't belong to you, I don't belong to anybody! Let me go—"

He held her, struggling. It excited him, and he laughed and bent his head to kiss her again.

"Aw, come on, Amity, I love you—"

She squalled like a cat and clawed his cheek. He let her go, and she was not pretty any more, her face was all twisted and ugly and her eyes were mean. She ran away from him down the path. The air was warm and the smell of roses was heavy around him. For a while he stood looking after her, and then he walked slowly to the house and up to the room he shared with Esau.

Esau was lying on the bed, half asleep. He only grunted and rolled over when Len came in. Len opened the door of the shallow cupboard. He took out a small sack made of tough canvas and began to pack his belongings into it, methodically, ramming each article down into place with unnecessary force. His face was flushed and his brows pulled down into a heavy scowl.

Esau rolled back again. He blinked at Len and said, "What do you think you're doing?"

"Packing."

"Packing!" Esau sat up. "What for?"

"What do people usually do it for? I'm leaving."

Esau's feet hit the floor. "Are you crazy? What do you mean, you're leaving, just like that. Don't I have anything to say about it?"

"Not about me leaving, you don't. You can do what you want to. Look out, I want those boots."

"All right! But you can't—Wait a minute. What's that on your cheek?"

"What?" Len swiped at his cheek with the back of his hand. It came away with a little red smear on it. Amity had dug deep.

Esau began to laugh.

Len straightened up. "What's funny?"

"She finally told you off, did she? Oh, don't give me any story about how the cat scratched you, I know claw marks when I see them. Good. I told you to keep away from her, but you wouldn't listen. I—"

"Do you figure," asked Len quietly, "that she belongs to you?"

Esau smiled. "I could have told you that, too."

Len hit him. It was the first time in his life that he had hit anybody in genuine anger. He watched Esau fall backward onto the bed, his eyes bulging with surprise and a thin red trickle springing out of the corner of his mouth, and it all seemed to happen very slowly, giving him plenty of time to feel guilty and regretful and confused. It was almost as though he had struck his own brother. But he was still angry. He grabbed up his bag and started out the door, and Esau sprang off the bed and caught him by the shoulder of his jacket, spinning him around. "Hit me, will you?" he panted. "Hit me, you dirty—" He called Len a name he had picked up along the river docks and swung his fist, hard.

Len ducked. Esau's knuckles slid along the side of his jaw and on into the solid jamb of the door. Esau howled and danced away, holding his hand under his other arm and cursing. Len started to say something like "I'm sorry," but changed his mind and turned again to go. And Judge Taylor was in the hall.

"Stop that," he said to Esau, and Esau stopped, standing still in the middle of the room. Taylor looked from one to the other and to the bag in Len's hand. "I've just spoken to Amity," he said, and Len could see that underneath his judicial manner Tay-lor was in a seething rage. "I'm sorry, Len. I seem to have made an error of judgment."

"Yes, sir," said Len. "I was just going."

Taylor nodded. "All the same," he said, "what I told you is true. Remember it." He looked keenly at Esau.

"Let him go," Esau said. "I'm staying right here."

"I think not," said Taylor.

Esau said, "But he—"

"I hit him first," said Len.

"That is neither here nor there," said the judge. "Get your things together, Esau."

"But why? I make enough to pay the rent. I haven't done any—"

"I'm not sure yet exactly what you have done, but much or little, that's an end to it. The room is no longer for rent. And if I catch you around my daughter again I'll have you run out of town. Is that clear?"

Esau glowered at him, but he did not say anything. He started to throw his things into a pile on the bed. Len went out past the judge, along the hall and down the stairs. He went out the back way, and as he passed the kitchen he caught a glimpse through the half-open door of Amity bent over the kitchen table, sobbing like a wildcat, and Mrs. Taylor watching her with an expression of blank dismay, one hand raised as though for a comforting pat on the shoulder but stopped in midair and forgotten.

Len let himself out by the back gate, avoiding the rose arbor.

Sabbath lay quiet and heavy on the town. Len stuck to the alleys, walking steadily along in the dust. He did not have any idea where he was going, but habit and the general configuration of Refuge took him down to the river and onto the docks where Dulinsky's four big warehouses stood in line. He stopped there, uncertain and sullen, only just beginning to realize that things had changed very radically for him in the last few minutes.

The river ran green as bottle glass, and among the trees of its farther bank the roofs of Shadwell glimmered in the hot sun. There was a string of river craft tied up along the dock. The men who belonged to them were either in the town or asleep below deck. Nothing moved but the river, and the clouds, and a half-grown cat playing a game with itself on the foredeck of one of the barges. Off to his right, further down, was the big bare rectangle of the new warehouse site. The foundation stones were already laid. Timbers and planks were set by in neat piles, and there was a sawmill with a heap of pale yellow dust below it. Two men, widely separated, lounged inconspicuously in the shade. Len frowned. They looked to him almost as though they were on guard.

Perhaps they were. It was a stupid world, full of stupid people. Fearful people, thinking that if the least little thing was changed the whole sky would fall on them. Stupid world. He hated it. Amity lived in it, and somewhere in it Bartorstown was hidden so it could never be found, and life was dark and full of frustrations.

He was still brooding when Esau came onto the dock after him.

Esau was carrying his own belongings in a hasty bundle, and his face looked red and ugly. His lip was swollen on one side. He threw the bundle down and stood in front of Len and said, "I've got a couple of things to settle with you."

Len breathed hard through his nose. He was not afraid of Esau, and he felt low and mean enough now that a fight would be a pleasant thing. He was not quite as tall as Esau but his shoulders were wider and thicker. He hunched them up and waited.

"What did you want to go and get us thrown out of there for?" Esau said.

"*I* left. It was you that got thrown out."

"Fine cousin you are. What did you say to old man Taylor to make him do that?"

"Nothing. Didn't have to."

"What do you mean by that?"

"He doesn't like you, that's what I mean. Don't come picking a fight with me unless you mean it, Esau."

"Sore, aren't you? Well go ahead and be sore, and I'll tell you something. And you can tell the judge. Nobody can keep me away from Amity. I'll see her anytime I want to, and do anything I want to with her, because she likes me whether her father does or not."

"Big mouth," said Len. "That's all you got, a great big windy mouth."

"I wouldn't talk," said Esau bitterly. "If it hadn't been for you I'd never left home. I'd be there now, probably with the whole farm by now, and a wife and kids if I wanted them, instead of roaming to hell and gone around the country looking for—"

"Shut up," said Len fiercely.

"All right, but you know what I mean, and not even knowing where I'm going to sleep tonight. Trouble, Len. That's all you ever made for me, and now you made it with my girl."

In utter indignation, Len said, "Esau, you're a yellow-bellied liar." And Esau hit him.

Len had got so mad that he had forgotten to be on guard, and the blow took him by surprise. It knocked his hat off and stung most painfully on his cheekbone. He sucked in a sharp breath and went for Esau. They scuffled and banged each other around on the dock for a minute or two and then suddenly Esau said, "Hold it, hold off, somebody's coming and you know what you get for fighting on the Sabbath."

They drew apart, breathing hard. Len picked up his hat, trying to look as though he had not been doing anything. Out of the corner of his eye he saw Mike Dulinsky and two other men coming onto the dock.

"We'll finish this later," he whispered to Esau.

"Sure."

They stood to one side. Dulinsky recognized them and smiled. He was a big powerful man, run slightly to fat around the middle. He had very bright eyes that seemed to see everything, including a lot that was out of sight, but they were cold eyes that never really warmed up even when they smiled. Len admired Mike Dulinsky. He respected him. But he did not particularly like him. The two men with him were Ames and Whinnery, both warehouse owners.

"Well," said Dulinsky. "Down looking over the project?"

"Not exactly," said Len. "We—uh—could we have permission to sleep in the office tonight? We—aren't rooming at the Taylors' anymore."

"Oh?" said Dulinsky, raising his eyebrows. Ames made a sardonic sound that was not quite a snicker.

Len ignored that. "Is it all right, sir?"

"Of course. Make yourselves at home. You have the key with you? Good. Come along, gentlemen."

He went off with Whinnery and Ames. Len got his bag and Esau his bundle and they walked back a way up the dock to the office, a long two-story shed where the paper work of the warehouses was done. Len had the key to it because it was part of his job to open the office every morning. While he was fiddling with the lock, Esau looked back and said,

"He's got 'em down there showing 'em the foundations. They don't look too happy."

Len glanced back too. Dulinsky was waving his arms and talking animatedly, but Ames and Whinnery looked worried and shook their heads.

"He'll have to do more than talk to convince them," said Esau.

Len grunted and went inside. In a few minutes, after they had gone up into the loft to stow their belongings, they heard somebody come in. It was Dulinsky, and he was alone. He gave them a direct, hard stare and said, "Are you scared too? Are you going to run out on me?"

He did not give them time to answer, jerking his head toward the outside.

"*They're* scared. They want more warehouses, too. They want Refuge to grow and make them rich, but they don't want to take any of the risk. They want to see what happens to me first. The bastards. I've been trying to convince them that if we all work together—Why did the judge make you leave his house? Was it on account of me?"

"Well," said Len. "Yes."

Esau looked surprised, but he did not say anything.

"I need you," said Dulinsky. "I need all the men I can get. I hope you'll stick with me, but I won't try to hold you. If you're worried, you better go now."

"I don't know about Len," said Esau, grinning, "but I'm going to stay." He was not thinking about warehouses.

Dulinsky looked at Len. Len flushed and looked at the floor. "I don't know," he said. "It isn't that I'm afraid to stay, it's just that maybe I want to leave Refuge and go on down-river."

"I'll get along," said Dulinsky.

"I'm sure you will," said Len, stubbornly, "but I want to think about it."

"Stick with me," said Dulinsky, "and get rich. My great-great-grandfather came here from Poland, and he never got rich because things were already built. But now they're ready to be built again, and I'm going to get in on the ground floor. I know what the judge has been telling you. He's a negativist. He's afraid of believing in anything. I'm not. I believe in the greatness of this country, and I know that these outmoded shackles have got to be broken off if it's ever to grow again. They won't break themselves.

Somebody, men like you and me, will have to get in there and do it."

"Yes, sir," said Len. "But I still want to think it over."

Dulinsky studied him keenly, and then he smiled. "You don't push easily, do you? Not a bad trait—All right, go ahead and think."

He left them. Len looked at Esau, but the mood was gone and he did not feel like fighting any more. He said, "I'm going for a walk."

Esau shrugged, making no attempt to join him. Len walked slowly along the dock, thinking of the westbound boats, wondering if any of them were secretly bound for Bartorstown, wondering if it was any use to go blindly from place to place, wondering what to do. He reached the end of the dock and stepped off it, going on past the warehouse site. The two men watched him closely until he turned away.

He was perhaps not consciously thinking of going there, but a few minutes more of wandering about brought him to the edge of the traders' compound, an area of hard-packed earth where the wagons were drawn up between long ranks of stable sheds and auction sheds and permanent shelter houses for the men. Len hung around here a good bit. Partly his work for Dulinsky required him to, but there was more to it than that. There was all the gossip and excitement of the roads, and sometimes there was even news of Piper's Run, and there was the never-ending hope that someday he would hear the word he had been waiting all these years to hear. He never had. He had never even seen a familiar face, Hostetter's face in particular, and that was odd because he knew that Hostetter went South in the winter season and therefore would have to cross the river somewhere. Len had been at all the ferry points, but Hostetter had not appeared. He had often wondered if Hostetter had gone back to Bartorstown, or if something had happened to him and he was dead.

The area was quiet now, for no business was done on the Sabbath, and the men were sitting and talking in the shade, or off somewhere to afternoon prayer meeting. Len knew most of them at least by sight, and they knew him. He joined them, glad of some talk to get his mind off his problems for a while. Some of them were New Mennonites. Len always felt shy around them, and a little unhappy, because they brought back to him many things he would just as soon not think about. He had never let on that he had once been one of them.

They talked awhile. The shadows got longer and a cool breeze came up off the river. There began to be a smell of wood smoke and cooking food, and it occurred to Len that he did not have any place to eat supper. He asked if he could stay.

"Of course, and welcome," said a New Mennonite named Fisher. "Tell you what, Len, if you was to go and get some more wood off the big pile it would help."

Len took the barrow and trundled off across to the edge of the compound where the great wood stack was. He had to pass along beside the stable sheds to do this. He filled the barrow with firewood and turned back again. When he reached a certain point beside the stables, the lines of wagons hid him from the shelter houses and the men, who were now all getting busy around the fires. It was dark inside the stables. A sweet warm smell of horse came out of them, and a sound of munching.

A voice came out of them, too. It said his name.

"Len Colter."

Len stopped. It was a hushed and hurried voice, very sharp, insistent. He looked around, but he could not see anything.

"Don't look for me unless you want to get us both in trouble," said the voice. "Just listen. I have a message for you, from a friend. He says to tell you that you'll never find what you're looking for. He says go home to Piper's Run and make your peace. He says—"

"Hostetter," Len whispered. "Are you Hostetter?"

"—get out of Refuge. There will be a bath of fire, and you'll get burned in it. Get out, Len. Go home. Now walk on, as though nothing had happened."

Len started to walk. But he said, into the dark of the stables, in a whispered cry of wild triumph, "You know there's only one place I want to go! If you want me to leave Refuge, you'll have to take me there."

And the voice answered, on a fading sigh. "Remember the night of the preaching. You may not always be saved."

## TEN

Two weeks later, the frame of the new warehouse had taken shape and men were starting to work on the roof. Len worked where he was told to, now on the construction gang and now in the office when the papers got stacked too high. He did this in a state of tense excitement, going through a lot of the motions automatically while his mind was on other things. He was like a man waiting for an explosion to happen.

He had moved his sleeping quarters to a hut in the traders' section, leaving Esau in full possession of Dulinsky's loft. He spent every spare minute there, quite forgetting Amity, forgetting everything but the hope that now, any minute, after all these years, things would break for him the way he wanted them to. He went over and over in his mind every word the voice had said. He heard them in his light uneasy sleep. And he would not have left Refuge and Dulinsky now for any reason under the sun.

He knew there was danger. He was beginning to feel it in the air and see it in the faces of some of the men who dropped by to watch as the timbers of the warehouse went up. There were too many strangers among them. The countryside around Refuge was populous and prosperous farm land, and only partly New Mennonite. On market days there were always farmers in town, and the country preachers and the storekeepers and the traders came and went, and it was obvious that the word was spreading around. Len knew he was taking a chance, and he knew that it was perhaps not fair to Hostetter or whoever it was that had risked giving him that warning. But he was fiercely determined not to go.

He was angry with Hostetter and the men of Bartorstown.

It was perfectly apparent now that they must have known where he and Esau were ever since they left Piper's Run. He could think of half a dozen times when a trader had happened along providentially to help them out of a bad spot, and he was sure now that these were not accidents. He was sure that the reason he had never met Hostetter was not accidental either. Hostetter had avoided them, and probably the men of Bartorstown had avoided using the facilities of whatever town the Colter boys happened to be in. That was why there had never been a clue. Hostetter knew perfectly well why they had run away, and he had spread the warning, and for all these years the men of Bartorstown had been deliberately keeping them from all hope of finding what they were after. And at the same time, the men of Bartorstown could easily, at any moment, have simply picked them up and taken them where they wanted to go. Len felt like a child deceived by its elders. He wanted to get his hands on Hostetter.

He had not said anything about this to Esau. He did not like Esau very well any more, and he was not sure of him. He figured there was plenty of time for talking later on, and in the meantime everybody, including Esau, was safer if he didn't know.

Len hung around the traders, not asking any questions or saying anything, just there with his eyes and his ears wide open. But he did not see anybody he knew, and no secret voice spoke to him again. If it was Hostetter, he was still keeping out of sight.

He would hardly be able to do that in Refuge. Len decided that if it was Hostetter, he was staying across the river in Shadwell. And immediately Len felt a compulsion to go there. Perhaps, away from people who knew him too well, another contact might be made.

He didn't have any excuse to go to Shadwell, but it did not take him long to think one up. One evening as he was helping Dulinsky close the office, he said, "I've just been thinking it wouldn't be a bad idea if I was to go over to Shadwell and see what they think about what you're doing. After all, if you're successful, it'll mean the bread out of their mouths."

"I know what they think," said Dulinsky. He slammed a desk drawer shut and looked out the window at the dark framework of the building rising against the blue west. After a minute he said, "I saw Judge Taylor today."

Len waited. He was fidgety and nervous all the time these days. It seemed hours before Dulinsky spoke again.

"He told me if I didn't stop building that he and the town authorities would arrest me and everyone connected with me."

"Do you think they will?"

"I reminded him that I hadn't violated any local law. The Thirtieth Amendment is a Federal law, and he has no jurisdiction over that."

"What did he say?"

Dulinsky shrugged. "Just what I expected. He'll send immediately to the federal court in Maryland, asking for authority or a federal officer."

"Oh well," said Len, "that'll take a while. And public opinion—"

"Yes," said Dulinsky. "Public opinion is the only hope I have. Taylor knows it. The elders know it. Old man Shadwell knows it. This thing isn't going to wait for any federal judge to jog trot all the way from Maryland."

"You'll carry the rally tomorrow night," said Len confidently. "Refuge is pretty sore about Shadwell taking business away from them. The people are behind you, most of them."

Dulinsky grunted. "Maybe it wouldn't be amiss if you did go to Shadwell. This rally is important. I'll stand or fall by the way it goes, and if old man Shadwell is fixing to come over and make me some trouble, I want to know it. I'll give you some business to do, so it won't look too much as though you're spying. Don't ask any questions, just see what you can pick up. Oh, and don't take Esau."

Len hadn't been intending to, but he asked, "Why not?"

"You've got wit enough to stay out of trouble. He hasn't. Do you know where he spends his nights?"

"Why," said Len, surprised, "right here, I suppose."

"Maybe. I hope so. You take the morning ferry, Len, and come back on the afternoon. I want you here for the rally. I need every voice I can get shouting Hooray for Mike."

"All right," said Len. "Good night."

He walked past the new warehouse on his way. It smelled fragrantly of new wood and had a satisfying hugeness. Len felt that it was good to build. For the moment he agreed passionately with Dulinsky.

A voice challenged him from the shadow of a pile of planks, and he said, "Hello, Harry, it's me." He walked on. There were four men on guard now. They carried big billets of wood in their hands, and fires burned all night to light the area. He understood that Mike Dulinsky came down there every so often to look around, as though he was too uneasy to sleep.

Len did not sleep well himself. He sat around talking for a while after supper and then rolled in, but he was thinking about tomorrow, thinking how he would walk through Shadwell to the traders' compound and Hostetter would be there, and he would say something to him, something quiet but significant, and Hostetter would nod and say, "All right, it's no use fighting you any longer, I'll take you where you want to go." He played that scene over and over in his mind, and all the time he knew it was only one of those things you dream up when you're a child and haven't learned yet about reality. Then he got to thinking about Dulinsky asking where Esau spent his nights, and sleep was out of the question. Len wanted to know too.

He thought he did know. And it was amazing, considering that he didn't care at all about Amity, how much the idea upset him.

He rose and went out into the warm night. The compound was dark and silent, except for an occasional thump from the stables where the big horses moved in their stalls. He crossed it and went up through the sleeping streets of the town, deliberately taking the long way round so as not to pass the new warehouse. He didn't want to talk to the guards.

The long way round was long enough to take him past Judge Taylor's house. Nothing was stirring there, and no light showed. He picked out Amity's window, and then he felt ashamed and moved on, down to the docks.

The door of Dulinsky's office was locked, but Esau had a key now, so that didn't mean anything. Len hesitated. The wet smell of the river was strong in the air, a presage of rain, and the sky was clouded. The watch fires burned, farther down the bank. It was quiet, and somehow the office shed had the feel of an empty building. Len unlocked the door and went in.

Esau was not there.

Len stood still for quite a while, in a black fury at first, but calming down gradually into a sort of disgusted contempt for Esau's stupidity. As for Amity, if that was what she wanted she was welcome to it. He wasn't angry. Not much.

Esau's cot had not been touched. Len turned back the quilt, folding it carefully. He set Esau's spare boots straight under the edge of the cot, picked up a soiled shirt and hung it neatly on a peg. Then he lit the lamp beside Esau's bed, turned it low, and left it burning. He went out, locking the office door behind him.

It was very late when he got back to the compound. Even so, he sat for a long time on the doorstep, looking at the night and thinking. Lonely thoughts.

In the morning he stopped by to pick up the letter Dulinsky had for him to take to Shadwell, and Esau was there, looking so gray and old about the face that Len almost felt sorry for him.

"What's the matter with you?" he demanded.

Esau snarled at him.

"You look scared to death," said Len deliberately. "Is somebody making you threats about the warehouse?"

"Mind your own damn business," said Esau, and Len smiled inwardly. Let him sweat. Let him wonder who was here last night, when he was where he had no business to be. Let him wonder who knows, and wait.

He went down and got on board the ferry, a great lumbering flat thing with a shack to shelter the boiler and the wood stack. A light, steady rain had begun to fall, and the far shore was obscured in mist. A southbound trader with a load of woolens and leather was crossing too. Len helped him with his team and then sat with him in the wagon, remembering what magic things these wagons had been to him when he was a boy. The Canfield Fair seemed like something that happened a million years ago. The trader was a thin man with a gingery beard that reminded him of Soames. He shuddered and looked away, down-river, where the slow strong current ran forever to the west. A launch was beating its way up against it. The launch made a mournful hooting at the ferry, and the ferry answered, and then from the east a third voice spoke and a string of barges went down well in front of them, loaded with coal that glistened bright and black in the rain.

Shadwell was little and new and raw, and growing so fast that there were half-built buildings wherever Len looked. The waterfront hummed, and up on a rise behind it the big Shadwell house sat watching with all its glassy eyes.

Len walked up to the warehouse office where he had to go to deliver his letter. A lot of the men who would have been building were not working today on account of the rain. There was a little gang of them bunched up on the porch of the general store. It seemed to Len as though they watched him pretty close, but then that was probably only because he was a stranger off the ferry. He went in and gave the letter to a small elderly man named Gerrit, who read it hurriedly and then eyed Len as though he had crept out of the mud at low water.

"You tell Mike Dulinsky," he said, "that I follow the words of the Good Book that forbid me to have any dealings with unrighteous men. And as for you, I'd advise you to do the same. But you're a young man, and the young are always sinful, so I won't waste my breath. Git."

He flung the letter in a box of wastepaper and turned away. Len shrugged and went out. He headed off across the muddy square toward the traders' compound. One of the men on the porch of the general store came down the steps and ambled across to Gerrit's office. It was raining harder, and little streams of yellow water ran everywhere along the naked ground.

There were a lot of wagons in the compound, but none of them bore Hostetter's name. Most of the men were under cover. He did not see anyone he knew, and no one spoke to him. After a while he turned around and went back.

The square was full of men. They stood in the rain, and the yellow water splashed around their boots, but they did not seem to mind. They were all facing one way, toward Len.

One of them said, "You're from Refuge."

Len nodded.

"You work for Dulinsky."

Len shrugged and started to push by him.

Two other men came up on either side of him and caught his arms. He tried to get free, but they held him tight, one on each side, and when he tried to kick they stomped his ankles.

The first man said, "We got a message for Refuge. You tell them. We ain't going to let them take away what is rightfully ours. If they don't stop Dulinsky, we will. Can you remember that?"

Len glared at him. He was scared. He did not say anything.

"Make him remember it, boys," said the first man.

The two men holding him were joined by two more. They threw Len face down in the mud. He got up, and when he was halfway to his feet they kicked him flat again and grabbed his arms and rolled him. Then somebody else grabbed him and then another and another, roughing him around the square between them, perfectly quiet except for the little grunts of effort, not really hurting him

too badly but never giving him a chance to fight back. When they were through they went away and left him, dizzy and gasping for breath, spitting out mud and water. He scrambled to his feet and looked around, but the square was deserted. He went down to the ferry and got aboard, although it was a long time before it was due to go back again. He was wet to the skin and shivering, although he was not conscious of being cold.

The ferry captain was a native of Refuge. He helped Len clean up and gave him a blanket out of his own locker. Then Len looked up along the streets of Shadwell.

"I'll kill 'em," said Len. "I'll kill 'em."

"Sure," said the ferry captain. "And I'll tell you one thing. They better not come over to Refuge and start trouble, or they'll find out what trouble is."

Toward mid-afternoon the rain stopped, and by five o'clock, when the ferry docked again at Refuge, the sky was clearing. Len reported to Dulinsky, who looked grave and shook his head.

"I'm sorry, Len," he said. "I should have known better."

"Well," said Len, "they didn't do me any damage, and now you know. They'll likely come over to the rally."

Dulinsky nodded. His eyes began to shine and he rubbed his hands together. "Maybe that's just what we want," he said. "Go change your clothes and get some supper. I'll see you later."

Len started home, but Dulinsky was already ahead of him, posting men to watch along the docks and doubling the warehouse guard.

At the compound Fisher spotted Len and asked him, "What happened to you?"

"I had a little trouble with the Shads," said Len, still too sore to want to talk about it. He went into his cabin and shut the door, and began to strip off his clothes, dried stiff with the yellow mud. And he wondered.

He wondered if Hostetter had abandoned him. And he wondered if Hostetter or anyone else would really be able to do much, when the time came. He remembered the voice saying, You may not always be saved.

When it was dark, he walked over to the town square, and the rally.

*Continued in Galaxy's Edge #21*